# BRIGHTBLADE SAGA

## BOOK ONE

## AWAKENING

LISA ARNOUX-BROWN

Martin and Bowman
1-855-921-1348

# CHAPTER ONE

I felt like I was walking for days. It might have been a few minutes, hours, I don't know, however it was endless. The funny thing about this excursion was that the streets kept repeating themselves like some weird time warp. Its July, but the air was cool, making me shiver. I pulled my little denim jacket tighter around me and clasped the strap of my bag closer, not because I was afraid of a purse snatcher or anything, it just made me feel more secure and warmer. I didn't want to walk anymore so I headed toward the pizza shop I passed a gazillion times on the corner. A blast of tomato sauce, peppers, sausages and onions hit me full on. My mouth began to water, and I head toward the refrigerated glass case in the back of the shop to get a cold beverage and –Whoa? My hand passed right through it!

I shook my head and tried again. Yup my hand passed right through the handle, and since I was already inside the case, I tried to grab hold of a can of soda. I grabbed nothing but air, so I pulled it out and turned around quickly to see if anyone saw what just happened.

No one even looked my way. A young girl and her mother walked into the pizzeria and the mother gestures toward the beverage case to her daughter. The girl walked purposely toward the case. She walked unerringly toward me and the case. I'm rooted to the spot, afraid to move. In fact, I couldn't move.

It tickled me when she reached right through me to get not one but two cans of soda. As if nothing happened and as if she hadn't violated me, she turned and walked back to her mother to wait their turn to order.

"Well excuse you." I said to her back. My heart started to beat faster and harder in my chest as more people walked through me. I couldn't breathe. My chest felt tight. What's happening?

I hightailed it out of the shop, forgetting to push the door open and realized that I couldn't remember if I opened it when I came in. I started to run then, not caring if I bumped into people. Mostly I'm plowing through them. Three or four blocks later, I stopped to catch my breath. I looked up to find myself standing in front of New York Hospital; you know the one in Flushing? I looked up and down the street. I didn't understand anything. How did I get there? I felt compelled to go in, so I did.

The pull was stronger once I was inside the lobby. I felt relieved and closed my eyes basking in it. It didn't last long however, because then I felt strange and when I opened my eyes, I was floating. I flapped my arms trying to get down, but no, my body seemed to have developed a mind of its own. I floated closer to the ceiling and then I began to accelerate toward the wall. I braced myself, but I went through it easily. Faster and faster I went, until I ended up in what looked like a trauma room, you know like on TV? I looked down and I saw myself lying on a gurney and three doctors and nurses were working on me.

Whoa! Was I in an accident? I looked like crap. My face was all bloody and my neck was a mess. I bled from everywhere, but mostly from my neck. A nurse or whoever was putting pressure on it while another tried to get an I.V. in my arm, while yet another was cutting my shirt open to place electrodes on my chest. I could see the machine bleeping as my heart, beat to tell the world that I was alive. I realized that I was having an out of body experience. You see these wackos on TV saying stuff like how peaceful it was and I can tell you that it's so not. I'm cheering for these guys to save my life. I didn't want to die and so I tried to float down to my body. I flapped my arms like a crazed dodo bird attempting to fly but nothing happens. Suddenly, I could feel pain and it was horrible, unbearable even and whatever they were doing to me made the pain worse. I wanted them to stop and to continue, you know? And, then I heard it, everybody in the room heard it. I flat lined. The doctor did his jumper cable thing and nothing. One of them called out 11:45 pm. They filed out and then the sole nurse left in the room with me was pulling out the I.V. and the other stuff they'd put on me or in me.

Finally, when I was presentable, this guy dressed in green scrubs came and transferred my body into a sunken gurney and covered me. He rolled me out of the room and down the hallway and into an elevator. We went down. Down is never a good sign when you're covered up like I am. For some reason, I can't leave them. Him and my body I mean. I hovered over us as we pass through a few sets of double doors, and finally we were at the morgue. He signed me in and parked me in the middle of the room.

He joked with the receiving attendant for a bit and then left us. The attendant picked up the paperwork the people in the ER trauma room stuffed into a plastic folder and then sat at the computer. Afterwards, he grabbed a toe tag, wrote my name on it, and looped it around my right great toe. Then he did the unbelievable. He lifted the sheet to get a look at my body. Thanks to the doctor going crazy with scissors upstairs, I was naked under there! If he touches me, I swear I will kick him in the nuts like dad taught me.

He doesn't, and I breathe a sigh of relief. He was just checking for jewelry.

"No jewelry." He said and went back to the computer. After that, he pushed me into another room and washed my body. He was a complete gentleman. He wore gloves. Then he toweled me dry and singlehandedly transferred me into the table draw, covered me up nice and snug and pushed the draw closed.

I couldn't recall how long after that, that my parents came to see me. It was heartbreaking watching them. They held each other while they cried.

When they were leaving, I tried to follow them and found that I could. I looked longingly at my body, but this time it felt okay to leave it. I followed my parents out of the hospital. I looked down at my body to find that I had clothes on. Cool.

They got in the car, but my dad just sat there behind the wheel staring out of the windshield. Giant tears slid down his face and then after a while, he wiped at his eyes, cleared his throat and started the engine. I followed him to our house.

"Oh God Gary, what kind of animal would do that to our little girl?" My mother asked as soon as they hit the living room. She collapsed onto the couch.

My father got busy pouring himself a drink at the bar behind her. "I don't know honey, it's a crazy world out there." He replied. He tossed the drink back like a pro.

Just then, my sister Laura burst into the house. She was in such a hurry, that she left the key in the door. My little brother followed her in more slowly with the keys in his hand, dragging his backpack behind him.

"Mom, what's the emergency? Why did I have to go get Jr. from his sleepover? What's happened?" She asked in that dramatic voice she used when she was annoyed.

My dad took her by the arm and led her to the couch next to mom. "It's your sister. Fiona's gone. She was attacked on her way home from the party with her friends." He told them. My brother Gary Jr. sat on the couch. Mom was sandwiched between Laura and him.

"What do you mean gone? She got hurt and is in the hospital, right?" She asked.

"No, it means that some deranged maniac killed your sister. Oh God!" Screeched my mom.

Gary Jr. leaned into my mom and she threw her arms around them both. They cried for a little while and then my sister, my sweet sister broke free and ran up the stairs to her room.

My father got up to pour himself another shot and then turned to my brother. "Jr. go upstairs to your room; we'll be up to talk with you in a little while." As soon as he was out of sight, my father sat next to my mom and cuddled her close. "We have to make arrangements quickly. No sense in prolonging it. We must contact everyone in the morning. It isn't right. Parents don't bury their children, it's just not right." He said shaking his head.

"I can't believe she's gone. It wasn't supposed to happen this way. She was supposed to grow up, have a career and family, grow old with lots of grandchildren." Mom sniffed.

"That's not to be honey. I'll make the calls in the morning, there's much to do." He stood up and looked lovingly at mom. "I'll go make you some tea."

That's so sweet of him, I thought. I waved my arms and floated up the stairs to my sister's room. She seemed so upset, I wanted to check on her. Wow, I had this going through stuff down pat. I tried to see if I could sit on her bed. No, I just hovered. Her eyes were red from the crying she did downstairs but she's on her cell phone now.

"Yeah, I know. It's so messed up. Dad said that she was attacked and killed. Mom is so sad. God, I know. Now they're gonna try to keep me locked up in here like a prisoner. I probably won't be able to go to Amy's party this weekend, but I can totally make it to Devon's next week and I won't have to beg Fiona to let me borrow her clothes either." She sniffed a little but then did this laugh cry thing. "I can let you have her Uggs, she's not gonna use them."

I'm not even buried yet and she's giving my stuff away! "What if I want to be buried in my Uggs you bitch?" I yelled, but it came out as a whisper.

"They're downstairs consoling each other. Dad is probably self-medicating with the scotch and mom is drinking a gallon of tea. I've been watering the bottle down for weeks. He ain't getting no buzz tonight." She laughed.

I waved my arms to float away quickly. My sister was making me mad. I floated down the hall to my brothers' room. Whoa, I haven't been in his room in a long time. It's kinda nice, for a boy, I guess. After the experience of my backstabbing sister, I braced myself for Jr. to be a royal jerk, but he's not. He's sitting on his bed looking sad.

"I didn't want Mom and Dad to know, but I can see you Fiona." He said and then looks straight at me.

"Can you hear me too?" I asked overjoyed that this being dead wasn't sucking so bad.

He nodded. "Yeah, I can hear you, but your voice is very faint. You look okay in case you were wondering."

"I don't know what to do, being dead and all. It's kinda cool that you can see me. I can come visit you a lot." I told him.

"I don't think it works that way. You've only just died, so maybe after we bury you, your ghost disappears. It's nice to see you though."

We stopped talking because we could hear our parents outside his room. They walked in and sat on either side of Jr. "Jr. things are going to change a lot now. Right now, I know it's a shock and you're probably feeling a lot of things. Anytime you feel you want to talk about Fiona, your mom and I will listen. If you want to cry, that's okay too."

"That's okay Dad. I can talk with Fiona whenever I want because she's still here with us." He told them. I waved wildly at him. I didn't want them to know that I was floating around the house. No sense in pushing Mom completely over the edge.

Mom moaned and took his hand. "Fiona will always be in our hearts too honey. The next few weeks are going to be very difficult for all of us. Your dad and I will be planning for her services in the morning. We're going to have family coming from all over, so be prepared to share your room with your cousins. Okay?"

"Okay." Jr. agreed. He looked at me sideways.

"Alright son, get ready for bed." After they left, I asked Jr. why he told them that I was still there.

"I was just checking to see if they could see you too. I thought that maybe Dad could, but they didn't even look your way."

"Well, for now let's just keep this between us. I don't know how long I can stay here but I'm going to try." I assured him.

I started feeling that pulling sensation again and before I could warn Jr, I started floating away. "Bye, gotta go!" I yelled quickly.

My body was traveling fast and once I oriented myself, I deduced that I was heading back to the hospital morgue. Sure enough, I'm back there floating beside my assigned draw. But I wasn't alone, I mean, there's this man standing there looking at the draw handle. In his hand was a metal-looking device he pointed at the draw and it opened. I could see my body in there covered in a white sheet. With his device he pulled the draw all the way open and then lifted the sheet.

"Wake up, Brightblade." He said. Immediately I felt a different kind of tug, I rushed into my body and I opened my eyes. The first thing I noticed was how cold it was in the draw, like I mean, really cold. I sat up and he helped me scramble out of the draw. So, there I was, standing in front of him completely naked. I did that cross your arms over your chest thing and he yanked out a white cape and threw it across my shoulders. That's when I noticed that he was wearing all white, even his boots. Boots? Who wears knee-hi boots in the summer?

The cape he threw around me suddenly did this bonding thing with my body. I looked down and I saw that I was wearing this bodysuit under the cape, and boots too.

I opened my mouth to speak but nothing came out. I lifted my hand to get his attention. He nodded at me and spoke, but I couldn't understand what he said. Then suddenly I understood what he was saying. "Speech will come momentarily, now step aside." He nudged me away from the draw and placed an object in it that looked like a nut, like an almond maybe? The nut started to move and wriggle, then it started to grow.

As I watched it, it took shape, my shape. Once it was fully grown, he instructed me to place my hand on it. I did as he asked cringing at the feel of the formless, clay-looking thing. It changed again to eventually look exactly like me. It even had the scars from the attack. He nodded and I removed my hand.

"What have you done?" I asked him as I wiped my hand on my pant leg.

He looked very pleased with himself. "They need something to bury." He answered and clasped my arm. "Now come along, we have a long journey ahead of us."

I wrenched my arm from his grasp and put my hands on my hips, like my mom did sometimes when she and dad argued.

"I'm not going anywhere with you. I want to stay here so I can be close to my family." I told him.

"That is not possible, you're dead." He responded, as if that answered everything.

"No duh, what did you do to me. Am I a ghost?"

He sighed. "I called your essence back into your body, but for all intent and purposes you are still dead, not a ghost." He explained.

"Can I still float and go through stuff? Are you a reaper or something?"

"Yes, and no, I am not a reaper. You and I are the same. I was sent here to retrieve you and to take you to the Elders."

I scratched my head. "I don't understand anything. If you aren't a reaper, then are you an angel?" I asked hoping that he was.

"Look, we are wasting time. Let me take you to the Elders and they'll answer your questions." He stated impatiently.

I nodded and allowed him to take my arm again. I decided that he wasn't an angel. He didn't act like one and he didn't look like the other one either. At the hint of a horn coming out of his head, I'm ditching him and taking my chances of being whatever I am alone. He kept looking at this little device thing in his hand and checking his surroundings.

His hand was gentle afterwards and he led me through the double doors and out of the morgue. When we got to the elevator bank, he tightened his grasp on my arm as we floated up going through concrete and metal. We accelerated until we got to the lobby. He pocketed the device and nodded to himself.

The sky was just turning pink when we got outside. He pointed up and I saw a space craft. It was a two-seater like on that cartoon show, the Jetsons. It was hovering just above the hospital. We floated up to it and he and I sat in it. As soon as we were seated, the lid came down and then it began to move.

I sat there fascinated as the space craft streamed through what looked like strings of different colors. Some were thick, and some thin. I wondered if we were in outer space, but I didn't see any planets or any kind of heavenly body. I wondered again about where we were going. The two-seater shook and jostled, and I held on tightly to the armrests. After what felt like an eternity, the craft slowed down and then it stopped altogether. We disembarked and then he led me through a door and into a room.

I couldn't make out where we were because it was just like stepping into a clean room for a super important experiment, all dazzlingly white. I felt dizzy and nauseous.

I turned to him and swallowed hard. "You still haven't told me your name."

"I am Jhael, now come along, Brightblade." I nodded and allowed him to take my arm once more. I felt less nauseous now and as I walked with him through a door that magically opened, I started to worry again. If Jhael was an angel and he came for me, did that mean that I was going to be judged or something?

Jhael looked like he was probably in his twenties. His face was smooth, not a hair in sight. His eyes were the lightest brown and his nose was so straight it could cut you. He wore his blond hair in a low ponytail and under his cape, I couldn't see his body.

We went through several corridors to finally come to a huge room. It was so big that the soft colored furniture looked like doll furniture in its center. He motioned for me to sit, and I did. The couch I sat in felt so nice that I wanted to sink my body deeper into it, close my eyes and go to sleep. Everything in the room was soft and comforting. The walls were a soft baby blue. The couch was a darker blue but just as soft. Even the lighting was soft. There were no pictures on the walls. Instead, there were shelfs built into them and as far as the eye can see, they held books. The ceiling was very high. If I were to guess, I'd say that the books numbered in the thousands if not millions.

A sound took my attention from the books to the door. An older man walked in. He was dressed in almost the same getup as me, except his was gold colored.

I watched him as he walked past me to the desk on the other side of the room. He sat behind the desk, clasped his hands together and stared at me. "Fiona Brightblade?" He asked.

I felt that I should stand, so I did, and I nodded at him. "Yes, sir I'm Fiona Brightblade."

"I understand that you have some questions dear." He said.

"Yes sir, I do. I'm not sure where I am, in fact I don't know where here is. If this is Heaven's judgement, will I have a chance to plead my case?"

"My dear, this is not heaven. You're here because you are a descendant of a race of beings that once took refuge on Earth. We are tasked with removing you from the Earth when you die."

I sat now because my knees had suddenly gone weak. "This isn't Earth?"

"No, it is not. We are on a planet parallel to Earth. It is called Anthora Two."

"I've never heard of it." I admitted.

"Earthlings have much to learn about the universe, my dear. Our planet sits side by side to it, almost occupying the same space but different dimensions. It is very similar to it, except for our special abilities. Anthorans are solid on it, but when we travel to other planets, we are like ghosts, invisible to others but ourselves."

"Okay let me see if I've got this straight. You say that I am a descendant of Anthorans, does that mean my family on Earth are descendants as well?"

"The genes we pass along don't always flow to every generation. Your parents are not Anthorans. Neither is your sister. Your brother however is very much Anthoran as you are because we detected his essence signature along with yours."

"What makes Jr. and me Anthoran? We have the same parents and you say that they aren't Anthoran, so how is that possible?"

"Your father's parents were Brightblades?' He asked.

"Yes."

"To answer your question, one of your fathers' ancestors was Anthoran. It is very rare that we get two in the same family." He explained.

"Can I ask some more questions?" I asked.

"That is why I am here dear. I will try to answer all of your questions."

"Good because I am confused. Will I be able to go see my brother soon? I kind of left him abruptly. We were talking because he could see me and then suddenly whoosh! I'm back at the morgue and Jhael is replacing my body with a pod person. If we are on another planet, why aren't we speaking another language? Why didn't I feel different when I was on Earth? What is your name?" I rapid fired at him.

"You can call me Boham." Boham answered with a slight smile. He looked to be in his seventies at a guess. His eyes were a crisp blue and his hair was nearly white. His smile was gentle. "We don't recommend going back and forth to Earth, but we might make an exception since your brother is Anthoran. We are speaking another language and since you are no longer on Earth, your Azel speech has returned. That was how you were able to understand Jhael. He doesn't speak any of the Earthling tongues. You were different on Earth; you just didn't understand your difference."

I shook my head and sat on the edge of my seat as if that made things clearer. "How was I different?" I asked.

"You were smarter, stronger. You rarely got sick and if in a fight, you defended yourself quite well." He explained.

I nodded. "Okay, I did really well in school. I didn't have to study hard to pass my tests. Jr. is smart too. I don't remember the last time I got sick. But you are wrong about defending myself. I didn't defeat whoever attacked me because I'm dead. I don't even remember the attack." I replied.

"That is why you are here Fiona. Your death was not natural, your body was brutalized excessively. We usually come for Anthorans after they die, but after old age or a fatal accident. You were murdered deliberately. We will be investigating your death to find the answers."

"I was murdered? Is that why I can't remember the attack? If my death is suspicious, does that mean that my brother is in danger too?"

Boham smiled. "You see? You are very astute. We will be conducting our investigation along those lines and we will be keeping your brother under surveillance. If your attack was because of race, then we must and will take action."

"How can I help protect my brother?" I asked. I was afraid for Jr.

"That is not up to me my dear. The Council of Elders makes those types of decisions. My path is understanding diverse cultures. I'm sure that as soon as you have acclimated to our world you will get your answers. Now if you have no more questions, I will take you to your room where you can rest. Dimension travel is hard on the body."

Boham stood up and beckoned me to follow him. I quickly join him at the door. Jhael must've left while we were talking, I didn't see him.

These corridors were not the stark white as when I first arrived. I wondered if that first room I came through was some sort of decontamination room.

Boham led me to a door and when he opened it, I swallowed hard. I was beginning to believe that I was no longer on Earth. Boham turned to me as I hesitated, and he smiled encouragingly. "I assure you that the bridge is completely safe." He said.

I took a deep breath and stepped out onto the bridge. It was encased in glass and to my surprise, when I stepped on it the floor moved, just like at the airport, I thought. I wondered briefly how long it would take to walk all the way across. We were headed to what looked like a city, but it was far away.

I looked behind me and all I saw was the doorknob and nothing else. Amazing! I faced forward again, and the city was getting closer. I looked down and I could see a body of water and what can only be boats and ships. The sky was blue, thank goodness.

After what felt like an hour, we reached the other side. The air tasted funny, but I didn't say anything. I was breathing okay and that was more important. The streets were very clean, and the cars were high tech. They had no tires and they looked like they were made of some sort of metal. They glided on cushions of air. The buildings were tall and made of what looked like glass, but I couldn't see through them.

As I walked beside Boham, we passed others on the sidewalk. They openly stared at me. I guess they knew that I was the new arrival. After several blocks, Boham turned toward a building. I quickly looked up to see if there were numbers on it so that I could remember it if I went out. There was only a symbol and I almost recognized what it meant. Inside the building was quiet. After the front door, we followed a corridor to another door with another symbol that I was sure meant the number nine. Boham opened the door and I stood there speechless. I was expecting something spectacular, but there was my room just like the one back on Earth. I went in to inspect everything. "Did you duplicate my room from Earth?" I asked him.

"Most of our recovered populace find it comforting to have the things they were familiar with from their former lives." He answered.

I hurried to the closet to find my Uggs just where I'd left them. I wanted to laugh at the absurdity of it all, but I cried instead. "Thank you." I said lamely.

"Once you're rested, someone will come for you." Boham said and left.

I opened another door thinking that I had another closet, but instead it was the bathroom. They thought of everything. Suddenly I felt tired and I quickly showered to change into my own clothes. I fell into a dreamless sleep.

A knock on the door woke me up. I sat up just in time to see a young woman come into my room. She was dressed in jeans and sneakers and she stood there staring at me. "Oh, good you're awake. I came for you earlier, but you were sound asleep. It's time for dinner if you're interested. You missed lunch." She said.

I scrambled out of bed, glad that I had changed into my jeans and tee shirt. I shoved my feet into my sneakers and hurriedly brush my hair. I didn't think I had time to do much with it, so I left it loose. Once I thought I was ready I went to her by the door.

She extended her hand out to me. "I'm Aisha Shamon come on we're going to be late." Aisha was African American. She was tall and thin. Her dark eyes sparkled, and she wore her hair in a bun on top of her head. She wore jeans, a tee shirt and sneakers like me.

"Nice to meet you, I'm Fiona Brightblade" I said as I hurried after her. We walked further down the corridor that led from my room and entered an elevator. I didn't know what I was expecting, but the ride was uneventful, only I didn't know if we went up or down. There were no buttons to push in the elevator.

Once off the elevator, I followed Aisha to what appeared to be a cafeteria. It felt like school. Was I in a dorm of some kind? We got in line and I grabbed a tray. I saw foods that I didn't recognize. I quickly grabbed a burger and some fries. Some of what was offered looked too different for me to experiment with.

I followed Aisha to a table. There were others sitting at the table and I waved as I sat down. There were two men and two women my age besides Aisha.

"Hi, I'm Fiona." I looked down at my food because no one answered.

"Don't worry about them. Give them a chance to get to know you better. They come from another planet, but I'm from Earth like you."

I started to eat my burger and fries. "How long have you been here?"

"Time moves differently here than on Earth. By my calculations, I've been here five years, but by Earth's calculations, it's been about fifteen years."

I choked on my juice. "I've been here a day I think." Quickly, I tried to do the math in my head. A day here would be about seven days on Earth, I think. "My family back on Earth have probably buried my pod body already." I said sadly.

"There isn't a day that passes that I don't remember my family." Aisha said wistfully.

"How old were you when you died there?" I asked.

"I was twenty-four. I'd been dating this guy and I thought he was Mr. right as they say. My father was a mechanic, a workaholic really.

He'd come home smelling of grease and gasoline. My mother hated that smell, but I loved it. My mom was a hairdresser. She was good at it too. I'd just gotten a promotion at my job at the Stop and Shop. I was shift manager. Things were going well and then out of nowhere, I was crossing the street and got hit by a car. It wasn't bad. I had a broken leg and two broken ribs. Ten days later, I died of a blood clot to the brain."

I made comforting sounds. I wondered if she became a ghost too, but I felt that I shouldn't ask. "Did you freak out when they came for you?"

Aisha nodded her head. "Yeah, but I calmed down once it was explained to me. I sort of wished that I could have said goodbye to my family. I was an only child and I know that my parents were devastated." Aisha shook her head. "How about you, what's your story?"

I swallowed more juice and nodded at her. "I'm twenty and the eldest of three. I have a sister and brother. I was a college student. I went to a party with a girlfriend of mine and once I got there, I found that I wasn't having a good time. The crowd was older than me and they were doing drugs. My friend didn't want to leave, so I left by myself. I don't remember much about my death. Like you I wanted to say goodbye but I didn't get a chance." I told her. Since she didn't tell me about whether she was a ghost for a while, I didn't tell her about visiting my family. Perhaps it was different for each person.

One of the two guys sitting at our table stood up and looked at me. "You died a dishonorable death. Where I'm from, we die honorably in battle." His eyes bore into mine as if he were trying to read something and then he walked away. The others got up and left too.

Aisha put her arm around my shoulders and squeezed a bit. "Don't worry about them. It took them a long time before they would even tolerate me at their table. They're all from the same planet. They consider Earthlings to be inferior, just because Earth is of another dimension and not part of the intergalactic conflict their whole galaxy had been involved in." She explained.

I was about to ask another question when Jhael suddenly showed up beside us. "Fiona, I'm here to escort you to the Elders' chamber." He said.

Aisha's whole face lit up. "Hello Jhael." She said.

"Good evening Aisha. I didn't see you this morning. Is everything alright with you?"

"Oh, everything's fine. I've been assigned to Fiona for a few days." I could tell she had a major crush on him.

"Fiona if you please, we mustn't keep the Elders waiting." Insisted Jhael.

I stood up to follow him. "Aisha would you take care of my tray for me?" I asked.

She nodded still making goo-goo eyes at Jhael. "No problem."

I turned to Jhael. "Okay, lead the way."

Without a word he turned and walked away. I hurried after him and once I caught up to him, I slowed down to match his pace. "Are the Elders the rulers of Anthora? Is that why they want to see me?" I asked him."

"The Elders are part of the government; they will explain how the government works to you, and its Anthora Two." Jhael explained.

He was no help at all. I decided that going to the Elders was a good thing. At the very least, I could get a better understanding of why I'm here and what's expected of me. We got on the elevator adjacent to the one Aisha and I got on earlier and then we started moving. I still couldn't tell if we were going up or down. The door opened noiselessly, and I followed Jhael out to a huge hall.

The ceiling was high, and the walls had murals on them. The wall on the right caught my attention. There was a drawing of what I could tell was of a galaxy and there were planets all around. Earth was right there like the beautiful blue and white jewel that it was. The other planets were either a dull green, red and orange with white or red swirls. The next mural depicted a battle of some kind in space. Triangular shaped battleships surrounded a blue and green planet and were firing on it as well as was a mass exodus of spaceships leaving the planet in different directions. The following mural showed the blue and green planet blown to bits, destroyed. I felt profound sadness at this and looked away.

We came to a door which opened as soon as were close enough and we walked in. The room was lit but muted, not soft like when I first arrived, just muted. The set up was like in a science fiction court room with judges seated up high. Three men and two women sat high above me. They were all dressed in hooded robes of different colors.

I stopped in the middle of the room. There were no seats and when I turned to Jhael, I found that he hadn't followed me all the way in, he was standing by the door. He waved and left me. Coward, I thought and faced forward to the Elders.

The one in the red robe lifted his hand to me. "Fiona Brightblade."

"Yes sir." I answered.

"On behalf of my brethren I reclaim you to Anthora Two." He said with a small bow of his head.

"Thank you." I said. I wasn't sure if I could ask my questions yet, so I kept quiet and waited.

"Fiona Brightblade it has come to our attention that you were not allowed to live out your life on Earth, that you were murdered. Is that so?" The one in the green robe asked.

"Yes ma'am. I don't remember much, but I was told that I was a victim of an attack."

"Have you any recollection of the act?" This question came from the one in purple.

"No sir, I don't remember anything prior to waking up in the hospital morgue." Again, I felt leery of admitting that I was a ghost for a while.

I watched them as they whispered to each other. Then the one in orange spoke up. "Fiona Brightblade, will you submit to a recall procedure? It will allow us to see how your life was taken and by whom."

I shrugged. "Will it hurt? I was also curious about my body, I saw the damage done to it, and yet I have no scars, I said showing them my arms. Back at the hospital, I had cuts and bruises all over my body and arms.

"No, my dear, it will not and when we retrieve someone, the body is restored to its original state before death." White robe said. She smiled at me.

"Okay. Before we do this procedure, I would like to ask some questions. Is that possible?"

White robe nodded. "Ask your questions, we will try to put you at ease."

I relaxed a little and blew out my breath. "Since my death seems to be of interest to you and the fact that my brother is also an Anthoran, I'm thinking that he might be in danger of being killed as well. If he is, I want to protect him, and I want to be able to visit him. Can you make that happen?"

Red robe looked across to his fellow Elders and nodded to them. "Fiona Brightblade, there are things that cannot be revealed to you yet while we are investigating your death. Rest assured that we will do this as quickly as possible. Your brother's safety is a concern of ours. One thing we can reveal to you is that your path is of the warrior persuasion. Once we can determine how and why you were killed, your training will begin. It is possible that you will be assigned to protect your brother."

"Excellent! Besides the training, what else am I allowed to do here? I feel like I'm in some sort of dormitory. Is the building that I am housed in a school?"

Purple robe answered. "The dormitory is necessary until you are fully trained and placed in your path. All those in your dormitory are being trained. We have retrieved a great number of Anthorans from different worlds recently. All are being sorted, trained and placed in their paths."

I nodded again. "When do we begin the recall procedure?" I asked.

"Boham will come for you in three days. Take the time to interact with your fellow trainees and acclimate yourself." White robe said.

Then as one, the Elders stood up and walked out through a door behind them.

Jhael appeared suddenly and indicated that I should follow him. We walked back through the corridor with the murals. I looked to the wall opposite me and I saw more murals of what I was beginning to understand was the history of Anthora Two. "Who painted these murals?" I asked Jhael.

He shrugged. "I do not know. They were here when I was retrieved. They are of some of our history. Our home world was destroyed by war. We were able to flee to different worlds. There is an archive of our history in the great library if you are interested in learning more."

"I would like that very much. Can you take me there now?"

Jhael nodded, and he led me to a different elevator from the one we rode on earlier. It started to move, and I wondered again how it worked. "How does the elevator know where we want to go?"

"There are different elevators, and each goes to a specific area or place. The one down the hall from your room goes to the cafeteria and the one across from it goes to the Elder's chambers. The one next to the Elders' chambers goes to the library and there's one other that is used only by the Elders from inside the chambers."

"How long have you been here?"

"I was born on Teah four. My existence there ended in a hunting accident. I was attacked by a wild zoyor. I have been here ten years"

"What's a zoyor?"

"It is like a saber tooth tiger on your Earth."

"You have tame ones?" I asked picturing a playful saber tooth tiger.

Jhael chuckled. "Yes, they are like your lions on Earth."

"How come you know so much about Earth?"

"My path is communication. I don't know much about Earth. I had a crash course in order to qualify to join the retrieval team. Your Earth has many languages that I find fascinating. On my planet, we spoke only one."

The elevator stopped, and the doors whispered open. We stepped off and walked a short distance to another door. This time it was a set of double doors and they opened automatically. I thought that I was starting to get the hang of how things worked here. Sensors on the doors made the doors to rooms or elevators open. At least that's what I thought.

The library was ginormous. "Holy moly I don't know where to begin." I exclaimed in awe.

Jhael laughed. "Everyone who comes here for the first time reacts the same as you. The library is big, but very easily navigated. The Keeper of Records will help you. I must go. Once you are done here. Let the Keeper know, and I will come for you."

"Okay." I watched him leave as the Keeper approached me.

"May I be of service?" She asked. She was medium in height and her jet-black hair was pulled back in a ponytail. Her eyes were brown and shown with intelligence.

"Yes. I wanted to know more of the Anthoran history. Jhael said there was an archive here. Can you direct me to it please?"

"It is this way." She turned to lead the way. There were books and scrolls upon aisles and aisles of shelves. "The aisle on the end contains our history. If you should need clarification, there is a communicator on the table. Ask your question and it will give you direction." She stated in a monotone voice, as if she recited that statement a million times a day.

"Thank you." I said to her back. The shelf held many books. I didn't know where to begin so I picked up the first one and sat down at the table. I hesitated to open the large tome afraid that it might be written in a language I didn't know. Well I guess there was one way to find out.

I opened the book and I wasn't surprised that I could read it. Boham explained that once I was among my own people that I would be able to understand the language. I guess it goes for reading too. The symbols were different from the American alphabet, but I could read the book just fine.

# CHAPTER TWO

Three days later, Boham came for me. He was so early that he had to wait for me to get dressed. That's another thing I needed a handle on. Time. I never carried a watch on Earth. Who needed one when you had a cell phone? Strange that the only thing they didn't duplicate for me was my phone. I'm gonna ask about that.

The medical facility was quite far. He came for me in one of those hover crafts I saw when I first got here. He said they were called Conveyors. I saw where that made sense. The drive took what I estimated to be an hour. As we drove, I watched the world go by. Everything was tall and shiny. After we left the city proper behind, we drove through endless stretches of road with trees on both sides. There were very few Conveyors on the rode we were on. There wasn't much else to see and the novelty of riding in the Conveyor had worn off.

The medical facility was bigger than any hospital I had ever seen. I really wasn't on Earth anymore, I thought. I kinda wished that this was all a dream and I'd wake up to my sister banging on the bathroom door for Jr. to hurry up.

Boham parked in an underground garage and we took an elevator up. I couldn't tell what floor we were going to. Boham spoke our destination. He simply said, 'Recall Station' and the elevator doors closed, and we were on our way.

Once off the elevator, I stayed close to Boham. The recall station was bustling. Men and women dressed in metallic tan jumpsuits were either sitting at a workstation or standing in front of one. The clicking sound of the computers and that of those other machines were constant. What stood out to me was that some of the men and women were truly aliens. Boham had to pull me along as I kept stopping to gawk at blue haired people, green or tentacled people. I made a mental note to go back to the library. I hadn't gotten far in my reading. The first book I took off the shelf was about some animal lost forever after the war. I asked the communicator on the table where I should start, and it directed me to another shelf. I read about two pages and had to quit. My eyes just wouldn't stay open. I called for Jhael to come for me and I didn't even want to hang out with Aisha. I just wanted to go to bed.

"Fiona Brightblade?" I was so glad this was a human asking for me. I didn't quite know how I would've reacted to someone blue haired or with tentacles asking for me. I raised my hand. The attendant beckoned to me and Boham waved me off.

"I'll be back for you when you're done." He said.

I followed the attendant to the exam room. The room was dimly lit and all I could see was a chair that resembled the ones back on Earth at the dentist office. On the walls were big screened monitors and standing beside the chair was a technician. "Hello." I said.

"Fiona Brightblade, please sit here." He said pointing to the chair.

My heart began to pound in my chest. I was suddenly afraid. I shook my head. "I'm nervous." I told him.

"That is quite understandable, but I can assure you that the procedure is perfectly safe." Said Elder White robe. I don't know where she came from, but I was glad she was there. She smiled at me as I settled myself onto the chair.

As soon as I settled in, the attendant approached me with a skullcap with electrodes which he placed on my head. White robe continued reassuring me with her presence. As soon as the cap was adjusted onto my head, I began to feel relaxed. The chair started to tilt backwards until I was almost reclining.

I felt so relaxed that I didn't feel the pin prick of the injection the technician gave me. "What is your name?" He asked a moment later.

"Fiona Brightblade." I couldn't help but answer.

"Good. How old are you?"

"I am twenty years old." Again, I had to answer truthfully.

"Do you remember the night of the party?"

"Yes, it was Friday night."

Then all at once I was there. At the party. Donna dumped me for Bill. He was the one who invited us. We were at his apartment. I watched as she danced with him. She had a drink in her hand, and she looked like she was having a blast. The music was nice, and I swayed to it until this guy approached me. He asked me to dance and I nodded. I walked away when the music changed to something else. I was hot, the apartment didn't have air conditioning. I saw a punch bowl on the counter in the kitchen and I went to get a drink.

The guy I danced with followed me into the kitchen. There was a couple in the kitchen kissing and groping each other. I ignored them. I ladled a cupful of punch, took a sip and gagged. It was pure alcohol. I spit it back into the cup and dumped it in the sink. The guy asked if I wanted a soda instead and reached for one in the fridge. I thanked him and took it from him.

"Hey, do you wanna smoke or something?" He asked me when we were back in the living room. He held up a joint to show me.

I shook my head. "No, I have to study later." I told him. He said cool and walked away. It was then that I noticed little pockets of people all over the living room smoking or snorting. What kind of party did Donna invite me to? I looked around searching for her because then I wanted to leave. I spied her in the corner with Bill. He was handing her a straw and was holding a book with lines on it. I couldn't believe it; Donna was doing cocaine.

I didn't care if she got angry at me or felt embarrassed. "Donna I want to leave, are you coming?" I asked her as soon as I was close enough.

She stared at me through glazed eyes. "What? Aren't you having fun?"

"No, I'm not. Are you coming or not?" I insisted.

"No, I'll call you tomorrow okay?"

"Fine." I answered, and I turned to leave.

I gave her a final glance as I walked out of the house. I'm pissed because she drove us and now, I needed to take a cab, bus or train. I wasn't sure which I'd need yet. Suddenly, the guy from the party was walking beside me.

"Hey, I saw you leave are you okay?" He asked.

"Yeah, I'm not cool with all that back there." I told him.

"Do you have a way of getting home? I can give you a ride." He offered.

"Nah, it's cool. I can find my own way home." I pulled out my phone and scrolled to see who I could talk into picking me up. My last resort was to call my dad, but I didn't want to hear the lecture I was sure to get from him.

The guy was still walking beside me. "It's cool if you don't trust me, but it's late and there are no buses around here."

"Can you take me as far as the closest bus stop?" I asked.

He smiled. "Yeah I can do that." He pointed to a car across the street. "That's my car over there."

We crossed the street to it, and he unlocked the door for me. I got in and immediately feel uncomfortable. There was another guy in the back seat. "Hi." I said.

"Howdy." He replied.

"I see you've met John. My name is Buck. The bus stop is about four blocks away okay?"

"Yeah, okay." Four blocks away wasn't that big a deal, I thought.

Buck drove at least ten blocks to a park. He pulled into a parking space and got out, then he came around to the passenger side. He pulled the door open and yanked me out. "Hey, what gives?" I screeched.

John got out also. It was then I realized that I was in trouble. Buck grabbed me in a choke hold and dragged me toward the park. I tried to scream but his hand was clamped tightly over my mouth. John followed behind us. He walked kinda funny and he was whistling a tune I didn't recognize.

When we got further into the park, John walked around me and Buck in a circle. "I've been on this stinking planet five miserable years searching for your kind. What were the odds that you'd just show up at our party playing right into our hands?" He asked no one in particular.

"We could smell you the minute you walked into the house." Buck said in my ear. I struggled but he was holding me tightly. Besides, the knife that suddenly appeared at my throat made me think twice.

John raised his arms high above his head and stretched. I heard a ripping sound and I stared in horror at him. His skin fell off clothes and all to the ground. I struggled harder. John wasn't human, and neither was Buck who also dropped his human body suit.

I felt adrenaline course through my veins and also felt a sense of calm. I took a deep breath to gather up my strength. Then I bent down pulling Buck with me. I could feel the knife as it cut at my throat, but I didn't care. Buck's hold on the knife and my arms loosened and I quickly turned to kick with my knee. I didn't get him where I wanted to, but he was having trouble breathing. I pushed him off to stand quickly and angled my body away from John's sudden lunge. I turned around and sent him flying with a kick to his back.

"Oh, you're gonna wish you hadn't done that Anthoran scum." Buck said behind me. I jerked toward him and he shot me with his weapon. Three projectiles landed in my abdomen, and chest. I could feel the blades moving inside me, ripping and tearing at my insides. I dropped to my knees trying to control the pain. It was then John came up behind me and slit my throat. The monitors overhead went dark.

I started screaming and kicking. The attendant and one other held me down while, another injected me with a sedative and then I knew nothing.

I woke up in my bed. At first, I thought I must've had a bad dream. I jumped out of bed and headed for my bedroom door. Across the hall, on my sister's bedroom door is a poster of Jack Sparrow. If it's there, then this was a horrible nightmare and I'm safe. I yanked the door open and there was a blank wall and no door. I shut my door quickly. Shit, it was not a dream. Those horrible creatures killed me. They knew what I really was.

I looked around quickly feeling like I wasn't alone in the room. "Get a grip Fiona, you've got this." I told myself. A knock on the door startled me and I gripped the doorknob hard and opened it. I nearly melted with relief; it was Aisha.

"Hey are you okay? I came to check on you because you missed breakfast, but you weren't here." She said.

"Boham took me to the medical facility. I was out of it when I came back. What else did I miss?" I asked her. I wasn't sure if I could trust her with what I've just learned yet.

"Are you sick?" She asked. There was genuine concern on her face.

"No, I wanted a tour and freaked out when I saw some of the others. I wasn't expecting that. I must've fainted or something."

Aisha grinned at me. "My first time seeing them, I screamed my head off. They had to sedate me. That's what they probably did to you too. Anyway, since you're feeling better, we can go out if you'd like."

I pulled her all the way into my room. "Hell yeah. I want to see everything."

"Great, until you're given your path and finish your training, you pretty much get a free pass. Everything is on them. I can take you shopping if you want. Some of the Anthoran fashions aren't too bad."

"Do I need to change?" I asked smoothing down my sweater. I wasn't sure what to wear earlier and figured I couldn't go wrong wearing a sweater with my jeans.

"You're fine. Come on, let's go." She led the way out of the dorm. Once we got outside, I felt a bit more relaxed. I realized that I was feeling cooped up.

"Do you wanna walk or take a Conveyor?"

"Is it far?"

"No."

"If you don't mind, I wanna walk. I didn't get to see much before. What did you mean by everything I get is on them, who's them?"

"The Anthoran government silly. What did you think I meant?"

"I don't know. Hey everybody keeps talking about paths, what is it?"

"You know how on Earth you go to school and learn a trade? Well it's like that. A trade is your path."

"Okay, that makes sense. What's your path?"

"Mine is healer. In a million years, I wouldn't have thought to go anywhere near medicine back on Earth. But here, all I can think about is ways to make people feel better. Did you find out what your path is yet?"

"My path is warrior." I said quietly.

"Oh, wow Fiona, that's mega cool!"

"It is?"

"Hell yeah. Warriors are revered here. They are the protectors of our people. Once you're trained, you get to go into outer space on patrol."

"Those guys we sat with the other night, were they warriors too?" I've been here almost a week and they were still snubbing me.

Aisha started to laugh. "They acted like they were big shots telling you that you died a dishonorable death, but here on Anthora Two, they aren't warriors. They are teachers and communication technicians."

I realized we'd been standing in front of our building just talking and wasting time. I grabbed Aisha's hand and started walking. "Don't you find it funny that none of us are doing what we did on the other worlds? I mean I was a student in college, but here they're telling me that I am a warrior.

"They explained it this way. On Earth our true nature was suppressed. Once we got here, it emerged. That's why we can suddenly speak and read our native language." She explained.

I nodded as I remembered when my essence returned to my body. Jhael spoke to me, but I couldn't understand what he was saying. A few minutes later I suddenly could. I hadn't thought it was strange then. I was still in shock. I was in a draw, cold and naked. I wanted to believe that all of this was really happening and that I was on another world, but I still felt that I should resist. Aisha showing up wearing Earth clothes just like mine, and her being able to answer all my questions was just too perfect. I kept thinking that something's up.

I could see other Anthorans as we walked; just people strolling and enjoying the balmy weather. They all seemed humanoid and normal. The buildings were all the same until a few blocks later. The scene changed, and I tried to take it all in. The shopping center, for that's what it was looked like something I've seen on television. Blue haired people were in the shops and some were outside the shops hawking for customers to come see their wares.

"Their path is customer service but some of them follow other paths. They are excellent shopkeepers and are very successful at selling." Aisha explained when she realized that I kept staring at them.

"What do they sell?" I asked.

"Come on and I'll show you." She grabbed my arm to lead me into one of the shops. At this point, I believed again that this wasn't Earth. The shop Aisha dragged me into turned out to be a restaurant. Behind the counters were more blue haired people wearing shimmering aprons. The food looked like nothing I've ever seen. In a steaming pot, something white churned and I glanced away quickly.

"What is that?" I asked Aisha.

"That's one of their delicacies. It's called Engee. It's kinda like tofu back on Earth. They are from a planet called Embeta Twelve, and they are vegetarians."

I looked at her. "How do you know all this?"

Aisha smiled widely at me. "It's part of my training as a healer. It is important that I know about all of our Anthoran refugees. I learn about their anatomy, so I can best treat them when they come to me."

We walked out of the restaurant and she led me to a clothing store. This time, human looking people greeted us. There were racks and racks of clothes. Some of the clothes didn't make any sense to me. Aisha explained that some Anthorans have more than four limbs, hence the extra sleeves and pant legs. I looked around trying to spot anyone with four arms or legs but didn't see anyone.

"Those clothes are for the Nozans. They are subterranean dwellers, very gentle people but hard to look at."

"I really need to get back to the library. I've got a lot to learn. I kinda understand that when the original Anthorans evacuated the planet, they had to find new worlds to call home. So whatever planet they landed on, they had to integrate in order to survive. It explains why we are all different on the outside but the same on the inside."

Aisha patted me on the back. "You're getting it!"

"I think I am." I admitted.

I bought a couple pairs of pants, a pair of boots that look like reinforced Timberlands from Earth and a dress. The dress was not something you'd find anywhere but on this planet. It was white, just above the knees in length and had bell shaped sleeves. What made the dress so cool was that it changed colors. It was a mood dress!

By the time we headed back to the dorm, it was starting to get dark and I was hungry. "Do you have classes after dinner?" I asked.

"No, I went to class today when I didn't see you."

"If you're not doing anything, can you come hang out with me? Or I can come to your room too." I suggested.

"We can go to my room. I have something to show you."

"Yeah, what?"

"You're just gonna have to wait and see. Come on, we don't want to miss dinner."

The atmosphere was different than the previous evening. We sat at the same table and this time the others were friendlier. The one who tried to shame me the other evening greeted me. "I would like to apologize for what I said to you. I am honored to meet you, Fiona Brightblade. My friends are Mingh, Druktar, Lylah, and I am Gorke. We are from Aveng Three."

I waved at them. "Pleased to meet you all. How long have you been here?"

"We have been here seven years. My friends and I were soldiers on Aveng Three. We were all killed in battle." Gorke informed me.

Aisha did not lie when she said that the Anthorans revered warriors. Gorke was a different person than the one I'd met a few nights ago. "How did you find out that I was a warrior?" I asked out of curiosity.

Gorke looked around quickly as if he wasn't supposed to know what he's about to tell me. "I overheard my former teacher talking with Master Tulle. When I heard your name, I started to pay attention. He said that you will be training with Master Tulle. He only trains warriors."

"You were all warriors on your world. Don't you want to continue doing that now?" I asked.

"Druktar, and Mingh are teachers. Lylah and I are communications techs. As soon as we came to this planet, we knew exactly what we were meant to do."

I smiled at them and tried to eat quickly. I was starting to feel like a bug under a microscope. Everyone was staring.

After dinner, Aisha and I rushed out of the cafeteria. She steered me to her room which was literally two doors down from mine in number seven. Her room was very girlie. The girl really liked her pink. She smiled widely at me when she opened the cabinet part of her bureau. There was a television set in it. I couldn't believe my eyes. "You've got a TV? What can you watch on it?" I asked.

"Somehow, they've managed to have all my favorite shows on it." She gushed. She clicked it on, and I could see the Danny Phantom cartoon show on.

"You've been here five years; don't you get tired of watching re-runs? I mean you're not getting new seasons, are you?"

Aisha clapped her hands and nodded. "Yes, incredible right? Somehow, Anthoran technology can tap into Earth's satellites and broadcast whatever I want to watch. Isn't that great?"

I looked at the TV and shook my head. "Why then couldn't I have my cell phone?" I asked her. I was getting angry. I guess I burst her bubble because Aisha stopped smiling and clicked the TV off.

"I had a cellphone on Earth too, but it didn't cross over. Besides, how was I going to use it here?" She reasoned.

"Aisha, do you mind if we do this tomorrow evening? I want to get some reading done. I want to go back to the library." She nodded, and we left her room.

From our dorm area, Aisha took a different route to the library than the one Jhael took with me. This place was so confusing. I was afraid that I would never be able to go anywhere without an escort. I made a mental note to ask for a map.

When we got there, she told me that she couldn't stay and left me with the Keeper of Records. I told the Keeper that I wanted to continue reading the Anthoran history. She nodded and led the way back to the history section. I steered clear of the animal book and picked up the early history of Anthora. I was amazed again that the words I was reading so fluently were not the alphabet I was used to. They were symbols, but my brain automatically deciphered them.

Anthorans were a race of peace-loving, highly evolved and cultured people. They originated in a galaxy billions of miles from anything known on Earth. This planet that I found myself on now, is Anthora Two as the original was destroyed in the galactic war between Anthora and a species known as Froagans. This race resembled what Earth scientists called Greys, only these Froagans were blood red. It is not known if they have a home world, but they planet hop and strip them of all their natural resources and enslave its inhabitants. In a last-ditch effort to rid the planet of their enemies, the ancestral Anthoran warriors fought back and won a grand victory by killing their leader. A bloody war ensued and the Froagans called for reinforcements. Their battleships came in from every direction, surrounding the planet. Anthora was given an ultimatum. They had to surrender, or the planet would be destroyed.

Unbeknownst to the Froagans, the Anthoran government had been formulating their plan B. While the battle waged between the bands of rebels and the Froagans, the Space Corps managed to gather all the planets' citizens and blasted them out into space in every direction possible. This was a great undertaking that took years of preparation. The Froagans occupied the planet for twelve long years and during that time, the Anthoran government had gathered all their greatest minds together to formulate a plan of freedom and escape.

In the book, I found a picture of the murals I saw on the walls when I went to speak with the Elders. The book doesn't give a numerical year. Instead, it stated that our people were saved during the reign of Lothar the Great. In a different book, I read about the plan to reunite the peoples of Anthora. The scientists were able to inject each original refugee with a gene preserver they'd devised. This enabled the species to survive no matter where they landed and no matter what other species, they inter-mingled with. This injection also enabled each person with foreknowledge of Anthora.

This was a lot to take in. I assumed that hundreds of thousands of years have passed between the war, the exodus and this reclaiming project. In yet another book I read more. The Froagans dealt a damaging blow to the planet rendering it inhospitable to life. While they thought the planet was dying, the Froagans gave chase to the fleeing populace, giving the government a chance to escape themselves with the charge of finding a new home. They were also able to save animals, and plants indigenous to the planet also.

Anthora Two, was a planet three-dimensional jumps away from the original. It was not ideal, but the scientists thought they could make it work. The air had too much sulfur, but they labored to eliminate it. Two thousand years later, the planet had been transformed into the paradise that it is now. From all the scientific jargon, I deduced that they found a way to terraform the planet. Anthorans have been reclaimed for thousands of years since.

I laid the book down trying to imagine how hard it was in the beginning. I imagined them wearing life support suits and erecting habitats to live in while they worked. I also reasoned that while they worked to make the planet habitable, they must've undergone some physical changes as well. The planet wasn't completely uninhabited. There was a humanoid species living on it. Their physiology was different from the Anthorans. They had gills along their necks and throat and noses on their faces. They lived on both land and water. It stood to reason that since the refugees integrated with whatever species they encountered, that these scientists did also. They managed to subdue them and took control which made it easier to take over the planet. That idea didn't make me feel good, but I guess survival of the fittest came into play there.

It was getting late, so I returned the books to their shelves and headed back toward the entrance of the library. Coming to the library earlier, I memorized the way. I should be able to get back to my room if I did it in reverse.

The keeper of records appeared in front of me suddenly. "Fiona Brightblade, did you find our history enlightening? Is there anything else I can help you with?" She asked.

"Yes, it was very enlightening and no I am through for the day thank you."

"Shall I summon someone to escort you to your dorm room?"

I shook my head. "I can get back on my own. Good night." Without acknowledging my words, she turned and walked away. When I got back to my room, I showered quickly and got into bed.

My brain wouldn't shut off, it was going a mile a minute. It replayed my assassination repeatedly. I realized that the Froagans were hunting surviving Anthorans. If I was found out and killed, then my brother was in danger of being killed also. Suddenly, I found myself committing fully to my path as warrior. I will fight to save my brother and I will fight to protect Anthorans.

The next morning, I rushed to get to breakfast early. I didn't want to miss seeing Jhael. I wanted to speak with the Elders again. I was eager to start my warrior training.

At our table, I found what I've decided was my crew. I greeted everyone quickly and ate while keeping a look out for Jhael.

"Hey slow down, what's the hurry?" Asked Aisha.

"I need to find Jhael. I want to see the Elders again."

"Oh. I guess you didn't know. Jhael finished his training. He is now working at the Space Corps." She supplied.

"No, I didn't know. I thought we were all trainees." I looked across at Mingh, Druktar, Gorke and Lylah. "Are you all finished with your training as well?"

Gorke nodded. "Yes. Since Jhael is new to the Space Corps, he must undergo additional training in the use of our computers." He explained.

"Do any of you know how I can make an appointment to see the Elders?"

Aisha touched my arm to get my attention. "You can put a request in at the Library. Why do you want to see them?" She asked interested.

I looked at her skeptically. It's weird questions like that, that make me suspicious of this whole 'you're on another planet thing'. "I have more questions and I wanted to know how long before I start my training." I explained guardedly.

"That's easy. They usually give you a few days to acclimate. Then you get a physical done and afterwards your training starts. I'm almost finished with my training. It was suspended so that I could spend time with you to help you since we are both from Earth." Aisha answered.

"Okay. I still would like to speak with the Elders again. Oh, before I forget, where would I get a map of the area, I don't want to keep you from your duties. I'd like to get around on my own."

"The Library is where you want to go. Almost all of the information you need is available there." Aisha said and stood up. "I have to go to my final class. Will I see you later?"

I nodded at her. "Yeah sure. Have a great day." I watched as the others got up to leave. I quickly dumped my tray and headed for the Library. Once there, the Keeper gave me a map when I asked for one. The elevators were situated on ends of every area forming a box shape. Each one goes to a different municipal building in the city except the medical center. The elevators either go up, down, across, and underground. They also space jumped. If I wanted to go across town to the Agricultural center, I could get there in a matter of minutes. The dorm was central to almost everywhere in the city.

I asked the Keeper to help me make an appointment to see the Elders and she showed me how. She then told me that I could either wait for the appointment or come back later for it. I decided to do some more reading while I waited.

This time I wanted to know the meaning of the different colors the Elders wore and who they were. There was only one book on the Elders. Of course, the ones I met weren't the original, because they too were reclaimed from other worlds as they became available.

Each robe signified a part of government. Red robes governed matters of security, which included the space corps, warriors and policing the populace. Green robes governed the environment. They oversaw power, such as electricity, and water. Purple robes saw to agriculture. All manner of foods was grown or manufactured by that department. Orange robes dealt with city affairs, such as schooling, and social concerns like housing and entertainment. White robes were all about the health of the populace and other scientific matters.

I guess when I finished with my training that I would be wearing red. I can't wait to be able to travel back to Earth. I wanted to make sure that my brother was safe, and I wanted to find those bastards that killed me. Buck and John have a lot to answer for. I had a life that I loved. I was going to be a Biochemist. I loved science or, so I thought. Now, all I want to do is kick Froagan butt. My family was everything to me and yet except for my brother, I don't feel any emotion for my parents or my sister. I think of them as acquaintances.

The Keeper announced that the Elders would see me right away. I got up quickly, put the book away and followed her to the chambers. At the door, she nodded to me and left. The door to the chambers opened and I walked in expecting them to be all high and mighty like the last time sitting up high. This time however, they were seated at a table in their robes and at my level.

Red robe stood up and extended his hand to me. I walked up to the table and placed my hand in his. "I'm Elder Chaktar, I oversee our planets' security, space corps, and warrior departments of our government. Elder Edwards in the green robe is also from Earth, she governs our environmental concerns and its needs. Wearing the purple robe is our Elder Ullah from Teah Four. He oversees the agricultural government. Elder Bitka wearing the orange robe is from the Detlam Belt system. He governs our day to day city life. Finally, we have in white Elder Sim. She governs our health care system and scientific research; she is from Embeta Twelve."

Each Elder raised their hand as they were introduced. I shook hands with them and tried not to feel intimidated. "Nice to meet you." I said respectfully.

"You made an appointment to see us. What can we do for you?" Elder Sim asked.

"Well, I wanted to know if you had come to any conclusions about my murder and I also wanted to know when my training starts. I am very worried about my brothers' safety."

Elder Chaktar nodded to me. "Warrior Brightblade, after reviewing your recall results, we are convinced that you were singled out. We are telling you this in the strictest confidence. Do we have your sworn oath that what we discuss here in these chambers will not be leaked to others? These matters are very sensitive."

I nodded. "Yes sir, I promise I will not tell anyone."

"Very well. You are among a group of newly retrieved Anthorans who have been murdered by the Froagans. As you know by now, we were at one time at war with them. It seems to us that they have figured out that we still exist on other worlds and have been hunting us. That is what happened to you and the others. We have erased the memories of the others for fear of the news spreading to the populace. We want to avoid a panic."

"I understand. Why didn't you erase my memory?"

"That's because you are a warrior, dear." Said Elder Sim. "This is information you need to know."

"Okay so when do I start my training?"

Elder Chaktar smiled. "Quite soon actually."

"How long will my training last?"

"Your fighting skills are a bit rusty, but we will soon rectify that. You also must go through weapons training and other forms of combat. I must say this in your favor, of the other warriors we've retrieved, you have the most skill." Elder Chaktar stated proudly.

"This afternoon, we will require that you have a full physical. Boham will come for you after lunch." Elder Sim said. She pulled down her hood to expose her blue hair.

"Once you are finished with your training, come see me about your new quarters." Elder Bitka added. Then as a unit they stood up and left the room through a door suddenly appearing behind them. Clear that they were done with me, I turned to leave out the door I came in.

# CHAPTER THREE

I went back to my room with a reeling head. I was right in my assumption that we were being hunted. They acted so calm about it. Weren't they worried that the Froagans would find us again? Weren't they afraid that war could be coming?

I couldn't sit still, so I pulled out my map and found my way to the shopping center. I walked aimlessly going from shop to shop. Nothing interested me until I saw a shop with a symbol I recognized. It was in one of the books I read in the library about the war. It was the symbol for weapons. The moment I walked into the shop, I felt at home. I even recognized some of the weapons and their use. Weird. The shop keeper was humanoid with silver hair, and she wore a red band on her arm. I asked her what the band was for, and she told me that it was a warrior's band. She introduced herself as Bel and is an officer in the Anthoran Defense Ground Division.

"My path is warrior as well. Am I able to buy a weapon here?" I asked her.

"I know who you are Fiona Brightblade. Once you finish your training, a weapon will be waiting for you here." She answered.

"How do you know who I am?" I asked her. It was getting annoying.

"The Elders didn't tell you?" Bel countered.

"No. What is there to tell?" I asked her.

"I do not know if it is my place to tell you." She explained.

"Tell me what?" I asked. Now my suspicions were coming to light, I thought. Something was going on involving me and no one wanted to talk. I got that vibe from the Elders, Aisha and the Aveng Three crew.

"Please, I cannot tell you much. As soon as you start your training it will become clear. All of us who are of the warrior path are special, but you are a Brightblade, you are the one we've been waiting for. That's all I can say."

I nodded at her. She seemed in distress over this big secret. "Is it the reason why everyone seems to know who I am?"

"Yes. It has been foretold that you would come. I cannot say more."

"Okay, I guess I can live with that. I know exactly where I'm going to get my answers. Thank you, you don't have to worry about what you've told me."

"I hope to see you again." She said as I walked out of the shop.

I nodded at her again and left the store. I was going to the library once more, that place was starting to feel like home away from home, I'm there so much. I believe that I am on another planet, but there is something else going on and it involved my murder. When I got to the library, the keeper of records met me with that irritating smile of hers. I wanted to ignore her, but I stopped myself. I told her that I wished to continue with the history of Anthora.

I seemed to remember mention of folklore in one of the books and I asked the communicator and it directed me. I sifted through all the legends until I found what I was looking for. It was the legend of the warrior who killed the Froagans' leader. There was a picture of her. I stared at her face and couldn't look away. She was me! Our hair was the same rich auburn, and we looked the same. Her name was Leena of the Brightblade clan. She was the warrior who killed Oftha The Vile. The Froagan nation suffered a terrific blow when he was killed, giving the Anthorans a chance for escape. The scientists enhanced her genes when they sent her away with the others. It got me thinking. They've been waiting for a Brightblade ever since. They knew that eventually they would be found out, evidenced by the subsequent assassinations of Anthorans found on other worlds. They've been waiting for a hero.

What did they think the Brightblade line had that other warriors didn't? What was the enhancement? I closed the book and stood up. After putting it back on the shelf, I called for the keeper.

"How may I be of service?" She asked.

"I want to know how to tell time here." I told her.

"Once you start your training, a chronograph will be assigned to you."

"Why haven't I been assigned one before?"

"A chronograph is only assigned to trainees."

I looked down her arm and saw that she was wearing one. "Are you a trainee?" I asked feeling annoyed.

She smiled and raised her arm to show me her wrist. "I completed my training a long time ago. A chronograph is given to a trainee as a sign that they will soon be a vital part of society."

"Okay, can you tell me what time lunch will be served?"

"The cafeteria will be serving lunch in twenty minutes." She answered.

"Thank you, I'd better hurry then."

I went back to my room to change. I had a physical scheduled for after lunch. I dressed in one of the outfits I'd bought on my first trip to the shopping center. It was a black pant with a red blouse. I was always fond of the color red. Now I know why. It was the color of my path. This time I wore white sneakers to complete the outfit. I threw my hair into a bun and I was done.

Lunch was a mixture of vegetables and a meat that resembled chicken. The first couple of days, the cafeteria catered to my Earthling preference but today, I had to choose wisely. The other stuff they had didn't look like anything I recognized. I chose a bottle of water since I didn't see any juice.

Aisha and the others were already seated, and they all greeted me enthusiastically.

"Hey guys." I said and took a seat.

"Hello, did you find out when you start your training?" Gorke asked me.

"Yes, I start soon. This afternoon I go for my physical."

"That is wonderful. I wish you the best of luck with your training." Druktar said sincerely.

"Thank you. I'm really excited about it." I admitted with a smile.

"You will be moving out of the dorm soon. Most of the warrior trainees are housed in the barracks on base." Jhael said as he sat down to join us.

"Hello Jhael, how's your computer training going?" I watched as Aisha sat up straighter and pushed her chest out. I wanted to laugh.

"It is going well. My trainer tells me that I am advancing quickly." He answered with a smile. Then he turned to Aisha. "I suppose you will be moving out to the Medical Facility soon."

"It was mentioned but I don't know when. I was told that housing will be near the facility." She answered.

"Are we all moving out then?" I asked.

"Most of us graduates usually move to be near where we work. The dorms are for the newly retrieved and trainees."

"Oh, I guess we won't be seeing much of each other then. You are the only people I know here."

"We can get together after work to socialize. Although the cafeteria is always open to us, we can eat elsewhere, or at each other's units." Aisha said.

"That would be great. It would be a wonderful way to unwind after a long day of work." I said.

"Let's wait until we all know where we'll be housed to make plans." Jhael said, and the others nodded in agreement.

"I'm afraid I must go now. Boham should be coming for me soon. If you all are available later, we can meet for dinner here." They agreed and I left them.

Boham was just arriving to the dorm when I came down the hallway. I waved at him. "Just give me a few minutes to brush my teeth and then I'll be ready."

"Take your time. Our conveyor isn't here yet."

"Oh, in that case come in and sit while we wait." I told him.

"Thank you."

I had a chair in my room, and I told him to sit while I rushed to brush my teeth and used the bathroom. As I was brushing my hair, Boham's chronograph chirped. He stood up saying that the conveyor was outside waiting for us. He left to go meet it and I hurried to join him outside.

The conveyor had no driver and I asked what happened to the driver. He said that conveyors can be remotely sent and driven. He likes to drive so he requested for one to be sent for his use.

Once we were on our way, I saw my chance to get some more answers concerning my famous ancestor. "Boham, what can you tell me of my ancestor Leena Brightblade? I read about her in the library today."

Boham chuckled. "We weren't supposed to tell you anything about her, even if you asked, but I suspect that you know some of the story. The Library only gives you a small portion of it. Leena Brightblade was a brilliant warrior. She was a general and in command of several fleets of space fighters. Her strategies were magnificent. Being a female of our species made her precious. She could carry the next generation of Le'ak wielders. So, when that final battle got too hot, another was sent in her place to keep her from harm.

Her first officer was sent in to finish the job, but he failed. His ship was destroyed. She got angry and commandeered a ship against orders and took to the skies. We had intel that Oftha was on the mothership and it was coming into range. Singlehandedly, she fired on the ship and destroyed it and everyone onboard." Boham recited.

"I don't understand, if her actions caused the Froagans to destroy the planet, how was she a hero?"

"The Froagans lost the only legitimate leader of their kind at the time. He was young and un-mated. He had no heir. Losing him, left them without leadership. It gave us time to re-group and organize our escape. By the time they had gotten an interim leader in power, we were ready. When they fired on the planet, none was left because the scientists had already implemented our escape plan. One thing about Leena's descendants was that they carried not only her genes but her superior intellect and strategy making abilities and the Le'ak. That is why every time we retrieve a warrior; we test them to see if those abilities will emerge."

"What is the Le'ak?" I asked. This special ability kept popping up and I was no closer to learning what it was.

"The scientists never said. It is a knowledge that is lost to us. We only know that only a select few of our men and women had the Le'ak. In thousands of years, you are the only warrior named Brightblade. Your clan is revered, and your brother is as valuable as you are." He answered.

"Do you know what the test involves?" Now I was worried that I'd disappoint everybody.

"No, I do not. The Elders believe that the only true way to determine that the abilities have emerged is to have the candidate be clueless of the history. Since you have cleverly discovered most of her history, it will be interesting to see how you will do on the test."

We drove in silence for a while. I needed to think. Even with all that I learned of Leena, I felt that I still didn't know much about her. She was a skilled warrior, who had some sort of superhuman ability. Boham mentioned that she was able to carry the next generation who could also have abilities.

"Boham, is there anything you can tell me about this special test?"

"I do not know much. What I do know is that you will be tested medically to see if you are healthy but as of the other, I am sorry."

"Thank you. I appreciate all that you've told me. I won't let on that I know anything more than I've read in the library."

"We're here." Boham said. He was all business again.

Once on the elevator, Boham commanded the elevator to take us to the Testing Center. The elevator went up and when we stepped off, Boham led me to the waiting room. There were two others in the room too.

"Hello." I greeted the man and woman sitting opposite me.

The woman answered, and the man inclined his head at me. Before I could say anything more, someone came for them. The room was a metallic yellow and the walls had friendly posters about exercising and diets to stay healthy.

After what I assumed was at least twenty minutes, I became bored and stopped reading the posters. I tried not to feel nervous; I mean I've had physicals before and apart from the blood tests, everything else was painless. What made me nervous however, was this special test that was supposed to bring out special abilities. What were they? Did I have super cool powers like telekinesis? Or maybe mindreading?

The door opened again. "Fiona Brightblade?" A woman dressed in a white uniform asked.

I stood up and walked over to her. "Yes, that's me."

"Follow me please." She was serious and never looked back to see if I was following. I followed her to an exam room. This time there's a bed in it and a crap load of instruments and machines. They looked harmless enough, I hoped.

"Fiona Brightblade, I require that you disrobe and to put this gown on. Take your shoes off as well. Once you have disrobed, make yourself comfortable on the bed. Master Physician Bolka will be in shortly to conduct the physical." Then she left the room.

"Aren't we the professional one." I said to the empty room. Mere minutes after I'd complied, the Master Physician walked into the room.

"Fiona Brightblade, welcome to Anthora Two. I will be conducting the medical part of the physical and then someone will come to escort you to the next portions of your tests." All the while he was speaking, he was scanning me with one instrument after another. The bed suddenly grew warm and on the monitors above me, I could see my skeleton. Then I could see all my veins, arteries and capillaries. Master Physician examined every inch of me. The only test that I remotely compared to that of Earth was the blood test and that was done robotically, and surprisingly painless. When he was finished, he stepped back with a bright smile. "Fiona Brightblade, as far as I can see, everything seems to be in order. The blood test will take a few more minutes but you may get dressed now." He left the room with an even brighter smile on his face.

As soon as I was dressed again, he came back with Elder Chaktar. I waved at him and he acknowledged me with a slight nod. "Fiona Brightblade I would like to be the first to formally inform you that all of the physician's tests came back satisfactory. Now if you will follow me, we will go on to the next phase of your tests." He said all businesslike.

I jumped off the bed and waved goodbye at the physician. He waved back and he had that adoring look everyone wore on their faces when they met me or heard my name.

Elder Chaktar took me to an elevator. He didn't say anything, but we were moving. He wasn't wearing a robe but a red military uniform. On his left shoulder were bands and symbols. It's funny that I knew what they meant.

"You're looking at my bands and insignias. Do you know what they are?" He asked proudly.

"You are Captain of the Air Corp Command, sir." I tried to answer meekly.

"Good, your understanding of warrior stations is growing. Now we will test your skill at space combat and strategy. Then you will spar with one of the advanced trainees." He told me.

The elevator opened to what could only be a space command station. I've only seen one on television back on Earth. There were techs at every station, and they all looked up at us when we entered the room and then they all scrambled to stand at attention.

"At ease. This is trainee Fiona Brightblade. She will be commanding for our simulation this afternoon." Elder Chaktar said. Then he turned to me. "The ready room is this way. I will give you a moment to prepare and to look over the scenario after which your test will begin."

I followed him quietly. I get that we were going to play at war. I didn't understand why this early on though. I thought if I was going to be tested, that it would be after some training. Throwing me to the wolves like this seemed rather presumptuous to me. What were they expecting?

"You will sit here and study the scenario, then you will come out to the simulation room and take command. Do you understand?" He asked.

I looked him straight in the eye and nodded. "Yes sir, I do." I put my hand out to take the tablet from him. He watched me as I read and then left me alone.

The scenario was straight forward. I have a fleet of fighters and we were 'under attack'. The scenario was to fight and destroy the enemy without losing any of my fleet. My fleet consisted of ten ships with captains on each. My goal was to lead them into battle with a strategy of my own devising and then bring them home alive. My ships were identified by numbers, one through ten. The captains were referred to by the number of the ships they commanded.

I stood up confidently to do battle and walked out of the ready room to the command center. Elder Chaktar's eyes widened in surprise when he saw me come out.

"You are ready?" He asked.

"Yes sir, I am." I answered. "Where is my command center?"

He pointed to the large console he was leaning against. He stepped aside as I pulled the chair to sit at it. Then he watched as I turned it on and activated all my fighters. I looked up at him. "Do I move the fighters myself or will the computer do it as I command it?"

"Each of these men here captain a ship. You speak your command and they will follow." He said of the men sitting at the consoles.

"Cool, let's begin then." I told them.

A big screen opened out in space. My ships were positioned facing the enemy in a straight line across. I commanded my ships to form the eagle formation, while the enemy continued to stay straight across. Behind them was the mothership. They didn't tell me that there would be one. So that's the surprise. Well, okay I thought.

The enemy fired first, and it came close. "Do we have shields?" I asked quickly.

"Yes sir," someone answered.

"Raise them." I commanded.

Multiple volleys struck the shields. "Advance ten kilometers and captains one and two fire on the end ships facing you and calibrate your distance, captains nine and ten do the same" I instructed. I watched as they did what I commanded and of the four shots, three hits true. I tried the same strategy again but this time with odd numbers and I got four hits that time. The enemy tried to compensate by copying our eagle formation. We both started with ten ships; the enemy presenting with their mothership made it eleven, but I was winning. They were down seven ships.

In my mind, I saw the opportunity to hit the mothership and I commanded the captain on ship number four to feint to the left, while the others fired on the ships they faced. When ship four got close enough, I commanded the captain to fire everything at the mothership. A cheer went up when the mothership burst into a ball of flame. I commanded the ships to continue firing until the enemy was destroyed completely. On my console, I helped move the ships into firing positions. They weren't doing it fast enough. When the last ship exploded, I stood up to clap and cheer along with everybody.

"That was most unusual, but impressive. We will keep record of this to teach to the Air Corps." Elder Chaktar said. He smiled but it didn't reach his eyes.

"Thank you, sir what's next?" I asked still feeling the thrill of victory.

"Hand to hand combat. I will take you to Master Tulle." He said and walked away. I hurried to follow him. I could sense his resentment. Wasn't I supposed to do a good job? Men and their egos. I guess they were the same no matter what planet or dimension they're from.

He took me to my next testing site. The arena was big, and the fight ring was well, round. I could see the other trainees sparring. They wore protective gear and red uniforms. I followed Elder Chaktar to the instructor who was shouting at a trainee on technique. "Do not hold back, you must go for the kill!" He was shouting.

"Master Tulle. I have brought our newest trainee for her sparring test. Fiona Brightblade, meet your new instructor, Master Tulle." Elder Chaktar said and he stepped away. I watched him go find a seat to watch. He was sitting next to an Asian man I've never seen before. Elder Chaktar leaned over to whisper something to him and they both laughed.

Master Tulle took my hand in his to welcome me. Then he instructed me to go change and then report back to him. I felt annoyed as I went to go do as I was told. I went to the changing area, where an attendant handed me a uniform and protective pads to change into.

Elder Chaktar seemed to have something against me and now I feel he's hoping to see me taken down a peg or three.

I returned to Master Tulle and he instructed me to put my hair in a ponytail. I do that, then he motions for me to get into the ring.

My opponent was much bigger than me and he was wearing the same uniform as me, but his was black to my red. I studied my opponent to see if I could detect any weakness and I saw nothing. It didn't matter, I guess since I've never seen him fight before. Master Tulle explained the rules which were to not hit below the belt and to always stay alert to each other. Feeling eyes on me I looked around to find that everybody had stopped what they were doing to watch. I guess they could tell that this was going to be a massacre because he was an advanced trainee and knew what he was doing, while I did not.

Master Tulle clapped his hands and stepped back. Immediately, my opponent began to bounce on his toes and circle around me. I bounced and circled as well watching him. When he made his move, I wasn't ready. A kick to my mid-section had me winded and almost on my knees. Twice more he attacked, and I couldn't hit back. I realized that although we were both padded for protection, the fight was no simulation. This was a real fight. His next kick almost got me, and I swerved to avoid it. Buck and John's faces swam before my eyes and I lost it. Suddenly, I felt like I was in a cocoon where I felt and saw nothing but victory. In this cocoon, I predicted every attack and countered it, and I did. When I hit him, I hit him hard, slamming him against the ropes. When he collapsed onto the mat, Master Tulle caught my fist and pulled me off him.

"Enough!" He shouted. I relaxed, drew a deep breath and stood up. I put my hand out to my opponent and he took it carefully and pulled himself up.

"How did I do?" I turned to ask Master Tulle innocently.

"I shall have to teach you proper techniques, but this wild untrained style will do in a pinch." Answered Master Tulle. Elder Chaktar caught my eye but didn't smile. Instead he said something to the man sitting beside him and stood up.

"Tomorrow you will report for warrior's training at sector four. Your first session will be on technique, followed by Air Corps combat training, weapons training and then you will have flight simulation."

"What time should I report sir?" I asked feeling excited that I was finally getting the training I needed to go protect my brother.

"Oh eight hundred sharp, trainee Brightblade, now go change."

Elder Chaktar was waiting for me by the exit. I went to him and he took me back to Boham.

In the conveyor, I asked Boham how I was getting to the warrior's training center. He said that conveyors take students to their various training sectors each morning. It was up to me to meet the correct one. I told him that I didn't have a chronograph and he pointed to a box on the seat next to me.

I reached for the box and opened it. It wasn't fancy, but I felt like I finally belonged, that I wasn't left guessing at every moment. I smiled at him as I fastened it onto my left wrist.

"Hey Boham, when will I know how my tests came out? I did the simulation spaceship fight, and then I sparred. Master Tulle only said that it would do in a pinch when I clearly was the winner. Elder Chaktar watched as I took down all ten enemy ships plus the mothership and all he said that was what I did was superior and wants to use it to train the Air Corps. I saw approval, but he didn't make me feel good about what I'd done."

When we finally arrived at the dorm, Boham stopped the conveyor to let me out. Just before I stepped out of it, he reached for my hand. "The fact that you will start training means that you have potential. Trainee Brightblade be careful from this point on. There are those who would wish to see you fail, just out of spite and nothing more. Your family's name has been revered for a long time and to finally have you here is a miracle. All Anthora wishes to survive, but jealousy may be our downfall. Keep your eyes open and be careful who you trust."

"Boham, I am way ahead of you on that. Elder Chaktar has already shown his hand and I know I will have trouble from him. Don't worry about me." I waved as he drove away.

It was getting late and almost time for dinner. I took a shower to relieve my sore body. Because I kicked ass today, I wanted to dress for the occasion. I pulled out my dress and it fit perfectly. I did my hair and applied make-up. I stepped out of my room with my dress glowing green.

The others were just arriving as I neared the cafeteria. "We heard you did well." Aisha said. She hugged me close and patted me on the back. The others weren't as enthusiastic but shook my hand as they too congratulated me.

"What did you hear?" I asked.

"One of my colleagues told me that he acted as captain on your war simulation. He said that you were brilliant." Druktar said.

"I thought I was too, but Elder Chaktar didn't make me feel like I did well. He said that it was good, but his smile said something else." I relayed to them. I watched closely for their reactions. I saw shock and disgust on their faces.

"Elder Chaktar resents anyone who is better than him." Druktar admitted.

"Too bad for him." Aisha joined in. "At the medical facility, I overheard Master Physician Bolka saying that you were in perfect health."

"Elder Ullah's son was your sparring partner, did you know?" Mingh asked me.

I turned to her in alarm. "No, I didn't. I won't be in trouble, will I?"

"Sparring was the objective, no one holds grudges." Lylah assured me.

"Well that's good. I really wanted to do well so that I can start my training. My family on Earth may be in danger and I want to be the one to protect them." I told them earnestly. For some reason, I didn't want to let on that it was only my brother that I was worried about.

"You are willing to go through those grueling sessions just for the sake of your family? What about glory? What about pride in your excellence?" Gorke asked. He had a serious expression on his face.

I smiled at him. "Gorke, my number one priority is the safety of my family, followed by the safety of all Anthorans. If we ever come to a battle, those ambitions, would only get in the way. On Earth we have a saying: pride goeth before a fall. It basically means that one will fail if glory is all they are looking for. I will be proud of any accomplishment I achieve, but I won't let it seduce me."

He nodded in understanding. "You are very wise Fiona Brightblade."

"Do you guys know how annoying it is to be addressed by my full name? It's a good thing you don't know my middle name. Just call me Fiona okay?" I looked around the table.

"Okay." They all agreed. I smiled at them because now I knew they were my friends. "I think I will call it a night. I'm sore from the sparring and I have to be up early for training." I stood up and they did too. As a unit we walked out of the cafeteria.

The Aveng Three crew and Jhael took the elevator with us but left the building while Aisha, Mingh and I continued to our rooms. I looked at them and waved before I went in and they waved back.

I quickly changed into my pajamas and absentmindedly planned what I would wear when there came a knock on my door. I opened it to Jhael. I smiled and let him in. "What's up." I asked him.

"I forgot to tell you that uniforms are expected when you are training. You are to report to your class in uniform, so I bought one for you. Master Tulle can be very cruel when he isn't obeyed." Jhael handed me a bag. In it was a red uniform and it was my size.

I looked up from the bag with a big smile. "Thank you so much. I owe you one."

"If that is so, will you have dinner with me tomorrow after class? We can go to one of the restaurants at the food court."

"Oh Jhael, that's really nice of you. I think you need to know that Aisha has a major crush on you. I've just gotten friends and I'd like to keep all of you. I don't want her to feel hurt." I tried to explain.

Jhael's face turned to stone. "You misunderstand Fiona. I wanted to have dinner with you because I need your advice concerning her. I know she has feelings for me, and I would like to return those feelings, however I'm not sure how to return them."

"Oh good. I don't know when my classes end but yes, I'd be very happy to help you."

"Thank you, I'll say goodnight then." Jhael murmured and let himself out.

Later in bed, I smiled. Aisha was going to be very happy to know that Jhael returned her interest. I wasn't seeing anyone on Earth and if I went out it was in groups. In high school I didn't date either. I've always wondered when or if I would ever find someone to crush on. Maybe once I've finished with my training and rescued my brother, I'll feel settled enough to think about the opposite sex. I wonder if Leena had a boyfriend or husband. I made a note to dig more into her personal life.

# CHAPTER FOUR

At dinner Druktar had showed me how to work the chronograph. I set it to wake me at six a.m. and when it went off, I got up eagerly. I wanted to make sure I didn't miss the conveyor. In my head I could hear my mother saying how important breakfast was, so after I was dressed in my uniform, I went to the cafeteria for the breakfast that does a body good. Of the others, only Aisha was at the table. She was dressed in white. I smiled at her when I sat down beside her. She looked beautiful.

"Wow Aisha, you clean up good." Her hair was in a soft bun and she wore makeup.

She smiled. "Today is my first official day at the medical facility."

"Good luck, I know you will do well."

We ate quickly. I hurried to go brush my teeth again and bumped into Mingh on my way out of my room. She had a worried expression on her face. Curious enough to give her a few minutes, I asked her what was wrong.

"I have to report to the school today and I'm not sure I will be any good." She lamented.

Mingh you are a teacher. It is your path isn't it?"

"Yes, it is. As soon as I arrived here, I knew that it was what I was meant to do. My fear is that I won't be able to teach the young ones." She explained.

I was in complete shock. For some reason, it never occurred to me that Anthora Two had children. "How young are they?"

"They are aged five through seven. I only trained with a simulator. These will be real live children." She wailed.

"Look, stop worrying. Children that age are very easy. You march in that classroom and teach them."

"You really think I can do it?"

"Of course, I do. You said so yourself, it is your path. Stop doubting yourself."

Mingh threw her arms around me to hug me tight. "Thank you so much, I knew you'd help me get my perspective."

I looked at my chronograph and pushed her toward the door. "Neither of us wants to be late for our first day. Come on, we don't want to miss our conveyors." We got outside just as they were arriving. It was then I realized that they came in different sizes. Huge conveyors pulled up looking more like trucks than buses. Each was labeled with their destinations. I waved at Mingh as I climbed into my conveyor and she waved back as she climbed into hers.

The ride to Sector four's warrior training center took a half hour. Trainees were hurrying to sit on the floor mats when I arrived; there were no mats available up front. I sat on the lone mat behind several rows of trainees. I tried not to feel that they took those spots on purpose so that I could sit in the back, but when I spied a free mat further up from where I sat, the trainee next to it quickly put his hand on it, saying that it was taken.

Okay, so that was the way it was going to be. That's fine I thought. Sooner or later, they were all going to have to spar with me. Once I learned the 'proper' techniques, it'll be on. I learned that as a trainee, my chronograph tracks me and tells me where I am supposed to be. Right now, it had me in physical combat training class, in Sector four.

"This morning we will be reviewing the basics of stance and the proper technique for offense and defense for the benefit of our new trainee joining us this morning. Partner up and take up your positions." Master Tulle instructed.

Of course, I was the only one without a partner. I raised my hand and started walking toward the front. "Master Tulle, I don't have a partner. Is it okay to partner with you?"

"Very well, come up." He agreed. I walked up to the front of the classroom and took up my position like the rest of the students. I learned a lot and mimicked him perfectly.

When it came to actual practice in hand to hand combat, Master Tulle suggested that I spar with another student. No one wanted to spar with me until he volunteered someone. Afterwards, things went well until the next class which was weapons training. We were given dummies to chop up with Anthora Two's version of light sabers. Again, no one wanted to partner with me when it came time to practice with live sabers. I took no offense as I asked the instructor to partner with me. Finally, the last class for the day was flight simulation.

The man who Elder Chaktar sat beside during my sparring test, was there. The more he pretended not to be watching me, the more I was convinced that he was. My instructor, Master Fontaine who was also from Earth was all business, but I could see that he took great interest in me. Since he allowed someone in his class to just sit to watch me, I didn't think I could trust him either.

No one befriended me in the classes, and I tried not to take offense, after all, I wasn't there to make friends. My brother was all that mattered. I could and would endure anything to ensure his safety.

By days' end, I was tired and sore. Flight simulation and Space combat training were the only classes where I didn't have to assert myself physically. The instructors I partnered with didn't hold back and I hadn't expected them to either.

On the way back to the dorm I had a revelation. Perhaps the reason they were all so hard on me was because they were expecting something else from me and also why they had someone watching me. This Le'ak thing they won't speak about. I may have to go to the library to see if I could find anything to shed some light on it.

When I got home, Jhael was waiting for me. He suggested that we eat at the food court. I asked him to give me a few minutes to change and he agreed to wait outside for me. He didn't want to bump into Aisha.

We walked to the food court and talked. Jhael was really a nice guy and shy too. For all the confidence he showed when he came to retrieve me, he had none when it came to women. I asked him to tell me about Teah Four.

"Teah Four is a planet much like your Earth, except it has two moons. The vegetation is a bit more complicated too. Some trees move while others bite, but that's all in the jungle parts. Our cities were magnificent, with tall buildings made from metal harvested from meteors. Falling meteors were a hazard our planet faced on occasion. Usually, the military handled their destruction, but sometimes one would make it through. There are six major oceans. Our race is unified speaking one language. My family and I used to go to the beach every chance we got. It was our favorite thing to do. I was an architect there. Anyway, my company had finished one particularly hard project for the city. The old sports arena had been destroyed by a meteor. My company was hired to build a new one. After we finished it, I took my family to the beach to relax. Later, I went with my colleagues to hunt. Hunting is another favorite pastime on Teah Four. The zoyor came out of nowhere and attacked me." Jhael fell silent as he got lost in his memories.

"How old where you when you died on Teah Four?"

"I was thirty." He answered. We were nearing the food court. There was a question I wanted to ask him, but I wanted to think about it and to choose my words carefully. I was still on the fence on trusting anyone fully.

We finally decided to try a little restaurant nestled between the weapons shop and what a sign said was a laundromat. It didn't look like any laundromats that I was familiar with from Earth, I had a pile of dirty clothes stacking up and now I knew where to go to get them washed.

Jhael assured me that the food was good and that I didn't have to worry about anything strange. I asked him to order for me and when our food came, I was relieved that it was vegetables in a meat sauce. It was delicious.

"Jhael, were you married on Teah Four?"

"How did you guess?" He asked with a guarded expression on his face.

"It was the way you spoke of your family. Did you have children?"

"My wife and I had a son and a daughter. Unfortunately, they are not Anthoran. I had hoped to see them again. I find that I want to have a family here on Anthora Two as well. Aisha reminds me of my wife. Our government encourages unions here because it will increase our people. I would like to start a new family here, with her if she is willing." He said wistfully. It made me wonder if he missed his family, like I miss my brother.

"I find that I don't miss my family as much as I thought I would, but they are still my family. It must be an Anthoran thing I suppose." I began. "What about you?"

"I think about them often, but not in a longing way. Sometimes I feel guilty for not missing them. It is an Anthoran thing as you say." He said confirming my suspicions.

Being Anthoran had completely changed my perception of family. I felt closer to these people than to the ones I left behind. Except for my brother, I don't miss them much.

"So, what is it that you want to know about Aisha?" I asked to move things along. It was getting late and I was tired.

"Since you are both from Earth, I thought you might suggest what she and I might do when we go out together. What was the mating ritual like on Earth?"

I smiled at him. "We don't have a ritual; however, we do have expectations. For example, if you were to ask her to come out with you. You are expected to pay for whatever it is you'll be doing. Dinner, dancing or whatever passes for fun here." I explained.

"It is almost like Teah Four. The man is expected to lead on an outing."

It took the better part of an hour to explain to him the mechanics of dating that Aisha was familiar with.

Finally, the evening was over, and we walked back to the dorm. I was relieved that Aisha wasn't around to see him dropping me off. It would have been too awkward and if I recalled how Earth women reacted to these types of misunderstandings, I would have lost a friend.

I had just showered when there came a knock on my door. It was Aisha and I tried to gage what she was feeling. She looked excited, so I relaxed. Just before she could say anything our chronographs chirped. Severe storm warnings were being broadcasted. We were to be extremely careful as winds were high and the air cold.

"What does high winds and cold air feel like? Is this storm unusual?" I asked her.

She shook her head. "There's a combination of weather happening all at once and I've only experienced one such storm. It has to do with the original state of the planet before we came here. The planet used to have severe storms all the time. That's probably why the originals lived alternately under water and land. They were adaptable that way. Normally, the weather is mild with the occasional rain. No snow at all."

"Will we be able to go to work and classes in the morning?"

"That depends on how long the storms lasts."

"How long did the one you experienced last?"

"Three long days, and it was scary. The ground shook, and the windows rattled. We had tornadoes, sleet and rain. We were assured that we wouldn't come to any harm, but I had my doubts."

Our chronographs chirped once more. This time it was to cancel training classes and only medical facility, Air Corps and Communications staff were to report to work. "In the morning, I'll be getting a conveyor to the medical facility. I'll be needed to help treat injured people."

That seemed strange to me. "Why would you be treating anyone, if we've been warned to stay indoors? Who in their right minds would brave such weather?" I wanted to know.

"It is because of the subterranean dwellers. They get hurt during the tremors. We also have Anthorans who live out in the wilds of the planet."

"Please be careful then." I told her.

"Not to worry. We have special conveyors in cases like this. They are armored for protection." She assured me.

"Great, what did you come to speak with me about?" I wanted her to think about something else. She looked worried.

Her bright smile returned. "Oh yeah, I wanted to tell you that Jhael asked me out. He messaged me through the chronograph. It's like texting on Earth."

"That's wonderful, I know you like him." She looked so happy, I thought.

"Now we'll have to wait until the weather is nice again, but I can't---- Wait, how did you know I liked him?" She asked, her eyes widened in surprise.

I gave her a look. "Really Aisha, a blind man could tell you liked him."

"It was that obvious? I feel foolish now."

"Don't be. He looks like a nice guy and who knows, you guys might end up getting married and starting a family."

"Oooh, I hope you're right." She squealed.

"Aisha, can you watch any show on your television?"

She nodded. "As long as it is still being played on Earth. Did you want to watch anything in particular?"

I nodded. "Yeah. Since coming here, everyone has treated me weirdly. It's like they are expecting something from me, but I don't have a clue. I used to watch this show about aliens that had powers."

"Oh, you mean like 'Star Trek'?"

"No, like 'Star Gate'. Have you seen it?"

"That comes on all the time, but I'm not a fan." She admitted.

"If the storms continue after work tomorrow, can I come over to watch a few episodes?"

"Yeah sure. You like shows like that?"

"I used to watch it all the time on Earth."

"What do you mean?"

"Have you ever heard of Le'ak?"

Aisha's face shut down, like she was caught doing something forbidden. "It is something we in the medical facility are trained to identify."

"How would you know if someone had the ability of Le'ak?"

"There's a legend about Le'ak. Supposedly, only a few men and women wielded it. The original Anthorans had a caste system which is why today we know our place in society. These people who had the ability were regarded almost like gods. They were different, couldn't be placed in any caste. They flowed through all the castes, but mostly in the warrior caste. As time wore on, the ability faded out because there were more women than men, so they married down, and the ability dumbed down until it was lost. Leena Brightblade was among the only remaining women who still had the ability when the Froagans came along."

Again, my suspicious nature reared its ugly head. "Why are you telling me this now? You knew all along why everyone thought I was special. Why didn't you tell me before?" We'd been sitting, me on my bed and she on the chair by the door. I stood up to approach her. She stood up too looking scared.

"You didn't ask. Fiona, you must understand that if we had a Le'ak wielder again, Anthora would be free from fear." She said quickly.

"Who are you?"

"I'm who I said I was. I'm from Earth like you. The only thing I didn't tell you was that I've been here longer. We age slower than on Earth, so I'm more like forty than twenty-nine. My path is healer like I said, but since I'm from Earth like you, I was instructed to stay close to you, to be on the lookout for your ability to wield Le'ak."

"What about Jhael?"

"What about him?"

"Is he watching me also?"

"No, he knows nothing of this. I only know because of my medical training."

"So, you really like him and stuff?"

"Yes, I do." She said. She approached me and took my hand in hers. "Fiona, I would be in serious trouble if they knew I told you everything. If you do have the Le'ak ability, you must let Elder Sim know immediately."

"Were you really killed by a blood clot to the brain?"

"No, I was murdered like you. Anthorans are being hunted and your ability is the only thing that can save us."

"I won't let on that you've told me anything, but I need you to be completely honest with me from now on, you understand?"

"Yes, definitely." She agreed.

"The reason I asked to watch that show is because I found it fascinating. The race of beings that controlled everybody else was something that always resonated with me. It's kinda hard not to think about special powers being on another planet and all. Since everybody is expecting it from me, I thought watching it here might trigger something. What do you think?"

She shrugged. "Is it something you think would help you?"

"I don't know, it couldn't hurt. The medical facility did a physical on me and took a blood sample. I don't think they found anything special about me, but I thought my blood might have some mutation perhaps. Suppose they took my blood to do experiments with to regain Le'ak?"

"You know, I wouldn't put it past Elder Chaktar to use your blood to his advantage. If you'd like, I can keep my eyes and ears open to that possibility."

I made an impatient sound. "Look Aisha, I don't care for all the subterfuge going on. All I care about is my family and the possibility that they might be in very real danger. Even though the idea of them being retrieved so that we could be together again, would be wonderful. However, I would like for them to live out a full life on Earth. I want my brother and sister to grow up, get married and have children of their own. Wouldn't that be beneficial to us? To have more Brightblades is better than just one or two and maybe one of us may have the ability everyone is looking for."

"I see what you mean. It's getting late. I have a hard day ahead with treating the injured tomorrow. When I get back later, we can watch that television show together. Okay?"

I nodded, and we said goodnight. Sleep took a long time in coming. I wasn't entirely sure that I should trust Aisha now. I didn't want her to know about my brother. Other than warriors, those who'd been murdered had their memories erased. Aisha is not a warrior. The Elders were clear that only warriors knew. Since I couldn't go to class tomorrow, I planned to spend it at the library learning all I could about Le'ak. Aisha neatly avoided telling me about how she would be able to determine if I could wield Le'ak. From the very beginning, I felt that she was too good to be true. Boham came to mind. He said that I shouldn't trust anyone and now I think he is right.

The storm raged harder if that were possible when I awoke. During the night, howling winds and sleet kept me up until utter exhaustion claimed me. Ground tremors woke me when stuff on my dresser were knocked down. The tremors didn't last long, but I was up.

Breakfast wasn't for another two hours so I got out of bed and occupied that time doing the strength building exercises Master Tulle instructed me to do. Once that was done, I was sweaty. I showered and dressed in a pair of sweats. We were instructed to always wear the red arm bands. I was given one and I slipped it on my left sleeve.

My hair was getting longer than I'd like. I must ask Aisha about hair salons. I braided it in a thick plait down my back. The last thing I did was straighten up my room before heading for the cafeteria. Aisha was just coming out of her room too and she waved. She was dressed in her uniform, so I gathered she was going to work.

"I don't have time to eat with you, but I'll see you later, okay?" She said as she headed in the opposite direction.

"Be careful out there." I called out after her.

The cafeteria was more crowded than usual. Jhael, Gorke and Lylah weren't at our table, but Mingh was and I joined her.

"Good morning Mingh."

"Good morning Fiona. I'm so glad to see you. I thought I'd be the only one here this morning."

"No. My classes were canceled. What about you and the others?"

"We don't have school today, and the others were called in to the communications center. Druktar teaches technical operations so he was needed there too."

"Is this your first storm?" I asked fishing.

She shook her head. "No, it isn't. We've been through two so far. They seem to get more severe each time."

"Really, how so?"

"The ground shook more than last time. The rain and sleet are more this time too. It's like the atmosphere is deteriorating or something."

"Don't we have scientists who maintain the atmosphere?" Perhaps the terraforming was reverting, I thought privately.

"I suppose we do, but I'm beginning to think, they no longer have control." She said with a whine, almost confirming my suspicions.

"The Elders would know if something was wrong. And I believe it is their duty to warn the populace if we were in danger." I told her, more for her comfort than believing it to be truth.

Sometime during the day, I was going to make an appointment to see the Elders again. I had a feeling that every time I asked to see them, they would make the time to see me. I felt that they were hopeful that I would be giving them good news. I didn't feel proud that I had them on a string, but it is what it is. We finished breakfast and Mingh told me that she was going to hang out with the other teachers.

The library had more people in it too than I had ever seen before. I was worried that I wouldn't be able to research what I wanted. The keeper approached me with her usual smile. "Hello trainee Brightblade, how may I be of service today?" She asked. I noticed that she now addressed me by what I was, a trainee.

"Hello Keeper, I would like to read about Anthoran folklore if you have it." I told her.

"Yes, we have a very small section. Was there something in particular you were looking for?" Her interest rose up a notch I noticed.

Aha! I thought, I wasn't going to give my hand away that easily. "I'm just curious about the legends of our culture. I already read about history and now I want something less serious. Do you have anything you could recommend?"

"Yes, of course. It is this way." She said and started walking.

I followed her to an aisle much further than I'd been before. There wasn't anyone there at all and the table had a communicator in case I needed to fine tune my search.

The Keeper pointed to two shelves and left. I pulled the first book and sat down at the table. Fortunately, there was a table of contents, so I was able to see what the book contained. The very last section of the book looked like it might be promising. I read about the fabled women of Anthora. These women were called the Shining Ones. They were healers, seers and were known for their bravery.

That one book led me to another on the shelf. In the second one, I read about the Shining Ones who had the ability to throw light by harnessing the sun's power. With the same light, they could harm or heal. I wondered if that was the Le'ak and what did throw light mean?

I went through three other books and none elaborated more on the Shining Ones. So, I asked the communicator if there were any books on Le'ak? I knew of course, that somehow someone would be alerted to my interest. However, the communicator did direct me to another aisle. There was a section on the mythology of Anthora. It was in one of those books that I found more on them.

Le'ak was an ancient skill only a few clans on Anthora possessed. This skill involved the worship of the sun. It was said that the sun imbued them with its power. They were able to channel or harness the light of the sun through their bodies and project it. Both men and women had that skill. Somewhere along the line, the male population lost their ability leaving only the women able to wield Le'ak and they had become the Shining Ones.

With Le'ak, these women healed the sick, and were oracles. Generations later, Le'ak was lost almost entirely except for a select few. The Brightblade clan retained their skills as well as a few others.

I returned to my room thinking hard on this skill lost to the ages. The Anthoran government preserved its peoples' genes when they blasted them into outer space with the hopes of one day retrieving them. Did they feel the need to preserve the genes simply because they knew one day, they'd be back to be a nation again? Or perhaps they hoped that in preserving the genes, latent abilities would re-emerge? I'm thinking it was more the latter. Why else would they go through all that trouble if they simply were trying to escape annihilation? I swear the more I dug, the more questions I had.

Could it be that when Leena destroyed Oftha's ship, that she used Le'ak? The ship she used was a fighter ship. Their technology probably was primitive compared to the Froagans who subdued an entire planet. I bet she used Le'ak. Flying up to the mothership brought her closer to the sun and she would have been able to call on its power, at least that's what I think, and I might not be too far off.

Aisha returned from work and she looked drained. I wanted to wait until after we had dinner before asking her about the injured. The storm raged all day and into the evening. Mingh joined us at our table full of news.

"I heard that there was a sighting of an unmanned probe and those who keep watch are worried. Who would probe a planet?" She asked no one in particular.

"Where did you hear this?" I asked her.

She pointed to a group sitting at a table to the left of ours. "Those guys over there, work in Sector X. That's where Druktar teaches."

I looked over at the table and didn't see anyone I recognized. Just then our chronographs chirped. The storms were still raging, and classes were postponed until further notice. All were warned to stay indoors. Mingh shook her head sadly. Aisha just looked horrified.

Mingh got up stating that she was tired and was going to bed.

"You look beat, you should go get some rest too. You'll probably have to tend to more injured tomorrow." I said to Aisha. She agreed and followed Mingh out.

As soon as Mingh and Aisha had cleared the cafeteria door, I got up and headed toward the table hosting the tech guys from Sector X.

"Hi," I introduce myself. "Do you guys have any more news about the cause of the storms?" Baby steps I told myself. I couldn't very well blurt out questions about the probe. These guys worked with sensitive equipment that kept our planet safe and hidden. They are not going to tell me everything. I have to be subtle. I learned that from the library.

They all turned to look at me. Again, I got the adoring gazes, but the one who seems to be the leader of the group nodded. He told me and the group that the storm would probably continue for a few more days. He also told us that there was a way we could all see the storm. We stood up to follow him as he led us to a door, I always thought led to the kitchen area of the cafeteria.

Three flights up later, we found ourselves in a dome-shaped room made completely of transparent glass. It was eerie to see all the way around us. The storm was frightening and every now and then lightning struck. It lit up the room and I could see where it touched down and scorched the earth and buildings. Fleetingly, I thought about all the clean-up that had to be done to make things look normal again. The buildings were all protected from the lightening, but trees were burned. Wollo told me that the probe was probably an Air Corps maneuver. The storms had nothing to do with it. Now where have I heard that before?

We pressed ourselves close to see everything. A lightning bolt hit the dome and bathed it in light. I watched as the strings of light danced across the dome. We laughed and squealed until another powerful bolt hit the dome. Somehow, it filtered through and we were all thrown backward.

I jumped to my feet to check on everyone. After a few seconds, Wollo started to laugh and the others joined in. Then they started to point at me and stare. I looked around thinking that maybe someone was behind me, and I caught a glimpse of myself in the glass. My hair had come undone and was undulating as if it had a life of its own.

I grabbed at it and braided it quickly. "I don't think coming up here was a good idea." I told the others. We jumped and ran as another bolt hit the dome. Running and laughing we parted ways when we reached the bottom. I thanked the others and made my way to my room.

I felt good and energized but my hair was still staticky. I went to the bathroom to wet it down in the hopes of ridding it of the static. Finally, I just wrapped a damp towel around my head and went to bed. The lightning was fantastic but scary. I could understand why they wanted us indoors. That bolt of lightning that somehow filtered through the dome was strange. It almost felt like it was targeting us. The others hadn't experienced the static I got. It probably had something to do with my being from a different planet from them, I reasoned.

Sometime during the night, I woke up from a nightmare with a start. I reached over to turn on the lamp and freaked out when streams of light struck the lamp shattering it. I started to scream and then I knew no more.

The light shining over my bed threatened to blind me. I sat up quickly. This wasn't my room or my bed. I was sure that I didn't have roommates, two others were on either side of my bed. Where was I? Was I still dreaming?

"Ah, you're awake, good." Elder Chaktar said as he approached the bed.

I grabbed the side of the bed to sit up. "Where am I?" I asked him.

"We brought you here after your accident. You used Le'ak." He answered excitedly. He pointed to the two in the beds on either side of me. "Mingh and Gorke are recovering from a memory wipe as they were the ones who came to your rescue. We can't afford to have your secret known."

"I really don't know what you are talking about. How could I use Le'ak when I don't even know what it is?" I gave him my best 'you're kidding stare'.

"And yet you did." He held up his hand and walked out the room to come back a few minutes later with two attendants who pushed my friends' beds out of the room.

"What's going to happen to them?" I asked.

"I assure you that they will be fine. The memory wipe they've undergone is precise. They will only remember coming to your room when you screamed and of calling for help after you'd lost consciousness."

"Did you wipe my memory also; I can't remember anything other than waking up with a splitting headache. I had a bad dream and tried to turn on my lamp and then----, Oh my God! There was a stream of light coming from my hand."

Elder Chaktar nodded knowingly. "You used Le'ak. Your friends came to your rescue. You were screaming about the light and passed out."

"I guess you're happy now. You've resented me from the beginning, so are we enemies now?" I asked giving him my best accusatory stare.

He shook his head and smiled. "Not at all my dear." He lifted his hands and faint beams of light flew from them.

"You too?" Ugh, I thought.

"You must understand that this must be kept secret. There are so few of us. Master Physician Bolka brought you here and performed the memory wipe on the others. We didn't dare bring you to the medical facility."

"So, what now?"

"We will help you control your abilities and train you in its usage."

"How can I trust you. You've treated me unfairly from the time of my testing."

"You must understand that things are very complicated. The other Elders aren't as trustworthy as they appear. I've had to be very careful around them. I wasn't retrieved like they were. I came to be an

Elder by birthright. I am a direct descendant of the original Anthoran scientists. I was born here on Anthora Two and my ancestors were of the few that wielded Le'ak. I've had to play the part of indifference toward you for appearances' sake."

"Is it supposed to hurt every time? I thought my head was going to explode." I told him.

He beckoned to me. "Come, the others are waiting." I got up and followed him out of the room. He led me to another room further down the hallway. He opened the door at the end of the hallway with a flourish.

I entered the room hesitantly, expecting to be ambushed or something only to find about ten men and women standing around. I watched Elder Chaktar walk up to the wall to place his hands on it. The wall was coated with a gel-like substance. His whole body started to vibrate and then his arms started to glow. The wall seemed to be absorbing his Le'ak. I looked around to find that they were all doing it. What the heck I thought. I approached a section of wall and placed my hands flat onto its surface like they were doing.

The wall felt mushy. I braced myself and automatically, I felt a vibration that started from deep inside my body. Then my arms both glowed almost orange.

I could feel power building up in my body. Suddenly everyone was thrown from the wall as power flowed from me into the wall. Elder Chaktar stood up and started laughing. The others joined in as they pulled themselves up. Master Physician Bolka came up to me beaming. The others surrounded me clapping. I noticed Bel from the weapons shop, two others that I vaguely remember and the man I was sure Chaktar had watching me.

Elder Chaktar gestured that we all sit down on the floor. I noticed it was made of rubber, to further protect others from harm I thought. We sat in a circle. They introduced themselves and when it was my turn, I told them my name.

"It is a pleasure to have you join us. We have been waiting for you for a long time. As I said before, my name is Lao. I am also from

Earth. I was born and raised in the mountains of Tibet. As a child, I listened to stories of people who worshipped the sun and who could harness its powers and project it. As an adult, I pursued those stories. I traveled extensively around the world gathering information. Some of our ancestors landed on Earth and those stories were about them. As an anthropologist, I had many speaking engagements and one man made it his business to attend as many as he could to try to get my attention.

He made an appointment to speak with me privately and he told me that he was a descendant of those people and that he was in hiding. He said that he was waiting for his people to come take him back to his home world. It took me a while to decide that he wasn't a nutcase. He told me that he could prove his claim. So, we arranged to meet in a place of his choosing so he could show me. I was late in meeting him, but when I arrived, it was to watch in horror as two men attacked him and then suddenly doffed off their clothes and skin before dealing the final blow. From my hiding spot, I was too afraid to do anything. After they left, I ran to his side. I started to call an ambulance, but he told me that it was too late. He told me that he and I were the same and then he died in my arms."

"Did you ever meet this man here on Anthora Two?" I asked quietly.

Lao smiled and nodded. "It was Boham. He prefers to keep to himself. What we all just did is expel excess energy. Fiona, you must do this almost every day so that you don't become overloaded. What happened to you during the night could happen again if you don't. We have rooms like this everywhere. The walls capture our energies and power the buildings they are in."

"Who is going to teach me to use Le'ak?"

"Master Tulle----," Elder Chaktar began.

"Master Tulle is here." He finished for him as he entered the room. He went to the wall to expel his energies and then joined the circle on the floor. "You must excuse me for being late. Elder Sim requested an audience with me. She wanted to know what progress you were making. She is especially interested in your combat skills."

"Elder Sim is one of those who is against Le'ak. She feels that it is an outdated skill. She would prefer our Air and Space Corps defend the planet should the occasion arise. For safety's sake Lao and I will conduct your training instead." Elder Chaktar explained.

"She was so kind to me, especially when I underwent my recall procedure. I was afraid but she stayed with me." I said in her defense.

"She was there to see whether your ability to use Le'ak would manifest during the procedure. If it had, she would have found a way to eliminate you." Chaktar said.

"How can you be so sure?" I argued.

"She's done it before. We had retrieved an older man from her own planet and when we had performed the recall procedure, the man started displaying Le'ak. At first, she acted overjoyed and insisted that the man be held over at the medical facility for studies. The man died days later of massive burns."

"Oh my God, what happened?"

"It was suspicious how it happened. She smothered his body while he wielded, and he was burned alive." Explained Master Physician Bolka.

"So she is suspicious of me because of my ancestry?" I asked

Lao nodded. "You mustn't let her know."

"Aisha insisted that I tell her at once if I found that I can wield Le'ak. Who am I to trust now?"

"If at any time you feel you need to talk with someone, find Boham. He is completely trust worthy, and he'll give you sound advice." Said Lao.

Master Tulle got up announcing that he had to leave. "Fiona, when classes reconvene, your lessons will be right after your regular classes."

The others got up to leave as well. I waved at Bel and felt that I had another friend. Lao hung behind to escort me back to my room.

I found that the room was in the dorm building tucked away in the lower levels. The entrance to the room was a door without doorknobs and the door itself was seamless. To enter it, one had to use Le'ak along the seams, otherwise it was just a wall.

"In a few days, Master Tulle will be advising the Elders of your progress. He will be telling them that you will be ready to travel to Earth in a few weeks to protect your brother. I will be assigned as your captain to help you." Lao explained.

"I really appreciate that. I fear for him and I want him to be safe." I said. We'd gotten to my room door and we stood there for a few minutes looking at each other. "Good night Lao, it was nice meeting you."

"Good night Fiona." He turned toward the exit and left the building.

# CHAPTER FIVE

The sky was just starting to turn pink. I wondered how it was that Gorke and Mingh were the ones to come to my rescue when Aisha's bedroom was the closest to mine? I knew she was tired, but if Mingh could hear me, how come she didn't?

Before I could change my mind, I left my room to go check on her. I knew that she was overly tired from caring for those that had been hurt. I knocked on her door and when she didn't answer, I tried the doorknob. It was not locked. I pushed the door open and peeked in. I spied a bundle under the covers, and as I was about to close the door, my eye caught something on the wall opposite her bed. Aisha was hanging on a hook on the wall. I clasped my hand over my mouth and pulled the door shut as quietly as I could and ran back to my room.

Aisha was a Froagan! I leaned against my door and locked it. That thing that ate with us and laughed with us was a monster. How could it be?

A clap of thunder lit up the sky surprising me. I don't dare let her/it know that I've found out. Poor Jhael is going to be devastated when it all comes out. In the morning, I'm going to contact Elder Chaktar and he'll take it from there.

A knock on the door startled me and I grabbed the doorknob with shaky hands to open it. It was Aisha. I stepped back to let her in.

"Was that you who knocked on my door a few minutes ago?"

I nodded. "Yeah, it was me. I had a nightmare and I didn't want to be alone."

"Oh, are you okay? Do you want to talk about it?" She asked with genuine concern.

I shook my head. "No, I'm okay now. It was a silly dream really, but I'm fine. Go back to bed, you still have to report to work in a few hours."

"Are you sure?"

"Yes, I'm sorry I woke you."

"That's okay besides, we're friends and we must look out for each other. Next time you get scared, you can come to my room, but you must knock harder and call my name. I sleep like the dead when I'm tired." Said the monster in Aisha's clothing.

"I'll keep that in mind." I said and closed the door behind her. I locked it again and looked quickly around my room. The lamp I shattered was replaced while I was gone. The Le'ak crew were an efficient group, I must say. They worked quick, I thought. Suddenly, I wasn't afraid anymore. I was freaked out, but not afraid. Whatever we had to do to expose Aisha for what she was, we will do.

I looked down at my chronograph to find a message on it. The storm was abating, and classes were back on schedule.

I didn't know how I was going to sleep knowing that thing was just a few short feet from my room. When my chronograph chirped a few hours later, I realized that I must've slept. I awoke slumped over on the floor against my bedroom door. I looked down at my chronograph to find that I had almost no time to get ready for my classes.

A short shower later, I was dressed and rushed out the door to make breakfast before the conveyors were due. This morning, the cafeteria was full as everyone had places to be. I met my group with a guarded expression. The others didn't know what I knew, so I schooled my features to be neutral.

"Good morning everyone." I said a tad bit over-cheerfully.

"Good morning." They answered.

Aisha was sitting next to Jhael. They smiled and waved at me. I waved back and sat beside Mingh. Gorke and she looked no worse for wear. He and the others sat opposite me. Everyone looked quite normal and I wondered a little fearfully, how many more Froagans did we have amongst us?

"This place is hopping this morning." I said to no one in particular.

"Most of us returned in the wee hours. The food was meager at the Air Corps mess hall." Gorke explained. Druktar, Lylah, Jhael and he were stuck at their workstations, unable to come back home while the storms raged.

"It must be good to be able to shower and sleep in your own beds for a change." I said.

"Yes, it is, and to see good friends too." Jhael said. Although he said the words friends, he only had eyes for Aisha. She giggled and snuggled closer to him. By now it was apparent to everybody that those two were an item.

"You two don't have to have your meals with us, you know. We'll understand and won't hold it against you if you go out to be alone together." Gorke said. He had a smile on his face as he watched the two lovebirds.

"That's okay." Aisha said. "We don't mind spending time with our friends, do we Jhael?" Aisha asked him.

"No, we don't mind at all. It is not to say that we won't miss some meals with you guys. Aisha and I will have plenty of time to be alone together. You are our friends." Stated Jhael. He clasped Aisha's hand in his as he spoke.

If the others knew what I knew, their stomachs would be turning just like mine was, I thought privately. I stood up announcing that I had a conveyor to catch. Mingh and the others got up as well, leaving Jhael and Aisha at the table. After dumping my tray, I headed for the door but stopped suddenly when I overheard Jhael speak. I turned around thinking that they had gotten up to follow us, but they were still at the table talking. I was a good ten feet from the table and the cafeteria still had many people seated yet. How was I hearing them?

I dropped down to my knees pretending to tie my shoelaces to listen some more. "Are you sure she didn't come into your room?" Jhael asked.

"Relax my love, she didn't. I went to her room afterwards. She was upset about some dream she had. If she had seen anything, her reaction toward me would have said it all. No, we are still safe. The listening device you've placed in her uniform should keep us informed of anything the warriors are planning."

"Yes, I thought I'd get something by now, but what comes through is static. I must find a way to replace the device, I think it is faulty. She is a Brightblade; I cannot stress how important it is that we continue to watch her and remain hidden. I am still new to the communications center, so I do not have access to Sector X yet. It is only a matter of time before I do and then I will be able to disable the jamming device and uncloak the planet." Jhael told her. He sounded so confident.

"Wonderful, and then you can contact the others. These Anthoran scum will finally be destroyed once and for all. I miss our children and I want to go home." Aisha said.

I got up not wanting to hear anymore. I had to hurry or else I'd miss my conveyor. Throughout the ride, all I could think about was how much danger we all were in. How could they have been retrieved? In some bizarre alternate reality, could some of our Anthoran ancestors have landed on their home world and integrated with them? Eww!

I tried to catch Master Tulle's attention, but he was busy. I waited until the session was over. I hung back until all the students were gone from the room to speak with him. "Master Tulle, can you make sure that everyone can gather later. I have some very disturbing news."

"I don't know. Lao and Elder Chaktar are the only ones training you."

I shook my head. "I have horrible news, please arrange it so that everyone is here later. I've gotta go, please try." I said and hurried out to my next class.

Knowing that later, I would be able to let everyone know about Aisha and Jhael, I was able to relax and focused on my training. Flight simulation took on a whole new perspective for me as I destroyed Froagan ships. The other students glared at me, but I didn't care.

Finally, I was able to return to meet with the others. Master Tulle was able to contact everyone. He met me and led me to the secret room where I expelled my energies into the wall and then went to sit on the floor with the others. This room was different from the one in the dorm building. Mechanized walls moved to reveal the energy absorbing one underneath.

"Well, we are all here. What news do you have?" Master Tulle asked. He didn't look pleased.

I looked around our little circle and told them what happened after I had gone back to my room earlier. "And what's more, I believe that Jhael is one also. He said that he placed a listening device on my uniform" I explained how he gifted me with it.

"Are you sure you saw the skin hanging?" Master Physician Bolka asked. There was a little whine to his voice.

"Yes. If you recall it was early morning when we met. The sun was just coming up and it was light enough in the room so that I could see it under the covers and the skin hanging on the wall."

"How can we make sure?" Lao asked.

"It is sad, but as a warrior Elder, it had fallen to me to keep our people safe. Our scientists had devised the cloaking device that keeps the planet from being detected by the probes the Froagans send into our atmosphere from time to time. I had only recently insisted that they devise a way to make sure that our people are truly Anthorans. Aisha Shamon and Jhael are considered new. The device hadn't been operational until very recently. It can detect DNA presently on Anthora Two."

"If they are wearing actual skin from an actual Anthoran, would it still detect alien DNA?" Asked Bel. She had been silent, but I could see that she was frightened.

"Yes, it will. All sentient beings sweat, and it will come through the skin. To us it'll come over as defective, not completely Anthoran. The Library is the only area that has been refurbished, but it hasn't come online yet. The refurbish project was only approved by the building committees just before you were retrieved Fiona. Once it comes online, it will be able to determine who is Anthoran and who is not." Elder Chaktar shook his head. "It is set to only send an alarm to the Air Corps and Warrior commands."

"What does Elder Sim say about it?" I asked.

"She has not been fully informed. All she was told was that the library needed attention as past tremors had caused structural damage. Elder Bitka suspects her too."

"You mentioned that you were able to hear their conversation while a distance away, this is great news. Your powers are growing. Apart from Le'ak, our ancestors used to have the ability to hear thoughts." Lao said.

I closed my eyes trying to remember the event. I opened my eyes quickly. "You're right. It was more in my head than hearing with my ears. How come I can't hear your thoughts?" I asked looking around.

"You must have a close relationship with those around you for your ability to manifest." Boham said. Everyone turned to watch as he entered fully into the room. He walked over to the wall to expel his energies. Once he was done, he sat down with everybody. "Once you establish a relationship with others, you can start to hear their thoughts. It doesn't work with us. Somehow we are shielded from each other." He explained.

"Hello Boham. I suppose you've heard." I said to him.

"Yes, by way of Elder Chaktar. It is very fortunate for us to have a Brightblade Le'ak wielder." He answered.

I shook my head. "No, I meant that I've discovered that Aisha and Jhael are Froagans. I saw Aisha's skin hanging on the wall in her room." I told him.

Boham's eyebrows shot up. "Oh my, that is bad news."

"How does the device detect Froagans?" I asked turning my attention back to Chaktar. He hadn't quite answered the question when Bel posed it. I wanted to know too.

"The Library attracts a lot of our people. We have sensors on the door, communicators and even the elevators that lead to the library.

You must understand also that this is a pilot project. If proven useful, all of our public buildings will be outfitted." He answered.

"What will the air corps and warrior commands do once they detect a signal?" Master Physician Bolka asked.

"These two are fairly well-known in our community; to have them disappear abruptly will raise suspicion and alert any other Froagans we may have in our midst. We must have an explanation in place after we do away with them."

Elder Chaktar's answers seemed to quell everyone's fears, but I alone knew exactly how important it was to catch those two. The others filed out leaving Lao and Elder Chaktar with me.

"Fiona, in light of recent developments, I think we ought to cut this session short. I would like to advise you to be careful around them and to listen carefully also. It is to our advantage that your ability to hear their thoughts has emerged; it gives us an edge." Lao suggested, and we ended the session.

I hurried to catch the last conveyor back to the dorm. I wasn't overly late, but I thought about an answer just in case I was questioned about not taking the earlier conveyor. I showered and changed into some sweats and went to meet the others for dinner.

Jhael and Aisha weren't at our table and I was relieved. The others told me that they had seen them leaving the dorm earlier. It was a good thing and a bad thing. They could be planning all sorts of things and I wasn't close enough to hear anything.

"Fiona, I heard you mention that you needed to do laundry the other day, were you able to do it?" Gorke asked suddenly.

"Not yet. I saw a laundromat in the shopping center. I'd planned to go there but haven't gotten a chance to go." I replied.

"You don't have to go to the shopping center, we have laundry capabilities here in the building. If you want, I can show you. I have a load to do myself." He said.

I nodded at him. "Great, apart from my uniform, I am down to almost nothing clean to wear. Can we go after dinner?"

"Yes. I must go collect my clothes first. We can meet later." He said with a smile.

"Oh, can I join you guys, I hate doing laundry by myself. It's so dark down there." Mingh said. She wore a pleading expression.

"Great, the more the merrier." I said. I got up to dump my tray and waved to the others at the table and followed Gorke and Mingh out of the cafeteria.

I told them that we could meet in fifteen minutes in front of my room. Mingh hurried to her room while Gorke left the building.

Minutes later, while I was still struggling with two pillowcases of dirty clothes, there came a knock on my door. I called out that it was open and continued to stuff the pillowcase.

"What are you doing?" Aisha asked.

I turned abruptly to her. "I am going to do my laundry, what does it look like?" I answered more than a little flustered. She keeps popping up unannounced, like she was trying to catch me doing something suspicious.

"You do know that you can arrange for it to be done for you, right?" She countered.

I dropped the pillowcase on the floor and gave her my best annoyed stare. "No, I didn't. I'm down to my last and you're telling me this now?"

Aisha shrugged. "Hey, sorry. I wasn't thinking."

"No, I'm sorry, I didn't mean to snap at you. How was your evening out with Jhael, I see you took our advice?"

Aisha's whole face lit up. "We had dinner and we went to a club we talked about trying. We had a wonderful time. Oh Fiona, I think he really likes me!"

"That's great. Have you two taken things to the next level yet?" I asked raising my eyebrows playfully at her but cringing on the inside.

Aisha stopped smiling. "He wants to, but I want to wait. What with all the rumors of the planet being probed and such, I'm afraid. Anthorans don't use birth control. Our people are so few, that we are encouraged to have families."

"Ah I see. You don't want to get pregnant while our future might still be in jeopardy." I said. Maybe it's because Froagans' gestational period is much shorter than ours. You'd be giving birth in less than six months, I thought privately. The library has such useful information.

"Anyway, we've sorted it out and he thinks that I've got good sense. Please don't say anything to him. He doesn't understand human women telling each other stuff." She turned to leave.

"I'm your friend, not your mother. What you two do is your business."

Aisha bumped into Mingh leaving my room. They said a few words and she went on to her room. "Is Aisha alright?" she asked.

"Yeah, she's fine. Are you ready?" I asked her.

She nodded. "Yes, my stuff is down the hall. We just have to wait for Gorke."

"Aisha was telling me about a service that does our laundry, did you know about that?"

"Of course, but I prefer to do my own because I'm kinda funny about strangers touching my things. My training on Aveng Three was strict. As soldiers, it was drilled into us. We did our own washing, cleaning and cooking. It was to make sure that the enemy didn't infiltrate to compromise us." Mingh informed me. It made me realize how hard it was being a soldier on that world. Out of the four of them, I bet she is the only one who probably doesn't miss that life.

I threw my arm around her shoulders. "I wasn't a warrior on Earth, but my parents insisted that we be independent. My mother taught me how to cook, clean and wash my clothes. My dad taught me about common sense, and how to be safe away from home."

"Are you ready?" Gorke asked suddenly appearing at the door.

He grabbed one of my bags and I dragged the other. Mingh and I followed him to the elevator down to the cafeteria with the rest. When we stepped off, instead of going left which would have taken us to the cafeteria, we went right. It was the door that led up to the domed observation room. However, we turned to the left of the stairs and went through another door.

The laundry room was nothing I was expecting. It was huge with what appeared to be cubbies every few feet. I expressed that I didn't understand how it worked and Mingh took over. She led me to one of the cubbies. She showed me how to place my clothes in the cubby. Inside was a conveyor belt that pulled the clothes along. On the door of the cubby's door panel had choices for what I wanted done to my clothes. The choices were, clean and press, or clean, press and fold.

Once I got the hang of how it worked, Mingh and Gorke moved on to the cubbies a few feet away. I realized that they were using laundry and me as an excuse to be together. I wanted to laugh, but I didn't.

The machines behind the cubbies made quick work of the washing and pressing. Thirty minutes later, all our clothes were washed, pressed and folded. They even smelled fresh.

I decided that I wanted them to know that I was on to them. "You really didn't have to use me as an excuse to be together. I can see that you like each other." I told them. I stood there watching them with my arms folded.

Mingh blushed crimson. "Oh no, you don't understand. We aren't lovers, Gorke is my brother. On Aveng Three, siblings weren't allowed to enlist together or be in the same regiment together. But here on Anthora Two we find that we must continue the charade. It's driving me crazy personally." She confessed.

"Wow, I wasn't expecting that. Do the Elders know?" I asked.

"They don't, but the one who retrieved us does. He suggested that we keep it to ourselves a little longer." Gorke explained.

"So why are you telling me?"

"That's because of this." Both Gorke and Mingh held up their hands to display weak streaks of light coming from their fingers.

I smiled and showed them my light. "Who retrieved you?"

"Boham retrieved us. He also told us that we shouldn't trust anyone, but the other night when you had your episode, we thought that you might be an ally."

"Didn't they wipe your memories?" Something didn't ring true.

"Master Physician Bolka intervened. He knows about us and only put us to sleep. I was in Mingh's room when you started to scream. When we saw what was happening, I tried to help you, but you were out of your mind with fright. I did the only thing I could. I knocked you out. I didn't want anyone else to see what was really happening." He explained sheepishly.

"That's why I had a headache. Good call by the way. I suppose I should thank both of you. Does Elder Chaktar know about you?"

Mingh shook her head. "We didn't know who to trust so we only expelled with Boham. This morning, he told us about Aisha and Jhael. He told us to be very careful around them. Gorke is supposed to watch him at the Air Corps and he asked that I pair with you to watch Aisha here."

"How do I know that you are trustworthy?" I asked. If Aisha and Jhael could fool everyone into thinking they were Anthoran, why not these two.

Just then Boham entered the laundry room. "Good, I see you were able to meet. Fiona, I know this is getting stranger by the minute, but I would like you to help these two keep their secret. The others do not know except for Bolka and he's sworn to secrecy. We have others also, however since these two are in the unique position to keep an eye on Jhael and Aisha, I thought they would be able to help you." Explained Boham. I looked at him and remembered how kind he was when I was first retrieved. He answered my questions and made me feel safe.

"Okay. Aisha and Jhael are trying to be very cautious so we must be as well. They are confident that no one knows their secret and if we are to keep them confident, what we are doing here right now, has to be few and far in between."

"You are right. We mustn't be seen together all the time except in the cafeteria." Gorke said agreeing.

"Does that mean we can't do our laundry together?" Asked Mingh.

"We can, but not together like this. One week I'll do it with your brother and the other time with you, okay?"

Mingh smiled. For a warrior on Aveng Three, she was a scared little rabbit here, I thought.

"You must forgive my sister; she's lost all her warrior instincts since our retrieval. As a warrior on Aveng Three, she was one of the fiercest of her regiment. I too have lost some of my instincts, but as I am male, it holds true that I have some bravery."

"It is so embarrassing. I feel like I'm incomplete and yet I know deep down that I may not be a warrior any longer, but if the occasion arises, I will be brave and do whatever is necessary." Mingh said with conviction.

"Look don't worry about it. I was nowise close to be a warrior on Earth, but my mindset has changed once I arrived here. We all must do what we must."

"Since we are all on the same page, I suggest that we not linger." Boham suggested. He led the way out. Mingh said goodbye to her brother and we entered our rooms lugging our laundry.

It had become my habit to check my room if I had been away from it for a while. I left it in disarray for a reason. Now as I put my things to rights again, I can tell that someone had been in my room. I found a strange stone in a corner of my room. I ignored it and finished straightening up. I tried not to look at it in case it was able to capture images. Now, I understood that while I was spying on them, they were spying on me.

The following morning, I greeted everyone cheerfully and ate my breakfast. I noticed that Aisha kept stealing glances at me and I pretended that I didn't notice. For operatives of the opposition, she was a poor excuse for a spy. Jhael had me completely fooled and I suspect that Elder Sim placed him in my way to keep her informed.

Two weeks later, I received a message from the Elders. They requested that I come to chambers immediately. Still in uniform, I made my way to the chambers. They were all seated up high again, signaling that the meeting was formal. I approached like I'd done before and waited for them to speak.

"Warrior Brightblade, Master Tulle has informed us that in a weeks' time you will be taking up your post. He also suggested that you are ready to travel to Earth. It is our ruling that Warrior Captain Lao accompany you. Your objective is to make sure that your brother isn't being stalked. If he is, you must neutralize the threat and once that is done, return home. Do you understand?" Asked Elder Green.

"Yes sir, I understand." I answered.

"Warrior Brightblade, congratulations and good luck. You will be contacted about your new quarters, soon." Elder Sim said. I scanned her features for signs of anger but found none. Her features were emotionless. I returned to my room quickly. Once there, I jumped up and down squealing. I was so happy. I couldn't wait to see my brother again. I've been on Anthora Two for a month and a half, but by my calculations, and Anthoran time it would be roughly about a year and a half since I'd last seen my family. They probably have gotten used to not having me around, I thought sadly.

That was okay though. All I cared about was my brother and how he was faring. The Elders said that in a couple of weeks I would be leaving to go on my first mission. Warrior Captain Lao would accompany me, and my brother's welfare would finally be secure.

Dinner later, was going to be hard for me. I didn't want to let on that I had would be off planet soon on my first mission. I needed to let Gorke and Mingh know that I had every confidence in their abilities to keep watch over Aisha and Jhael. In a sense, they were on a mission too.

I ate with my friends and we chatted about work and teased Jhael and Aisha about their relationship. Everything was kept to an even keel. Just before we decided to say goodnight, my chronograph chirped. Elder Bitka messaged me about my new quarters.

"Hey guys," I announced. "I've got my new quarters. I'll be moving in a few days."

"You'll still be able to have at least dinner with us, right?" Mingh asked.

"Of course. Master Tulle assured me that after my duties are done, my time afterwards will be mine to do whatever I please."

"You are also graduating if that's the case. I say we party, go out and paint the town red!" Aisha gushed.

The others looked confused. "Painting the town red means having a good time back on Earth." I clarified for them.

"Oh well then, we must go and paint the town red." Lylah said. She had been so quiet that I almost forgot that she was there. Out of all of them, she'd been a mystery to me. I realized that I didn't know much about her. She and Gorke work in communications and that's all I knew about her.

"We probably will see each other more than you think, Lylah. You are working in communications and me at space corps, we're bound to run into each other." I told her.

"That's right, we will." She said a little dejectedly.

"Is everything alright?" I asked sensing her discomfort.

"It's just that Gorke and Jhael work in a different part of the communications sector, I work in the data part. I don't see them at all. The people I work with are kind of cruel to me." She said quietly.

"Is someone bothering you?" I asked ready to go kick ass.

"Some of the men say things that make me feel uncomfortable, especially after they find out that I'd been a warrior. I'm afraid that I cannot defend myself." She said with tears in her eyes. Lylah was a knockout, with blond hair and big boobs, however she wasn't the dumb blond known on Earth. She was intelligent and worked with important data.

"Why didn't you tell me?" Gorke asked. He got up to go sit next to her.

"I don't understand why it is so difficult for me to stand up to those men. I used to kill without thinking about it, but now it scares me to death."

Gorke put his arm around her shoulders and pulled her close. "The next time any of them say something to you and you feel uncomfortable, come find me or better yet message me and I'll come." It didn't escape me that Gorke wanted to do more than protect her. He'd been eying her for a while now.

"Me too." Said Jhael.

"You can count on all of us to come to your aid Lylah." I told her. Workplace drama were the same no matter what planet or dimension you were in, I thought.

Later, in bed, I thought about Lylah and her situation. Men were pigs wherever you go, I thought. It made my blood boil thinking about how awful it had been for her to work with those men and having to endure their probably sexist remarks. Mingh came to mind and her confession of losing her warrior instincts since coming to Anthora Two. The same must've happened to her.

Graduation was a few days later, and it wasn't the elaborate affair it was on Earth. The graduates were gathered in the assembly hall of Sector Four and each trainee was called to the front where Elder Chaktar stood at attention. He saluted each of us and removed our chronographs and replaced it with another and pinned our ranks and badges on our lapels. When my turn came, he even smiled a little.

Later, at a small reception, he told me that my chronograph was a little different from the others he'd handed out. Mine had an extra feature. Mine would alert me to alien DNA as his was. He said that because of my Le'ak abilities, it was important that I know who I dealt with.

After classes I went home to find everyone waiting for me. They informed me that we were going out to celebrate. How could I say no to that? They waited while I showered and changed. I wore my white dress and some boots that I recently bought.

I noticed that while Mingh and I walked together, that her brother stuck close to Lylah. He seemed very protective of her.

"He'd been trying to find a way to express his feelings for her and he told her today. She seems happy about it." Mingh told me.

"That's great, what about you? Who's your secret crush?" I asked.

"Like you, I don't feel the need to pair off with anyone yet. This new existence is different from what I knew back on Aveng Three. I want to settle into it. It is not to say that I haven't been approached by someone. I just don't feel I need someone else in my life now. Can you understand that?" She asked looking at me intently.

"I know exactly what you mean. I can't think of anything else right now. All I can focus on are my warrior duties and protecting my family. My brother is very young, he's only eleven years old and helpless. I feel that having a boyfriend would mess with my focus." I explained.

"Exactly. I spoke with Gorke and he feels that it is okay for him. I warned him to not trust her with our secret, because we just don't know how the Froagans are infiltrating us or how many there are yet."

"Master Physician Bolka says that he was going to do some research. Perhaps it's our skin and not our blood that contains all that is needed to identify us as Anthoran. Why else would they clothed themselves with it?" I suggested.

"Perhaps you are right." She agreed.

"I found a foreign object in my room the other day. It was a small stone. I think Aisha or Jhael put it there to spy on me. I think my Le'ak spazzed out the listening device they placed in my uniform. You should check your room too. They might want to find out why Gorke is in your room so much."

She looked at me with wide eyes. "I have to tell him to search his room as well. We talk about everything when he comes over." She looked worried.

"Be careful and search thoroughly."

Mingh nodded and we continued in silence. Aisha and Jhael were watching us and I reached out to squeeze Mingh's hand. "The game's on now. They are watching us; you must check your room." I let go of her hand and looked straight ahead.

The rest of the evening was spent eating, laughing and then dancing. This was the most fun I've had since coming to Anthora Two. Weren't for the fact that Aisha and Jhael were the enemy, the fun would have been even better. The club we went to serve a beverage that was close to beer on Earth. Aisha and Jhael drank that exclusively. I tried it and almost spat it out. It was bitter and made my stomach churn instantly. Aisha and Jhael enjoyed it immensely.

"How can you drink this stuff?" I asked after taking my second sip.

"It is an acquired taste. I was pleased that Aisha likes it too. We are finding that we have a lot of things in common." Jhael said with a sloppy grin on his face. I looked at Aisha and she wore the same grin.

Just because they liked the drink, I pushed mine away. I went over to the bar to order something different. I asked what the Bizah beer was made of and the bartender said that it was made from the Bizah flower. He said that it used to grow wild on Anthora and almost became extinct because the Froagans used it as a drug. The beer itself did not affect Anthorans like it did the Froagans. Anthorans used the flower as a salve on rashes, while the Froagans got high crushing it into a paste and ingesting it.

I thanked him and brought a bottle of Siklag wine back to our table. I leant over to Mingh and told her to stop drinking the beer and she told her brother. We watched Aisha and Jhael and Lylah just get wasted. I didn't have the heart to tell Gorke that Lylah might be a Froagan too. Druktar looked disgusted with the drink too. Mingh squeezed my hand and I squeezed hers back.

I stood up with my glass of wine raised. "I'd like to make a toast. It is something we did on Earth. I want to thank all of you for celebrating with me and bringing me here to have a good time. I hope that this is just one of the many times we will do this!" I chugged my wine and let out a whoop.

The others followed suit and then we called it a night. As we walked, Jhael and Aisha hung back. Mingh and Gorke walked with me, Druktar and Lylah. I couldn't say what I wanted to say with Lylah around, so I waited. We came to their building and watched as Druktar, Jhael entered the building. Aisha rushed over to me to tell me that she was going to spend some time with Jhael, and she rushed back to him. Lylah waved at us as they all entered the building.

Gorke told them that he would walk Mingh and me to our dorm.

"I think Lylah is a Froagan. She got just as drunk as they did on that beer. The bartender told me that during the Froagan occupation, they used the Bizah flower as a drug and the beer is made with the same flower."

"Could it be that she just likes it? I mean, if she was a Froagan, why would she be frightened of the people she works with?" Gorke asked. He was trying hard to defend her.

"We may have to make sure. I don't know of any other way to test her. She's always been standoffish with me, so I hadn't had any real connection with her to hear her thoughts. Just be careful around her. I know you like her, and she likes you, but really, be careful. Okay?"

Gorke nodded. He touched foreheads with his sister and left the dorm. I decided that I was going to help Mingh search her room. She gave me her earring and we were to pretend to look for it.

"You're so nice to help me look, Fiona."

"Think nothing of it." I told her as I got on my hands and knees to look on the floor. It was covered with some sort of animal skin, like bear rugs back on Earth. As I pretended to search, I spied the odd-looking stone under her wardrobe. So, I deduced that it didn't record images only voices. "I found it!" I announced and got up.

"Oh, thank you." Mingh said as she nodded at me. She understood that the stone was under her wardrobe.

"This was a great night. Thank you for celebrating with me." I said as I hugged Mingh.

"It was a pleasure. Thanks again for helping me find my earring. Good night."

"Good night." I let myself out and went to my room. My eyes strayed to the corner. It was still there. I quickly showered and got in bed. My first real day of work wouldn't start for another day or two. Moving day was certainly soon too.

So much has happened since I died on Earth and I knew that more serious stuff was coming. To find that I was surrounded by the very enemy that killed me made my warrior blood boil. My murder was still fresh in my mind and it made me want to make things happen faster. Master Tulle and Elder Chaktar insisted that we wait to gather more intel on them. It was certainly a stroke of luck that we went out to that club, otherwise, I wouldn't have discovered that Lylah might be an enemy as well. I must remember to ask that they investigate the club too. Why would they serve Bizah beer?

I fell asleep with a mind full of strategies for routing out the enemy in our midst. Sometime in the wee hours of the morning, I awoke. Something woke me up. I quickly scanned my room and found everything just like it was before I fell asleep. Still, I felt something was wrong. I felt anxious.

As quiet as I could, I slipped out of bed and shoved my feet into my slippers. As I approached the door, I could hear voices outside it. I put my ear on the door, not even sure I would be able to make out what the voices were saying. I mean you see stuff like that on television and the voices are exaggerated so that even the studio audience can hear what's being said.

I couldn't quite make out who was talking but suddenly, I could. It was like a switch turned on in my head. It was Aisha and Lylah.

"Lylah, we are counting on you. You're in position and you've gained their trust. Jhael is still too new, but you've been there long enough. No one will suspect you. You have access to the codes."

"It is not as simple as you say sister. I may have access to the codes, but they cannot be activated by one person. It is done sequentially by an Elder, a warrior and a communications technician."

"We know that already. Just get the codes and we'll take it from there. Thank you for walking me back, but you need to get back before someone suspects. Good night."

"I'm glad you found that bar. How is it that these filthy Anthorans know to make Bizah beer?"

"Our people used to force them to make it when we occupied them. They never really knew what it meant to us. I don't think we have anyone in that club, but you never know. You must hurry back before someone sees you and be careful sister."

"I will, good night." Lylah said. I listened for Aisha to get to her room before I could tiptoe back to my bed.

I almost laughed. These had to be the worst spies ever. I heard everything they were saying, and they talked so loudly, I'm sure that if Mingh had been awake, she would have heard them also. They are either new to the game or so drunk from the beer that they're careless, I thought. The other possibility was that I heard their thoughts and not actual voices. It was hard to distinguish whether I'm hearing with my ears or my mind. And could they really be sisters?

One good thing came out of it, however. I now have proof that Lylah is a Froagan. And had it not been for our impromptu celebration, I wouldn't have known. I tried to go back to sleep, but it was difficult. Aisha was forcing Lylah to steal the codes to the cloaking device that kept our planet invisible to the enemy. I wasn't completely sure how they would get the codes out to their waiting ships, but I'm sure Elder Chaktar can thwart their plans. I'll be working with the warriors soon and I will make it my business to keep a closer eye on her. Lylah has made it very easy to watch her especially after she'd expressed her discomfort with the men she worked with. I could drop by her workstation periodically without her being suspicious.

I must've slept, because my chronograph chirped, startling me out of sound sleep. This morning, I didn't mind getting out of bed to start my day. This was my first day on the base. I wouldn't be working yet, I still had additional training to do there.

I met Mingh and Aisha for breakfast and wasn't surprised to find Lylah and the others at the table as well.

Jhael sat opposite me, sandwiched between Lylah and Aisha. They looked hungover, while the others appeared well rested. Served them right, I thought.

"You don't look well Aisha, are you okay?" I asked. I put my best concerned face on.

She made a face. "Ugh, I think I overdid it with the beer last night. My head feels like it might explode."

"Is that why I feel so bad?" Lylah asked with a pained expression on her face.

"I guess the next time we go paint the town red, we'll listen to you Fiona. You look ready to do battle in your new position." Jhael stated with a weak smile.

"I hope you've learned your lesson. Perhaps you should invest in aspirin or whatever passes for that here." I told them.

"What's aspirin?" Druktar asked.

"It is a pain medication. The wonder drug back on Earth." I explained.

"I'll be sure to ask for something when I go in to work today." Aisha assured them.

"Well, I'm off to my first day. See you guys later." I announced. The others got up also, leaving the hungover trio to their misery.

"I think Fiona might be suspicious of us. She might know about the Bizah flower and its effects on us, you saw how she made the others stop drinking it." Lylah said.

Hearing her voice so clearly made me stumble. I dumped my tray and walked out of the cafeteria. I stood just outside the door as an experiment to see if I could still hear them.

"You might be right. She used to live in the library when she first got here. There's no telling what she's learned." Aisha agreed.

"You are both being paranoid. She may be a descendant of the original Brightblade, but she is not as cunning. I'm still waiting to see how long it will take for her to notice my listening device that I personally placed in her room. She hasn't noticed it." Jhael interjected with a chuckle.

"I don't know. She seems intelligent to me. Most of the time she doesn't notice me, but I watch her. She watches you very carefully. I will take advantage of this." Lylah said.

Someone bumped into me standing at the doorway. I hurried away before I attracted more attention. I hurried to my room and took in a deep breath. This was getting more complicated. I'm was no spy, but here I was plotting against beings who have been hunting my people for eons.

As I hurried to put finishing touches to my hair and uniform, I vowed that I would personally rid Anthora Two of this vile threat.

The ride out to the base was not long, however the route was different than the one I was used to. We rode through a part of the main city that I wasn't familiar with. The buildings were not as tall as the ones on the other side of the city. These buildings were no more than four to five stories tall and had almost no windows. As we entered the main complex, I noticed signs for the barracks, mess hall, armory and bunkers. I realized that this was just like an army base back on Earth. We drove past a huge hangar where I spied real live space cruisers.

I didn't know what I was expecting, but this surpassed it. I was looking at true alien technology and I was part of it, a vital part of it.

The conveyor dropped us off at a large open area. Warriors of every description stood at attention. For the benefit of newbies, like I and some of the others were, sergeants directed us, mine was Sergeant Veena. Suddenly, a loud whistle sounded, and everyone stood at attention in their designated ranks, including me. My new rank was Second Officer Warrior of the Anthoran Space Corps. It just meant that I was a crew member of the space corps.

"Today begins a new chapter in the lives of many of you. Our world is constantly vigilant of the ever-increasing threat of invasion. It is left to us to keep our world and our people safe. A lot is expected of you and you will not take it lightly. Many of you have seen some combat, while the rest of you dream of it. Our task is to make you ready to fight to keep Anthora Two safe for future generations. For those of you that are new graduates, welcome to the A.D.B. (Anthoran Defense Base)." That glowing speech was given by Imperial Commander Podge. Standing next to him was Elder Chaktar.

We were dismissed and instructed to go to our stations. I was stationed at ground command for the time being. I was to be trained in the protocols and defense plans for the city. In the next few days, I would be expected to learn the procedures and defense plans for each sector of the city. After which, I would advance to the Anthoran Air Defense command and so on so forth.

In a private meeting, Elder Chaktar assured me that as soon as I completed the training, that my mission on Earth would take place. Assigned to me and Captain Lao was a space cruiser ready to take us to Earth.

The mess hall was full and lively with men and women from every corner of the universe. We even had Nozans. They were outfitted in special suits. Because of their special survival needs, they could only serve as ground defense. They sat together in a separate area, almost cave like to eat. I was surprised to see so many.

Captain Lao joined me at my table. For some reason, I was still being treated with esteem. My name still carried a lot of weight. I had the table to myself.

"This is going to take a lot to get used to. In the dorm, we were all trainees and I guess in the same boat, but now I'm a warrior, able to fight to defend us. I just wish they'd stop putting so much stock in my name. I'm not Leena and I feel that they expect me to perform miracles."

"Give them time. You'll be surprised how quickly your table will fill up with comrades," he said looking around. "You said you had news?"

"Yes, I do. Yesterday, they took me out to celebrate at a club in the shopping plaza. As you already know, Jhael and Aisha are Froagans and I discovered that Lylah is one too. At the club, they got wasted on a beer the bar served called Bizah beer. They could hardly walk by the time we were ready to leave. Jhael has placed a listening device in my room and Minghs' as well."

Lao's eyebrows shot up. "What do these devices look like?"

I described what they looked like and further filled him in on how I got confirmation that Lylah was a Froagan. I also asked if there was a way to have the club investigated. I told him of the plans they had to get the codes from the air corps. I told him everything including my fears that this was getting too big for us to contain alone.

"I will speak with Elder Chaktar. My advice to you is to continue to gather information and to also keep doing whatever you are doing." He got up and left.

I don't know how he thought I could continue doing that way out on base. I'm gonna ask Mingh and her brother to keep their eyes and ears open.

# CHAPTER SIX

Later, Elder Chaktar approached me. He suggested that I stay in the barracks while my quarters were being prepared. My new apartment unit was within walking distance of the base. The buildings I saw on our way in were living quarters for those who worked on the base. I told him about all I was feeling.

I could tell that he was trying to be sympathetic, but his effort didn't fill me with any sort of comfort. I guess emotions come across differently when you're from a different dimension.

The barracks were not what I was expecting either. I've gotta stop comparing things to Earth. In fact, I wasn't expecting to move so soon either, but needs must. They sent a detail with me back to the dorm to get my stuff. They waited patiently while I packed and when I was done, they loaded them unto the conveyor. This conveyor looked like a moving truck and my stuff barely filled it. I felt a perverse sense of accomplishment leaving the stone behind.

Once my stuff was delivered to my quarters, I packed necessary items for my stay on base. I walked around familiarizing myself with my new apartment. The floors were done, and the light fixtures were being put in. I came upon another listening stone purely by accident. The bedroom was completely done, and while I was helping the movers push the bed into position, I spotted it. This time it was so pale looking that I almost missed it because it blended with the wood grain of the flooring. It was in a corner of my bedroom. On a hunch, I went to the other rooms and found stones in those too. It seems that keeping me under surveillance was a top priority. Not only did I have to worry about listening devices in the dorm, now I had to worry about them on the base too.

Elder Chaktar will not be pleased to know that there may be Froagans on the base as well. I really didn't know who to trust now. Apart from Captain Lao, and the Elder, I didn't know anyone. My only clue to who is friend or foe is in how they treated me. My name continues to illicit adoring attention, so if I get that from someone, I know that he or she is a friend. They just couldn't help themselves it seemed. They hear my name and immediately, I am a hero.

The barracks were mercifully segregated. Women in one row on one side of the base and the men in the other side across from them. I wasn't sure how many women warriors there were, but an educated guess tells me that we were few. The female section of the barracks had four large units with each housing ten to fifteen women. I couldn't tell how many were in each, but if I were to guess, we numbered about fifty-five. My barracks had fifteen beds in it and by my count, only ten were occupied.

As I made myself at home, I found a stone wedged between the mattress and the frame of my bed. Wow, I thought. Someone really wanted to know my every move. Who was I gonna talk Froagan stuff with? They must think that I felt confident enough to spill my guts to whoever just because they were warriors like me. How monumentally stupid.

I can safely bet that my quarters will be fully outfitted with listening devices and even video surveillance. Just who was Leena Brightblade?

"Second Officer Brightblade!" Sergeant Veena announced loudly. She was standing at the entrance of the barracks.

I quickly stood up at attention and saluted as I was trained to do (fist to chest and then straight out) "Sir!" I replied.

"You will accompany me to Command Sector Zed." She said.

I grabbed my little red beret and followed her out. Eyes were fixed on me as I walked past the other women who also stood at attention.

Our trip to Command Sector Zed, demanded a small conveyor ride outside of the base. The Sergeant sat rigidly beside me in the back while a private drove us. She didn't speak nor did she look at me. That made me nervous.

Luckily, the ride ended, and I jumped out to follow her into Command Sector Zed. Being new, I couldn't help gawking at everything. In my head, I was oohing and ahhing at all the shiny metal all around me. The Sergeant took me to Imperial Commander Podge's office. When I entered the office, I quickly stood at attention and saluted.

"At ease Brightblade." He said sitting behind his desk. He looked even more impressive up close. I was too afraid to stare at him when he congratulated me at the graduation ceremony. His hair was silver, a color I had encountered only once since coming to Anthora Two. What planet was he from, I wondered?

"Second Officer Brightblade, Elder Chaktar and a few others will be having dinner with me later. I will send someone to come collect you at nineteen-hundred sharp." His features didn't give anything away as he spoke.

"Sir, yes sir!" I saluted and turned to leave when he didn't say anything more. The Sergeant was waiting for me in the waiting area. She gave me a curious look but refrained from asking me anything. I could tell that she was dying to though.

The barracks was empty when we got back. Sgt. Veena told me that they were out on an exercise. She suggested that I hurry to catch up. I ran back outside to see them running off. I pumped my legs to catch up and fell in line. This was something like Earth, but I could be wrong. A run on Earth and a run here could be different. A few minutes later, I was proven right. In a clearing near where we came to a stop, were supplies waiting for us.

Our names were on each backpack. The packs contained a coil of rope, a knife, a bottle of water, a small pouch of rations and a camouflage blanket.

"Attention!" Drill Sergeant Koop shouted. "This exercise is to help you familiarize yourselves with an ambush method used in combat. Around you are the trees that you will climb to hide yourselves in. Your blankets will take on whatever plumage, bark, and limb you are on. It is activated by shaking it and then throwing it over what you wish to hide. Shake and test your blankets by dropping it over your feet and the ground."

We did as we were instructed and I was amazed by how the blanket suddenly looked like the dirt on the ground, the black of my boots and the red of the hem of my uniform trousers. The drill sergeant further instructed us to pick a tree to climb in the wooded area near the clearing.

Drill Sergeant Koop had blue hair as did Sergeant Veena. Although I didn't get any bad vibes from either of them, I decided to be extra careful around them simply because they originated from the same planet as Elder Sim. There were a few warriors with blue hair too and I noted that they stayed to themselves.

We were split up into groups of three and assigned a captain for each group. Unfortunately, I was captain and my two team members were blue haired. Odd thing about them was that they wore the 'I adore you' expression on their faces. Okay, so they were friends.

Pua and Lippi were their names. I instructed Pua to find us a good tree while Lippi and I carried our packs. Pua found a rather large tree around the trunk and tall enough so that once climbed we'd be at least ten feet off the ground.

"Any idea how we're going to climb this tree?" I asked them.

"We used to climb trees all the time back on Embeta Twelve. The ground wasn't safe, our homes were high up in the trees." Lippi supplied. I watched as she demonstrated how to loop the rope around the tree trunk and then braced her legs on the tree on one side while simultaneously inching the rope around the tree up inches at a time and then feet as she got higher. Once she got onto the first limb, she tied one end of the rope around it and let the other end dangle to the ground.

Pua caught the end and fashioned an elaborate loop which she inserted her foot in and then pulled herself up. Once she was with Lippi, she let down the rope and asked that I attach the packs to it. I watched as they worked together to pull our packs up. Then it was my turn to climb up. I only slid back down once, and then I was sitting atop the huge bough Lippi picked out. I looked around us to see the others either already up in their tress or still down on the ground struggling.

When we were all finally up in the trees, Sergeant Koop announced that the enemy was approaching. I was surprised to see all of us 'disappear' under our camo blankets. I looked on the ground as 'Froagans' approached. Instinct took over as I uncovered myself and threw my knife into the enemy below our tree. I was the first to engage the enemy. The others followed suit and only when all the enemy was lying dead on the ground, did Sgt Koop tell us to come down.

Coming down was easy enough and I couldn't wait to examine the enemy on the ground. They were androids of course but they looked so life-like that once I was close enough, I wanted to kill it again.

"Good job!" Beamed Sgt. Koop. He held the remote control in his hand to activate the androids once again. "Froagans have a weak spot and for every one of you that targeted it, well done. Their weak spot is their heads. Once the brainwaves are interrupted, they become incapacitated and can be killed easily."

I watched as the androids came to life again to stand at attention. Our next exercise was to engage the enemy in hand to hand combat. Keeping in mind that the androids were also armed, each team was to be careful not get tagged by the light beam of the android's weapon.

Pua, Lippi and I circled around our android keeping well away from its weapon, a gun that projected a red-light beam. Pua threw her knife. It missed the head but landed on its shoulder. The android turned to face her, while still trying to target Lippi and me. I threw my knife and grazed the side of its head. Lippi quickly went in to stab it in the heart. We watched our android fall to the ground convulsing.

Sgt. Koop came to inspect our work. He grinned at us but didn't approach the android. I saw why when it suddenly got up and tried to attack me. Lippi pushed me out of the way, and it shot Lippi in the abdomen with a loud burst of its gun, then fell back down.

"Lippi!" I screeched and rushed to her side. She was on the ground holding her abdomen as blood oozed out from around her fingers. She lay there whimpering and I looked around wildly for a way to help her.

Sgt. Koop knelt beside us and using his chronograph called for a medic. Within minutes, a medical conveyor arrived and transferred her carefully on board and took off again. I wanted to go with her but didn't know if I'd be back in time to await the driver Commander Podge was sending for me. Pua went with her instead.

"Why were the androids outfitted with live ammo?" I asked him horrified.

"They weren't supposed to be, the weapon was supposed to give off colored light beams to indicate that you'd been hit." He explained. He looked shook up enough to convince me that he had nothing to do with it. It also dawned on me that, that attack was meant for me; had Lippi not pushed me out of the way, it would have been me the medics came for.

Sgt. Koop pulled out the remote and deactivated the androids who all at once stood still and shut down. Another conveyor came to collect them. All the androids were bound with the ropes as a precaution. Sgt. Koop ended the exercise and we headed back to the base.

On the run back, some of the other women kept well away from me, giving me these puzzling looks. Once we got back, I headed for my bunk. I needed a shower as I had Lippi's blood on my uniform. I ignored the others. I didn't care what they thought of me. From the corner of my eyes I could see them gathered together whispering. Then they sent their spokesman to approach me.

I was in such a mood that Sgt. Veena might have to call for another medic.

"Hey Brightblade, we just wanted you to know that we saw what happened and that we also know that, that attack was meant for you. We want you to know that we've got your back, we just don't know why." Her name embroidered on her shirt said Larson, S.

I snorted. "Take your pick. My name is Brightblade, I'm a warrior and a woman. I'm just so tired of the snide remarks, the dirty looks, the adoring looks. I am not Leena Brightblade. I am Fiona and that's all I will ever be. Whatever she may have done, was her gig not mine. I just wish everyone would just leave me alone." I hadn't meant to cry, but the tears came just the same. Suddenly I was surrounded by comforting women who patted me on my shoulders and back.

"Stop worrying about all of that. I don't know about the others on the base, but we know who you are. You're Fiona Brightblade." Sue Larson said.

I smiled weakly at them. "Thanks guys, I really appreciate it."

The others dispersed after making sure that I was okay. Sue hung back. She had a huge smile on her face. "I wanted to introduce myself before, but I was a little bit in awe. I'm from Earth too." She began to tell me about herself. She was only eighteen when she died. She didn't remember how she died, and she'd been on Anthora for seven years.

After she told me her life's story, I excused myself to go shower. I dressed in a clean uniform and stepped outside just as the driver came for me.

The driver drove off the base and passed my apartment building. Although the commander wasn't from Earth, his house was a mini mansion modeled after Earth's design. Elder Chaktar was standing in the doorway waving me in.

"Good evening, Elder Chaktar." I said respectfully as I got near.

"Good evening, Fiona. Come in." He replied as he stepped back to allow me in. True to its design, the formal foyer was stately complete with fresh flowers on a round mahogany table in its middle. The Elder led me to the dining room where everyone sat at the table.

"Good evening everyone." I said as I sat in the only seat left.

The commander was seated at the head of the table and he inclined his head to me. "Fiona, welcome to my home. This is my wife Micha, and I assume you are familiar with everyone else." He said touching the woman sitting beside him lightly on the arm.

I smiled at her. "Pleased to meet you, Mrs. Podge."

She smiled back and looked around the table and then back at her husband. She seemed to be communicating something that only he understood.

"Fiona, do you need to expel some energy, or can you wait for after dinner?" Mrs. Podge asked.

"Oh yes, if you don't mind." I answered quickly. Being outside most of the day made for a massive build-up.

"I'll take her Mother." Bel volunteered.

I did a double take. Bel was the commander's daughter? I didn't see that coming, especially since I'd only seen her as a store clerk. She led me to the basement of the house and into a room no bigger than a closet between the washer and dryer. As I expelled, I imagined the lights flickering upstairs. I came out of the room and smiled at her and she led us back to the dining room. Commander Podge and everyone at the table were wielders. I wanted to relax but after what happened today, I needed reassurance that I wouldn't be killed in my sleep.

"Commander Podge, may I speak freely?" I asked. A server rolled a trolley up to me where I chose what I wanted to eat. After she served me, she left the room quietly.

"We're all friends here. What is on your mind?" The commander asked. He even wore a sincere expression on his face. I looked around the table to find everyone watching me.

"Sir, it seems that I am a concern to our common enemy even here on the base. I'm assuming that Elder Chaktar filled you in on the happenings at the dorm, however, I found listening stones in every room in my apartment. There's even one wedged between the mattress and frame of my bed on base. Today while participating in a drill in the woods, an android malfunctioned and attacked, hurting one of my teammates. The attack was clearly meant for me. Why is all this happening?" All of it came out in a rush.

I looked around the table and found astonished expressions on almost all their faces. The commander's wife clasped her husband's hand and Bel stood up.

"Father, you have to do something!" Bel exclaimed.

"Fiona I must clarify one thing for you. The stones you see in your apartment are not listening stones, they are for your protection. They jam any listening devices that may be in your rooms."

My eyes grew like saucers. "Then what do the listening devices look like?"

"They usually are attached to things you already have." Bel answered.

"Oh, thank goodness I'm relieved the stones are something else, but I guess Jhael was right when he said that I was too dumb to find the listening device he put in my dorm room."

"I neutralized it. It was in your hairbrush." Elder Chaktar said.

"I'm sorry to bring my problems here and spoiling your dinner, Commander Podge. I've just been so overwhelmed lately." I confessed.

"This is a safe place for all of us and especially you. Now finish your dinner. We have more to discuss." Said the commander.

After dinner, Mrs. Podge and Bel gave me a tour of their home. It made me a little bit homesick, but I was able to brush it off. I couldn't dwell on the past and on things I couldn't control. I was an Anthoran and there was the matter of my mission to Earth coming up. That should be all I dwell on.

After the tour, the ladies took me to the living room. Mrs. Podge told me that in her younger days, she was part of the retrieval team. She especially liked going to Earth. She loved the homes she'd seen. After marrying the commander, she insisted on having a home just like the ones on Earth. Now she counsels the newly retrieved.

I asked about where the commander was from and she said that he was from Embeta Twelve. At my confused expression, she realized that I didn't understand, because she went on to explain that Embeta Twelve had two races of people. Silver haired people were the ruling class while the blue haired were the working class.

The living room was huge. Two couches and two loveseats left plenty of room for comfortable side chairs. They even had a fireplace. Commander Podge picked up a remote and pressed a button. I was expecting a television screen to pop up from somewhere but instead, a blank screen did. Another button activated a projector. The commander had a presentation prepared for us. In it he detailed all that was happening on Anthora Two that was a concern for our people and the planet in general.

It had become apparent that the Froagans had infiltrated the planet. Only recently, since my retrieval had the scientists and military began to discover how it was being done. It was on a retrieval mission to Teah Four. The team were picking up a group of Anthorans who had been killed. The Froagan who had killed the group was able to watch as the Anthorans were retrieved.

They then reported back to their superiors who've devised a way to masquerade as an Anthoran. Our scientists had captured one such imposter and examined it and wiped its memory of the capture and allowed it to enter the planet. Jhael was one of the few imposters who had successfully infiltrated Anthora Two. Much to the frustrations of Jhael and the others who are on the planet, they aren't able to report to their superiors. The jamming defenses of the planet has been keeping all communications off/on-planet from being delivered.

After the presentation, the commander looked around the room at us and announced that the scientists have discovered how the Froagans are taking over the bodies of Anthorans.

"Anthorans have a rather unique physiology. Our skin contains all there is to know about us even memories. When the scientists enhanced our genes all those hundreds of thousands years ago, it wasn't quite certain that our survival would succeed. The Froagans have had millennia to study us and they have succeeded in using our skin to bypass our sensors. By putting on our skin, they found that they could passed as Anthoran." He stopped speaking to look each one in the eye. It made me feel uneasy when his eyes bore into mine.

"Commander, was Jhael an Anthoran when he came to retrieve me?" I asked.

"Jhael is an imposter. The original was overpowered on his mission to retrieve another. We captured and examined him. His memory had been wiped and has been under surveillance since. We were able to secure the real body and keep it in suspended sleep." The commander answered.

"With a specialized laser the Froagan cut into all the layers of skin and dressed itself. They can put on and take off this skin. They cannot sleep in it which is why you were able to spot the Aisha skin."

I was horrified to think of how horrible is was for the real Aisha and Jhael to die. "I remember being told that we were invisible to others when off planet. Jhael couldn't see me as I hovered over him in the morgue. He could only see me when my essence was back in my body. He never once looked up at me as I watched him."

"That's right. That is the only thing they do not know about us. And it is something they mustn't know. Considering what happened on the base today, we now know that you have become a target. If they were to capture you and use your skin, they would be able to try to bring about our destruction."

I sat back in shock. My ancestry has made me a target. If they succeed in killing me for a second time, they would be able to use my skin to their advantage. Most of the planet see me as a hero and probably would not refuse me anything. It would be so easy to fool everyone, I thought.

"We will have a back-up vessel following closely behind you when you go off planet. As we speak, the space corps and communication centers are being outfitted with the Froagan detectors. Anyone who doesn't pass the detection will be removed from duty and destroyed." Elder Chaktar said.

"What happens to those whose skin was stolen? Are they completely dead and gone forever?" Bel asked.

"Their essence is still aware, but without a body, it is not certain how long they can survive. Aisha, Jhael and a few others' bodies and essences are being held in sleep capsules until our scientists can successfully return them to their bodies. The problem is that we are not certain where some of those bodies are." Commander Podge explained.

The silence in the room was pregnant with the knowledge that those precious Anthorans might very well be lost forever. I didn't see how any of those whose skin was stolen could possibly be restored. It was my understanding that an Anthoran was retrieved almost immediately before the body was processed for burial or decomposed.

"Commander, when I go on my mission to see about my brother, am I to assume that I will have orders to capture a Froagan in order to gain new intel?"

The commander turned to regard me with a sadness in his eyes. "Fiona, we have no other opportunity to capture one. You are a lure they cannot resist. What we ask of you is very dangerous and we have no way of knowing if they mean to kill you or use your skin."

"What use is it to capture one when we have several on the planet already?" I asked angrily.

"Froagans are connected by a mind link. Those on the planet cannot connect to the hive mind. As imposters they cannot communicate with the skin on, and because of the planets' jamming devices, they still cannot communicate with the skin off. That is why they are after the codes to disable it."

"That means we can only capture and interrogate it off-planet, but being part of the hive mind, they would immediately contact their ships and we'd be surrounded." I deduced.

"Father, that is too dangerous." Bel interjected.

"That is where Le'ak comes in. Our intel has discovered that their leader travels with the fleets. They have no home world that we know of. They are still planet hopping and destroying whole galaxies. They must be stopped. We are being joined by leaders of other worlds to put a stop them."

"What other worlds?" I asked. I looked around me at the others sitting with me and realized that there was a diverse group.

"Fiona, the Froagans have been plundering the galaxy for a long time. Every planet that our ancestors landed on, have either been visited by the enemy or is at present being occupied by them. Earth and a few others have been lucky to escape occupation, but it won't be long before they face that danger as well." Elder Chaktar said.

Later, I lay in my bed thinking how much danger I was about to expose myself to. Even with an edge I still faced danger. My ability to wield Le'ak wasn't all that great. I hadn't had enough training to use it effectively if I had to defend myself. Commander Podge insisted that my training continue on the base and Elder Chaktar agreed and so did Captain Lao.

# CHAPTER SEVEN

Morning came much too soon for me. I almost forgot that I was in the military or on base for that matter. I only awoke when one of my fellow warrior-mates shook me awake. I still can't seem to act like I'm a mindless military drone.

I hurried to shower and dress. I only had minutes to spare before Sgt. Veena came to inspect and scream at us. We had weapons maneuvers this morning and after that I was to report to Elder Chaktar and Captain Lao for Le'ak training.

Le'ak training was off base and I felt all eyes on me when the conveyor came for me. Sooner or later, one of the women will ask me where I go, and I wish I knew what I'd answer.

Elder Chaktar led me into the training room. I immediately walked to the wall to expel my energies, but Captain Lao stopped me. Weapons training was outdoors, and I could literally feel my body absorbing the sun's energy. I needed to expel.

"I'm vibrating here." I told them.

"Today you will expel by using your energies to defend yourself." Captain Lao said. He walked further away from where I was standing and took a stance. I looked over to Elder Chaktar; he too was positioning himself.

I dropped my jacket and shook my arms. These guys looked like they weren't kidding. To prove my point, Chaktar activated his Le'ak and raised his arms. I followed suit. I felt the power gathering in my body and my fingers tingled.

Captain Lao threw a warning shot over my left shoulder. It was so close that I could feel its heat. Elder Chaktar threw one as well, this time across my right shoulder.

"Two against one, that's not fair!" I screeched.

"The Froagans aren't known for fairness. Defend yourself!" Chaktar insisted. He threw another stream of searing light at me. I ducked and threw one back. It went wide, but I threw it.

"Sad, try again!" Chaktar shouted condescendingly.

I nodded and targeted Lao. He scrambled to get out of my streams' way, but I got him. Then I felt sorry because I burned him, and I could smell his scorched flesh. I hurried to his side, but he threw a stream at me. I jumped away but not fast enough. I felt the heat along the side of my right thigh. I dropped to the floor, but Chaktar powered up to fire at me again.

I went to inspect my thigh and realized that it was healing. I looked up at Chaktar and smiled. I rolled away from his stream and fired back at him. This time I got him. His right ear lobe blackened. He didn't even flinch as he powered up.

Lao got my attention with a hit to my left flank which sizzled. I grunted and faced him. I knew that this was just training, an exercise, but damn that hurt. As I felt the healing begin on my burns, I let loose from both arms streams of angry heat at them both. The force of it knocked them off their feet.

The stench of scorched flesh filled the air. I dropped to the floor and crawled over to first Chaktar and then Lao. They were breathing thank goodness. Moments later, they started to stir as their bodies healed itself. All the pain from my burns was gone and I watched as Lao's skin started to turn pink again.

Elder Chaktar was the first to sit up. I watched him closely. He checked his body quickly and then turned to look at me.

"I think you have learned all you need to learn from us." He said.

"That was a lesson? If I'm not mistaken, you both tried to hurt me."

"It was necessary. You must learn to defend yourself and to protect others." Lao added.

"Why didn't you tell me that my body would heal? The books in the Library said that we healed others not ourselves."

"Those books were wrong. There is nothing stopping you from confronting the enemy should the occasion arise." Lao interjected. He had sufficiently healed and was sitting up against the wall.

I stood up because my thigh was feeling better and so was my side. "What else about Le'ak was wrong in the books? Seems to me that you guys are grooming me for more than just going to see about my brother."

"Your only mission is to go to Earth to protect your brother. Our intelligence says that he is safe for the moment. Your killers have not made any advances toward him." Chaktar told me.

I said nothing and walked over to the wall to expel the rest of my energies. I noticed that Chaktar and Lao didn't need to.

I had a lot to think about as I changed into a new uniform Chaktar furnished. I had fleetingly wondered how I was going to explain my ruined uniform and now I didn't have to. A conveyor was waiting for me when I left the building.

I thought hard on what I'd learned this evening. Elder Chaktar and Lao didn't have to spell it out for me. They said that my killers hadn't approached my brother, which translates to that they may. Did they know that my brother was Anthoran?

They also said *my* killers. John and Buck were still on Earth hunting. If they are targeting my brother, I will have the chance to hunt them. Well, that is if they aren't aware that I came back.

The next morning, Lippi came back to the barracks. She didn't look worse for wear. Anthoran medical technology was able to patch her up. She, Pua and the others sat with me at my table pulling another table so that we could all fit. I realized that I had a new crew. The rest of the week was uneventful as we progressed from ground defense to air defense.

Most of our exercises were virtual simulations. I thought that after the incident in the woods that they weren't taking any chances of having another malfunctioning android. In the simulations we are in space to confront or defend against attack by Froagan battle drones. I wondered if outer space will look as awesome. Drill sergeant Rim was a hard task master as he put us through endless scenarios, and I was frustrated on one level and appreciative on another. I thought it was a little bit overkill to have so many ships firing at us. I mean, come on, unless we were in actual war, there shouldn't be so many ships coming at us like this.

It dawned on me that they've been training us for such an eventuality. A Brightblade finally being retrieved is giving Anthorans a fighting chance. Whoa! These people really should get a grip. I am not Leena, I am not a hero.

They still see me as one, however. How can one person singlehandedly fight off a single fleet? Oh, wait a minute. Are they thinking that I will repeat history and kill the new Froagan leader? Even if I could perform such a miracle, what would it accomplish? I'm sure that subsequent Froagan leaders from that time has learned from history that he or she should have an heir or heirs. Should he be eliminated, his heir would step in and they'd be back to business.

Every time I start to relax and get comfortable, I get hit with reality. All the wielders are not warriors. Those that are, are few in numbers. Commander Podge had spoken of other worlds occupied by the Froagans and some alliance forged to fight them off. Chaktar and he seem to think that Le'ak is the answer to everything. I will do my part but only to make sure that my brother is safe. Whatever else they have planned is on them, I thought selfishly.

Air defense maneuvers was a breeze and now it was on to actual stations and assignments. Most of the women in my barracks had been assigned to ground defense. Only Lippi, Pua and Sue and I were assigned to air defense. I had been promoted to First Lieutenant of Air Defense. Captain Lao was our immediate supervisor. When we go off planet, they would crew with me.

Elder Chaktar told me they were to undergo a final check to make sure they were truly Anthoran before we take off into outer space. If they pass, they'll be able to get full disclosure on what the mission was.

Two days later, Commander Podge invited me to dinner. I had no choice but to go. I guess it was short notice for everyone, because no one at the table looked dressed for dinner.

"It has come to my attention, that your mission to Earth had come under scrutiny by Elder Sim. She is insisting that we have a representative of the Medical Facility accompany us. To what end, I don't know, but I suspect that it is to not only compromise the mission, but also to be able to finally get message out to the Froagans. Elder Sim is a Froagan who we'd captured, and memory wiped. We cannot deny her or else she will become suspicious. You must find a way to eliminate it as soon as you are out of Anthoran range."

"Do you know who she is sending?"

"She said that it will be one of her more experienced healers. Your crew must consist of a healer in case injuries occur. I am not sure who it is yet."

"How long will communication last between our cruiser and the planet?" I asked. My heart was beating fast and hard in my chest.

"Communications between the planet will disconnect as soon as the cruiser is out of orbit. The spy among you will be able to alert the hive mind almost at once as well if there is a ship close by." Commander Podge answered.

"What can we do to counter this?" It all seemed so hopeless now. Suddenly I thought of when Jhael retrieved me. He could've made contact then.

"Wasn't Jhael able to contact the hive mind when he came for me?"

"There is only one complication with having the skin on. They cannot mind link. They either must remove the skin altogether or partially. The skin hinders them just like our cloaking device blocks the probes." Elder Chaktar explained.

"So, the only way to identify the spy among us is to catch them without the skin on?" I asked trying to picture it.

"Yes, you must be vigilant of your crew members. Ensigns Lippi, Pua and Sue and this one other person will be on board, and it will be up to you and Capt. Lao to identify and neutralize it quickly."

Sleep was getting harder and harder to fall into these days. In the morning, I will be getting intel on my crew members to determine if they were legit or not. What's more incredible was that if any of them failed to be Anthoran, they would still be allowed to go on the mission. It would be up to Capt. Lao and me to deal with them once we escaped orbit. That last Le'ak session with Elder Chaktar and Capt. Lao came to mind. One of us would have to deal with the enemy quickly.

More intel on the Froagans came to me in bits and pieces. They couldn't sleep in the skin or communicate with the hive mind. They didn't have any special powers other than the hive mind which gave them rapid reflexes. If one didn't know something, the information would immediately be relayed from the collective minds. Out of disguise, they were formidable fighters. That made sense, since when they assassinated me, they had to doff off their skins. They were able to fight better.

I was informed that when I returned from my mission that I would be able to move into my apartment. After maneuvers, I took a stroll to see the place. I had asked Mrs. Podge if she would see to it that my place looked more Earthlike in décor. I was relieved that she hadn't gone all out like her place. It was beautiful, however. The simple and functional pieces from my dorm room were enhanced with drapes, and wall hangings. She even thought of my age and had a variety of music discs that I knew and liked.

Sue, Lippi and Pua and I went out to dinner with the rest of the women from the base. I had a hard time being cheerful because Sue was a Froagan. She was the one who I had to eliminate. Lippi and Pua were okay. The healer they were sending with us was also a Froagan. Sue was the only one who had moved to her own apartment right after our training. I wondered how she slept while on base. It must've been torture.

"Sgt. Veena is getting a new group while we are gone. I hope they give her hell. That woman was a pain in my ass." Sue said suddenly.

"She didn't scream at you as much as she did me. I know for a fact she goes to bed at night thinking of ways to make my life miserable." I told her.

The women around our table laughed. "I think we were the best group she had. To us!" She announced and lifted her glass of Siklag wine. We followed suit and then we danced the night away with the men who weren't too shy to ask.

The following morning, we were escorted to the pre-flight station. There we performed a safety checklist on the cruiser and did inventory of our supplies. The techs double checked the cruiser and we signed off on it. The healer was finally introduced to us as Healer Gruha. He was a massive man with pale green skin. His was a species I had not been introduced to before.

"How do you do?" I asked him as I openly checked out his green hue.

"I am well, thank you." He replied.

"I don't believe I've ever met someone like you before. What planet were you retrieved from?"

"I was retrieved from the Botan Star System. My planet was the fourth planet from the star called Armayah. I have been here since I was a child." Gruha supplied.

"Welcome aboard. I'm sure we will work well together. Hopefully we won't need your services and you get to have a vacation.' I said to him.

"I'm sure it will be as you say." He replied.

Sue came up to him and smiled brightly at him. "Hi, I'm Sue Larson. I've never seen anyone from your planet before, what was it like?" She asked and took his arm to go talk away from us.

Smooth, I thought. She wasn't wasting any time I saw. Well, plot away, Captain Lao and I will be killing both of you later, I thought.

At fifteen hundred hours, our team was brought aboard the cruiser. We each took our stations and a final check took place. From my seat beside Capt. Lao, I turned to look back at the rest of the crew. Sue was navigations officer and sat at her station behind the captain. Lippi and Pua sat at their stations as security and communications officers. Behind me was Healer Gruha.

I clicked on my com link and turned on the privacy mode. "Capt. Lao once we're free of orbit, I think I know of a way to deal with our problem."

"Do not tell me." He answered curtly and disconnected his com.

I looked quickly behind me to catch Sue watching us. I waved at her and gave her a thumbs up. She waved back and clicked on her link. "This is the most exciting thing I've ever done. I can't wait for us to be off already."

I was about to answer her when the command center began the count down. It wasn't exactly like on Earth but similar.

It was almost an hour before we broke orbit. I turned to see how our crew fared since we'd only done it in simulation. Sue looked green and held onto her stomach. She got up to go to the lavatory and the healer assured me that he would look after her.

I nodded and turned back to my console. I waited a few minutes and then got up to go to the back. I motioned for Lippi and Pua to stay put. I tried to calculate how long it would take them to remove their head skins so that they could communicate with the hive mind. I gave them a three-minute window and then I threw light at the door lock and burst in.

Healer Gruha was almost done taking off his head skin when I burst in. I threw a wave of heat at them enough to melt their heads and watched as they fell to the floor. I heard a scream behind me and turned to Lippi screaming and Pua holding her.

I closed the lavatory door and ushered them back to their stations. Lippi had calmed down to just whimpering.

"I'm sorry you had to witness that, but now that you've seen this, I guess an explanation is in order. We've had a rash of retrieved people who are masquerading as Anthorans. Those two are only a few of them. Their mission is to take down our protective shields to send messages out to their ships who will then come down and annihilate us." I explained.

Captain Lao walked past us to go see for himself that the deed was done.

"What kind of weapon did you use on them and why weren't we given weapons as well?" Lippi asked in a shaky voice.

"That's because it isn't a weapon. Fiona is special. She has special powers." Capt. Lao told them.

"I knew it! Didn't I tell you that she was the one?" Pua said.

"What? No!" I started. "I am not special. I have these powers, but it can't save everybody. Those two were easy because they weren't expecting it." I said in my defense.

"So, what do we do now?" Asked Pua.

"We continue with our mission. This was only part of it. Commander Podge and Elder Chaktar will be glad to know that our enemy has been dealt with." Capt. Lao told us.

"Wait, this was part of the mission all along? What if I couldn't do this?" I asked annoyed. I hate that they were still plotting behind my back.

"I am sorry we kept this from you. Sue Larson has been suspected for a long time, but we couldn't prove it. She must've been higher up in ranks of her battle unit. We couldn't catch her out of her suit. She has mastered sleeping in it. We thought it best to have you react instinctually, since you've been so leery of doing anything more than practice your Le'ak." Capt. Lao explained.

I sat down in my seat and stared out into space. I didn't even get a chance to look around the vastness of it before my attention was taken away. I looked now and it was breathtaking. We didn't jump yet, so this was real space. There weren't any planets in sight, but I could see some stars in the distance.

"We have only one lavatory, so can we get rid of the bodies?" Ensign Lippi asked.

I stood up. "Come on Pua, help me clean up." I said. I led the way back to the lavatory. The bodies were still laying one on top of each other. There was a hole inside of Sue's head that my fist could go through. The side of Gruha's head had a hole in it too. Because the method of their death was by Le'ak, their wounds were cauterized. There was almost no blood and Pua and I merely had to drag them out of the lavatory and bag them. The bodies had started to decompose, turning into a gel-like gooey substance. We stored them in the baggage area. I made a note to go back later to wipe everything in there with disinfectant.

Lippi looked more composed now and she was at her station keeping us on course. It's a good thing that she's able to perform Sue's duties. We'll need a navigation officer for our return trip.

"Get ready to jump," Capt. Lao announced. "We are far enough from Anthora, fasten your seatbelts and hold on."

Sitting up front, I saw the strings coming at us, or rather us going through the strings. When Jhael retrieved me, I was too out of it to appreciate it. The cruiser shook and jostled us as it navigated the jump route. It was beautiful to behold. The strings were beginning to thin out which meant that were getting ready to come out of the jump.

The other side of the jump landed us in Earth's orbit. Immediately, Capt. Lao re-engaged the cloaking device to keep us from being detected not only by Earth's satellites but also from any Froagan ships that might be close by.

"Ensign Lippi plot a course to the Brightblade residence. Ensign Pua, prepare our communicators." Capt. Lao ordered.

I turned to watch them do as ordered. Sue was our navigator, but Lippi was doing just fine. Pua was our science slash communications officer and I watched as she pulled out a small box containing a device that we would use once we stepped foot on Earth. It would enable us to communicate with each other and for others to understand us. Pua placed one on her neck close to her voice box and instructed us to do the same.

Since our ship was cloaked, we had it hovering over the house. I was excited and scared at the same time. This was my house we were floating into. Just like when I died and floated through the walls, we floated right through the walls and entered my old home. It was early evening and we could hear voices coming from the living room. We entered from the roof, so we needed to float down to the main floor of the house. Our special uniforms allowed us to control gravity, so we wouldn't be floating without control.

My mother was sitting on the couch reading a magazine while my dad and brother were at the desk to her left on the computer. I didn't see my sister. I wasn't sure what day it was, so for all I know, she could be out with her friends.

"Thanks for helping me with my homework Dad. I'm going to put my books away. Do you wanna play Call of Duty with me?" Jr. asked our dad.

"No thanks, I've got some work to finish up. Go on up and get ready for bed son." Dad replied.

My brother gathered his books and turned to find us hovering just beside the stairs. In his surprise he dropped his books on the floor. He could see us, I thought. He stooped down to pick them up and I signaled him to go upstairs and he nodded.

He hurried up and we followed him. Jr. watched us file into his room and then he closed his door. "Fiona, you're back!" he exclaimed excitedly.

"Yes, and I've brought friends." I pointed to each member of my companions and stated their names.

"I didn't think I'd see you again. You look great."

"I missed you so much, I've got so much to tell you but first I want to know how you're doing."

Jr. couldn't keep his eyes from straying to Lao, Pua and Lippi. They're walking around his room, checking out his things.

"I'm fine, I guess. It's been almost two years since the funeral and stuff. Mom and Dad are doing good, except sometimes I catch Mom crying. Laura is still a pain in the neck, and she keeps going into your room to take your stuff. Mom goes nuts when she sees her wearing your clothes."

"That's fine Jr. I have to ask you something. Has there been anyone new around lately, like hanging around school or coming here to the house?"

"No just the regular stuff. Laura's dating this new guy though, a real douche. He says mean things to me, and Mom and Dad don't like him either."

I perked up. "Yeah? What does he look like?"

"He's tall with dark hair. He talks funny like he's a cowboy. He doesn't say hello when he comes over. He says howdy like a dork."

"Oh, what's his name?" I ask with a squeak to my voice.

"John and his friend is even creepier. They are always together. Laura doesn't seem to care that Buck is always along on their dates either. She's a dork too."

"Omg Jr, this is bad, very bad. John and Buck are the ones who attacked and killed me. They're bad news. You must be very careful around them. Now I'm going to tell you a story about you and me. You and I are descendants of a race of people from another planet. Somehow, Dad and Laura got excluded from being what you and I are. When we die, we go back to Anthora Two; that's the planet we come from. I've been training to come back here to protect you. And get this, we have superpowers. John and Buck are aliens that have been hunting people like us and killing us. John doesn't care about Laura, he's only around so he can get his chance to hurt you." I explained to Jr.

"I sorta knew they were bad guys. I didn't understand why Laura couldn't see them for what they are and why she could stand to be around them. Do I have superpowers too?" He asked.

It was then that I realized that my baby brother didn't fully understand the danger he was in, after all, he was only eleven years old, well twelve now.

"I don't know. My powers only showed up when I left Earth, so maybe when you go to Anthora Two, your powers will show up then." I explained.

"How long are you staying this time?"

"I really can't say. We're here to make sure that you are safe." I told him. I couldn't bring myself to tell him that we were going to kill John and Buck. I couldn't tell him that there was a chance that we could fail in protecting him and that John or Buck might succeed in killing him too.

"Did you come to take me back with you?" He asked excitedly.

"Why don't we just play it by ear for now?" Lao answered for me. I threw him a grateful glance.

"Jr. did Laura go out with John tonight?"

"Yeah, you missed them by a half hour."

"Does Laura still have a curfew?" I asked him. If she still had one, we might be able to set a trap for John and Buck.

Suddenly, we heard voices in the hall behind Jr's. door. Dad came in looking around the room, as if to catch people in the room.

"Who were you talking to?" He asked still looking around.

"No one Dad. I was just rehearsing my plan of attack for when I play Call of Duty with Calvin. He doesn't stand a chance against me."

"It's late son, I don't think you have time to beat him tonight. You have school in the morning, get ready for bed."

"Ok Dad, good night." Jr. told him. He grinned at us when my father left the room closing the door behind him.

"I'm going to brush my teeth. You'll still be here right?" He asked in a mock whisper.

I nodded and watched him leave the room. Lippi and Pua were still inspecting one object in the room to the next. They were fascinated by his collection of action figures. It seemed that the collection had grown since I'd been gone. He had all the marvel superheroes strategically placed on the shelves across from his bed. Now it looked like he's added other heroes from other comics.

"So, what's the plan?" I asked Lao.

"We know that John and Buck can't see us, so we have to find a way to trap them. Elder Chaktar and Commander Podge wants us to capture one of them to bring back with us."

"How do you propose we do that?" I asked agitatedly.

"We know that they have to come back here, so we'll be waiting for them. Lippi has a special drug that will paralyze them. Once we have them on board the ship, we can secure them and jump back home."

Jr. came back smelling minty fresh. He even had his Pjs on. "Are you staying the night in my room?"

"No, we'll be back in the morning to make sure you get to school okay." I told him. I reached out to touch him, and I tried to ruffle his hair. Not being solid kinda sucks when you want to touch a loved one.

"Dad's been listening outside my door a lot. I thought that if I started talking to you, you'd show up. They think I'm crazy, so he's been very protective since you've been gone." Explained Jr.

"I'm sorry but I really was gone until now. Okay kiddo time for bed. We'll see you bright and early. Okay?"

"Good night Fiona. Night Pua, Lippi and Capt. Lao."

"Good night." They chorused.


The others returned to the cruiser, while I went downstairs to where my parents were sitting on the couch talking. Dad had a few more gray hairs on his head now and mom just looked tired.

"I caught him talking to himself again. I really think we ought to take him to see a therapist, just to see if he's okay. He misses Fiona." My dad said suddenly.

"Honey I don't think that's necessary. Some people process grief that way. They talk to their loved one as if they were right there with them. My mother used to talk to my dad after he died. It's just a coping mechanism. He just needs time." Mom answered.

"Funny how Laura just bounced back. She hardly ever talks about Fiona."

"She won't admit that she misses her. She wears her clothes and that's her way of keeping Fiona's memory alive."

I snorted at that. Laura was a selfish bitch. She doesn't miss me at all. I floated out of the house and up to the cruiser.

Our quarters were small but comfortable. Lippi prepared a meal for us and as we ate, we plotted the best way to capture John and Buck. We threw ideas around until it dawned on us that Laura was out with aliens and that she could be in danger as well. Granted she wasn't Anthoran, but she was still my sister. Those Froagan hunters may be doing all kinds of things to her to give up her brother.

"Do they possess any kind of mind control?" I asked Lao.

"I don't know."

"Don't you think it's a possibility given that they mind link with each other? Couldn't it stand to reason that they could also control minds?" Asked Pua.

"Yeah, that makes perfect sense." I added.

"It hasn't been our experience with them. However, if they can control minds, your sister is being used to get to your brother." Capt. Lao reasoned.

I cocked my head as I heard the roar of an engine. I looked down from the cruiser and spied my sister getting out of a car. I recognized the car. It was the one they drove me around in before they killed me. We floated down to them, ready to act if need be.

Laura was laughing as she stepped out of the car. "John you are such a kidder."

"I am not kidding Laura. Tomorrow morning, I want you to drive your brother to school. We'll meet you there." Buck said. He got out to stand in front of her. He placed his hands on either side of her head. "You will drive your brother to school in the morning."

"Yes, I'll drive my brother to school in the morning." My sister repeated. Buck dropped his hands and Laura stepped back and smiled up at him. "What time am I meeting you at the school?"

"No need to make him suspicious, bring him at the regular time to the dumpsters."

"Oh okay. Are we going out again afterwards?"

"Probably not, I have stuff to do."

"Okay, I guess I'll say good night then."

"Yeah, you should." Buck answered.

I watched my sister walk robot-like toward the house. Buck and John watched her also. I held my breath and only let it out after she was safely inside.

"What a stroke of luck, we can follow them and end it right now. Your brother won't be exposed to whatever they have planned in the morning." Pua whispered.

I turned to them and nodded. Capt. Lao was already heading back up. He was at the helm when we joined him. We were going to follow them. "Ensign Lippi enhance our listening capabilities; we need to hear what else they are planning." He commanded.

Lippi got on her console to comply. Almost immediately, we could hear everything outside the cruiser. It was a matter of finetuning before John and Buck's voices came in loud and clear.

"I don't know why you let this drag on for so long. We could've done away with the little brat ages ago." Buck complained.

"There's a rumor that Anthorans come back. Our intelligence tells us that they come back as spirits to gather their dead. I wanted to make sure that the bitch was truly gone. I kept watch over the body at the morgue. I trailed it to the funeral home, and I watched them embalm the body. When we killed her, we did a lot of damage and when they took her organs out, they were cut to bits. That was her body. I watched for almost a week at the cemetery to see if anyone came to disturb the grave. She is dead. They didn't come for her. And even if they still wanted to, it's been over a year. Her decomposed body is of no use to them now."

"Fine, but we still have to kill the boy before our mission is over. I am done with this planet." Buck insisted.

"No problem there. Tomorrow when the sister brings the kid to school, we snatch them both and finish the job." John said.

"We're killing the girl too?"

"Not before I have me some fun." John said laughing. Buck joined him and it was all I could do to keep from killing them right there on the street.

"That was gross to listen to." Pua said sadly as she reached over to turn down the volume on the console.

"So, do we hit them now or wait until the morning?" Lippi asked. Capt. Lao and the others all stared at me.

I took a couple of deep breaths before I could answer her. I felt power gathering in my gut, but I damped it down.

"We have a job to do. We have to gather more intel on them and the hive mind. If they are planning something, this is our chance to find out what it is. Already we have more on them than we had previously. They can control minds and they also believe that I am gone for good. I say we follow them and listen in some more."

"You're right. We follow to determine if there are more of them and then we strike." Capt. Lao said.

"It also occurred to me that we could also be going into a trap. Is there a way we can determine if there are any Froagan ships around?" I asked. I had this nagging feeling that this couldn't be as simple as it seemed.

"Zortaiyh! There are four Froagan cruisers in orbit now. They weren't there before." Lippi screeched. I could appreciate her cursing. I must remember to ask her at a later date what it meant.

"Check to see that our cloak is still intact." Ordered Capt. Lao.

"We're still cloaked." Pua assured us.

I looked down to see, John and Buck's car speeding. "Turn up the volume."

We could hear the static of radio signals. John and Buck can't communicate without taking off their skins. They have to do it the old-fashioned way. They were communicating by way of coms. "Yes sir. It will be done. Is there any way we could get off planet for a little while? No sir, I am committed to doing my part sir. Yes sir, we will be ready to go to our next post as soon as it is done." The static cut off and John and Buck continued driving.

"Why the *chitak* are there so many Anthorans on this freaking planet?" Buck wailed.

"At least we get to go somewhere else. Who knows, after this mission we could be the ones giving the orders." John said.

"We did what no other has done dude. We got all the Brightblades, the kid is the last of them. No one can take that away from us. This is going on our record and we might not even have to stay here for another mission. I bet we could put in for a promotion and get it." Buck insisted.

"Yeah you're right bro. We killed the bitch's legacy. Oftha's life force can rest at ease. You remember training camp? Man, they played that recording over and over again, drumming it into our heads until I heard it in my sleep dude. Leena Brightblade's voice telling Imperial Leader Oftha that she was going to kill him, just before she blew up the mothership."

"That voice gave me the creeps. They never did find out what kind of weapon she used. It was because of her that I became a fighter. I wanted to kill every Anthoran I came across. Being able to do it now is the best job in the world."

"Our families will be so proud of us. I think we deserve to have some fun before we get down to business tomorrow. You wanna go back to the club we took Laura to last week? The females there were wild, and I could use a bit of fun." John suggested with a laugh.

Buck made an impatient sound in his throat. "I don't know how you can do that with these humans. Their bodies are disgusting."

"Don't knock it til you try it bro, besides, that's how we found the Brightblade bitch. Her odor was all over that girlfriend of hers. Bill was so easy to manipulate. He invited the girl who brought Brightblade right to us."

"Even so, you remember the time you caught that illness from one of them. You were lucky a cruiser was around to get to; otherwise, you'd be dead."

"I know better. I've been inoculated, so nothing can hurt me now."

"Whatever man, while you're getting your rocks off, I'm gonna find me some weed. It ain't Anthoran Bizah, but it will do in a pinch."

We followed our Froagan quarry to a club on Queens Boulevard. Leaving Pua and Lippi to keep monitoring Earth's orbit, Capt. Lao and I followed them into the club. It bought back memories of the few times I'd ever been to a club. The music was loud, and the people were dancing, drinking and having a good time.

John and Buck had no trouble entering the club after doing a little mind controlling. They took seats at a booth and immediately, two women joined them. I was brave enough to get close to listen to what they were saying to the women.

"Hi, I'm Buck and this is my friend John."

"I'm Caitlyn and she's Brittany." Caitlyn said of her friend.

"Wanna have some fun?" John asked them.

"What'd you have in mind?" Brittany asked. She was the blond dumbass who was probably going to get herself killed, I thought.

"Well I was thinking that we could dance a little, drinking a little and see where that goes. You game?"

"Yeah sure." Brittany stood up and starting jiggling. "Come on this is my jam!" John nodded and got up to go join her on the dance floor.

That left Caitlyn with Buck. "What are you into?" He asked her.

"I don't dance, if that's what you're asking. I'm here for the weed. The bartender's got the good stuff. Buy me some and I'll share it with you."

Buck stood up and put out his hand. Together they made their way to the bar. Soon they were holed up in a dark corner smoking. I assumed no money changed hands as Buck mind controlled the bartender. I looked around to see if I could find John and they were still on the dance floor.

# CHAPTER EIGHT

John and Buck didn't leave the club until the wee hours of the morning. I was tired and so was Capt. Lao. When they headed back toward their house, I was relieved. We waited until they had entered the house before we flew back to my house for the night; good thing our yard was big enough to set down.

We didn't get an opportunity to capture them as they were in a crowd. These days there was always someone who's recording something. YouTube and Facebook would've had footages of them being dragged away by an invisible force in minutes. I wasn't too much worried that it would be believed, however there were those four Froagan ships in orbit to consider.

I set my chronograph for seven and that came early. I had never been a morning person and no amount of military training was going to change that. Don't get me wrong, I can do discipline with the best of them, but only when I chose to.

I left the crew to have breakfast while I went over to check on Jr. He was eating his breakfast and my sister was rushing him. I overheard her telling our parents that she would drive him to school. I signaled to him that he should be cool when he started protesting that he didn't want Laura driving him.

"That's very nice of you Laura." Dad said with a smile. I looked across at Mom and she wore a smile too.

When Jr. hurried upstairs to get his school bag, I followed after him. "Why do I have to go with Laura, I hate the way she drives." He complained to me.

"I know. You don't have to worry; I'll make sure you get to school okay. Now hurry up before she makes a fuss." I told him. I really felt for the little guy, but there wasn't anything I could do about that.

I waved at him and headed back to the cruiser. Capt. Lao and the others were waiting for me. We took off and kept pace, to have an aerial view of Laura's car as she drove toward the school. When she arrived, she parked and headed toward the teachers' parking lot urging Jr. along with her.

I quickly disembarked and headed toward the lot to find that John and Buck were there waiting for them by the dumpsters.

Laura was practically dragging Jr toward them. It was a sunny morning and I welcomed as much of the sun's rays as possible. I could feel my Le'ak building up inside me.

"Good morning John, Hi Buck." Laura stated cheerfully. She wore a stupid smile on her face as if dragging her little brother toward those creeps was something big sisters did to their little brothers.

"Howdy." John and Buck chorused together.

I hurried to face Jr and motioned for him to be quiet. He gave me a quick nod that he understood. Laura finally stopped pulling on him and just stood there with a blank expression on her face.

"Laura, you can go now. I'll see you later." John told her.

His voice echoed and I realized that he was using his mind control power on her. Buck was holding Jr, while John reached into his jacket. He pulled out a switch blade knife. The smile on his face was devious. Buck had been speaking to him too. Jr. was in a trance and wasn't struggling as the blade came closer to his throat.

I let out a scream as I blasted Buck with a stream of light. One minute he was standing holding Jr. still, and then the next he was on the ground with a fist sized hole where his eyes used to be. I turned to hit John, but Capt. Lao appeared behind him. He injected him with a syringe full of the paralyzing agent they'd prepared. John fell to the ground face first.

"We still need one to take back with us. Good job by the way." Capt. Lao said pointing at Buck on the ground.

Just then, Jr broke free of the trance and jumped back from the men on the ground. "What happened?" He asked looking scared.

I wish I could touch him. He looked like he needed a hug. "They hypnotized you and Laura. They sent her away so that they could hurt you. You don't have to worry about them anymore." I told him. I wish that I could keep him from seeing Buck with the gaping hole in his face. Suddenly, Buck's body started to steam and melt until it was a gooey mess on the ground. That's new and gross I thought.

"Fiona, I don't feel well; I want to go home." Jr. whined. It must be the aftereffects of the trance he was in. He looked a little green after watching Buck's body melt like it did. I didn't see how we could take him home when we weren't visible or solid for that matter.

"We'll take care of them, escort your brother home." Capt. Lao urged me. I could see Lippi and Pua coming toward us with a huge camo blanket and trunk to put the bodies in.

"Come on Jr. I'll walk with you." He nodded and started walking. I could tell that he was in shock. Poor kid.

I had a decision to make. Somehow, I had to try to communicate with my parents about Jr. and me. I was able to eliminate the immediate threat to his life, but I wouldn't be around forever. They would have to be vigilant to keep him safe. As we walked, we tried to come up with ways to convince our parents that I was still alive and needed to explain things to them.

Laura's car was parked in front of the house when we arrived. She was in the car staring into space. Whatever trance they put her in was still in effect. How she drove home without causing or getting into an accident was beyond me. Jr. got her out of the car and into the house.

It wasn't until she was in the house that she came to her senses. First off, she began badgering Jr to hurry up to finish his breakfast, that he was going to make her late for school. Almost two hours had passed since she had brought him to the school's lot to be killed. It would seem that she didn't remember any of it. Jr was a little bit fuzzy about me killing Buck, thank goodness.

"Laura, we already went. Don't you remember taking me to school? You left me in the teachers' parking lot with your dorky boyfriend." Jr responded.

"Why would I do that?" She asked stupidly.

"Fiona saved me from them. They were going to hurt me. They told you to go and you left me there." He accused her.

"What's the matter with you? I don't have a boyfriend." Laura looked around with a determined expression on her face. "Mom, Dad?" She called out.

"They left for the office already, check the time. Why don't you remember anything?" Jr asked.

"I don't know what kind of sick joke you're playing here, but it's not funny. You've been acting weird ever since Fiona died, you need to get over it. She's gone and she's not coming back." She told him cruelly as she checked her cellphone.

"That's not true, she's right here. Don't you see her?" Jr screamed at her.

At this point, I figured that I should step in before things got out of hand. I told Jr to stop and let me try to convince Laura that I was indeed there with them.

Laura watched him as he cocked his head to listen to me.

"Fiona says that she's going to prove to you that she's here." He told her.

"Jr. you have to stop this, you're scaring me." Laura said softly.

Jr. cocked his head to listen to me again. "Go get a sheet from the laundry and bring it to me." I told him.

"Laura, I'll be right back. I swear, if this doesn't convince you, nothing will." Jr. took off running to get the sheet. He came back a few minutes later with a white sheet. Here goes nothing I thought. I had him lay the sheet on the floor and hoped I wouldn't burn the house down as I used Le'ak to burn my message on it.

"How did you do that?" Laura asked Jr. He was standing beside her looking just as surprised as she was.

"Laura, I didn't do that. Fiona did."

Laura looked around wildly. "Fiona, is it really you?"

I scorched the word yes on the sheet. I waited for her to freak out, but she just stood there looking at the sheet. Suddenly, she started to cry. I wanted to comfort her, but I didn't know how.

"Laura, Fiona wants you to try to calm down and she also wants you to call Mom and Dad. She has something to tell us."

It took a few minutes, but she finally complied and called our parents. From our end, Jr. and I could tell that neither were pleased that their kids were home. It took a lot of Laura's skill at convincing to get them to agree to come home.

By the time they finally showed up, Capt. Lao, Pua and Lippi had come to see how I was faring. I filled them in and asked for advice. Revealing that I was still alive and that I lived on another planet was big. I wasn't sure that I was doing the right thing.

"My advice to you is to tell them as little as possible. We may have gotten John and Buck, but there could be others. Remember there are those ships in orbit right now. If they can't reach John and Buck, they will send others to investigate." Capt. Lao said.

"Alright, I'll figure something out." I told them. I asked them to go back to our cruiser and I'd join them as soon as I was done.

Dad was the first one to come through the door and he wasn't happy.

"Laura, you had better have a pretty good explanation calling me away from the office. I was in the middle of an important meeting." He said.

Mom came in wearing a worried expression. She rushed to Jr. feeling his forehead looking for fever. When she deduced that he was fine, the questions began. "What's the matter with you?" She asked him. "The principal called me. She said that your teacher saw you and Laura arrive, but you both went to the dumpsters and then she left you there. She was going to call the police when she saw you with those men. She went to get the principal and when they got back, you were alone and was leaving the school grounds. Were you buying drugs? Tell us the truth Jr. We can get you help; won't we honey?" Mom looked to my father.

I asked Jr. to tell our parents and Laura to sit down. Once they were seated, I asked him to also tell them that I was there.

"Is this what this is all about? Son, you've got to accept that Fiona is gone." My dad said sadly.

"Dad, she really is here. Fiona show them." Laura said. Her face was pale as she spoke.

I concentrated to write the word hello on the sheet. For some unknown reason, the burn marks didn't go through the sheet. Mom made a sound in her throat and placed her hands on her chest. Dad stood up quickly looking around wildly.

"Alright you two, how are you doing that?" He asked pointing to the sheet on the floor.

"Dad, it's really Fiona." Jr. tried to explain.

"Fiona, is it really you?" Mom asked. I thought dad was going to be the one to accept this, while she was going to be the one curled up on the couch drooling. On inspiration, I tried to concentrate on lifting the sheet and found that I could drape it over me briefly. Now I looked like a Halloween ghost.

"Oh my God, Gary it's our daughter. She's really here!"

"How is it possible?" He asked no one in particular.

"How are you sweetheart?" Mom asked.

"Jr. tell her that I am fine. I can't write any more, it's very tiring. You speak for me okay?" I let the sheet drop as I kept going through it.

Jr. nodded. "She says that she's fine."

Half an hour later, after telling them what happened to me and how Laura was being manipulated by Buck and John to get to Jr. My parents finally believed, especially after Laura swore that she didn't have a boyfriend. Both my parents have seen and met John and Buck while she had no recollection of them.

Dad excused himself to go upstairs for something. He came back down carrying a strong box that he had on the top shelf of his closet.

Growing up, I'd always wondered what he kept in it. Now he held it in his arms. With tears in his eyes, he told us about grandpa Brightblade.

"My father kept this box in his closet, and he gave it to me when I turned 21. He said that his father gave it to him on his 21st birthday. He said it had been in his family for generations. He showed us what was inside and told us the story behind it. He said that a long time ago, our ancestor Leena Brightblade was a warrior from another planet called Anthora. There was a war and that her planet was destroyed. She and a group escaped to Earth to live until her people could come for her." He pulled a key from his keychain to unlock the box.

In the box was a picture of Leena Brightblade, several pages of a letter written in a strange language, that only I could read. There were pictures of her and her human husband and children. Her arm band was worn but still as red. She wrote instructions to pass the knowledge down to every child but especially to the males. For some reason, it was rare in the Brightblade clan to produce male children. The contents of the box were to be passed down from father to son.

"I kept that box out of respect more than anything else. I didn't believe any of it, although my father swore it was true. I promised him that I would pass it on to you Jr. when you turned 21. I can't believe this is happening."

"Dad, Fiona says that she is glad that you kept the box. She says that she had spent months trying to learn about Leena. On Anthora Two she is a hero and her descendants are revered. She says that she is treated as if she were the actual Leena because she looks a lot like her."

Mom raised her hand to speak. She kept looking around as if trying to pinpoint where I was because I wasn't wearing the sheet anymore. "Fiona, did you come back just to protect your brother?"

I nodded and Jr. told her that I did.

"So, what now? Is the threat to him gone?"

"Tell her that I can't say for sure." I tell Jr.

"Mom, she's not sure."

"Will you come back to check on him from time to time then?" Asks Dad.

Jr. cocks his head to listen to me. He told them that I came to eliminate the immediate threat. I wasn't sure if there would be more attempts on him. I told them that I would try my best to come back to check on him.

"Are you leaving soon?" Laura asks.

"Very soon." Jr. conveys.

"Why do you have to go? Why can't you stay here to protect us?" She asks.

"Laura doesn't understand that only Jr. is Anthoran honey. There's no threat to the rest of us, right?" Dad asks.

I nod and Jr. tells them that I nodded.

"What does the letter say?" Mom asks suddenly remembering the letter in the box.

I ask Jr. to take it out and to hold it open for me. It was ten pages long. I read some of what it said to the family. Leena hopes that we are well, that we get a chance to see how beautiful Anthora is. She wishes that she could've seen her home world again but knew that it was destroyed by the Froagans. She tells of the narrow escape she and the rest of the people on her ship experienced. A Froagan ship followed them after the jump to Earth. Fortunately for them, she had been vigilant and used the last of her Le'ak to destroy that ship and they were able to land safely on the planet. She tells of how hard it was at first to co-exist with the Earthlings, that they were afraid of her and the others.

She had learned to Limit her use of Le'ak. She learned their ways and she had found acceptance in a special man. Most of the people who came with her had found mates and settled down. Of the 80 on board the ship, she was the only one who had the ability to wield Le'ak. For a while, she was their leader until they were fully accepted. The settlement they founded was small, but it suited them.

They were lucky that the mountain people agreed to keep their existence a secret, although when she went back years later, she found that they had left drawings about them in their cave walls. She decided to leave them untouched as they were really beautiful. Besides, who would believe that people from another world lived among them?

She didn't know when her people will come but knew that they would. She wants all of us to be ready and to never forget Anthora. Oftha The Vile may be dead, but she knew this one thing about our enemy, they will rise again, and they will continue to hunt us.

She kept the manifest of the people aboard the ship. She hopes, they will continue to remember and to tell their children of home.

The letter ended with her name and the year 1866. At the bottom of the box was the coordinates for where the ship could be found and the deed to a home the family used.

I had tears in my eyes, and I asked Jr. to fold it back up. The papers were fragile, and I was afraid that they might rip. I asked my dad if he would allow me to take the letter back with me and he agreed. I told him that it would be held in the hall of records on Anthora Two.

Leaving was bittersweet and I promised that I would come back as soon as I could. I also asked that they keep the secret for a little while longer. Laura said that she would never tell a soul. I believed her. My parents agreed as well as Jr. I realized that I still had feelings for them, not as strong as what I felt for Jr., but I now know that I would always think of all of them as my family.

When Capt. Lao came to check if I was ready to leave, I told him that I was. It was hard to leave, but I had to. We had caught a Froagan and we needed to bring him back with us.

As we prepared to leave orbit, I thought of how understanding my family was and how they would now do whatever it took to keep Jr. safe. My dad promised that he would do his best and so did Mom.

Although our cruiser was cloaked, we were especially careful to run silent to keep from detection. We didn't take a deep breath until we were far enough away to make our jump. The trip was uneventful. John was heavily sedated, and I didn't rest until we were landing. Elder Chaktar was there to meet us at the landing pad. He and Commander Podge were there to relieve us of our cargo.

Elder Sim was given an alternate arrival time for our ship, so we had to 'land' again for her sake. Capt. Lao gave her the report we'd rehearsed. Healer Gruha and Sue Larson were among the casualties. Lippi agreed to play injured and was taken to the medical facility to recuperate under Master Physician Bolka's care.

Elder Sim asked that I report to her. Again, making sure that my story matched Capt. Lao's I told her what happened. We were attacked almost as soon as we arrived. I was in the process of trying to communicate with my brother, when we were attacked, I told her. Sue and I were pinned down and couldn't get to safety. Once we saw our chance, we made a run for it, but Sue got shot and when Healer Gruha ran to her aid, he got shot too. I was especially happy to relay that the weapon they used melted their bodies. I even asked what kind of weapon would melt bodies. She didn't reply but had a horrified expression on her face at that. I also reported that Lippi got hurt trying to help me get to safety.

"It was as if we were expected. They'd been keeping my brother under surveillance just so they could catch us. How could they know?" I asked. I didn't have to pretend to be upset.

"Were there any casualties on their end?" Elder Sim asked looking pale.

"We fired back, but I couldn't be sure. It all happened so fast. Elder Sim, you must convince the other elders that it is important that I be allowed to go back to make sure that my brother is okay. When the dust settled, we decided that it was too risky to try to get to him."

She nodded. "Yes of course, we will be meeting shortly to discuss the merits of another trip. Now you must go get some rest and I insist that you go see the physician yourself."

I smiled weakly at her. "I'm fine, I'm just so upset that I didn't get to see my brother."

"If you're sure, then I suggest you go home and rest just the same."

"Of course, Elder. Do you think I could speak with Elder Chaktar? I think if I can convince him, then the others will agree along with you and him."

"Warrior Brightblade, you are starting to sound hysterical. Go home and get some rest. We will contact you once we've met. Is that clear?"

"I'm sorry, I understand." I answered.

I turned to leave and knew that I had convinced her without a shadow of a doubt.

My apartment was freshly aired thanks to Mrs. Podge. The Commander has given me a few days leave before we were to meet to discuss the mission. I had time to go over everything that occurred and despite what I told Elder Sim; I really did want to go back to Earth. There was the matter of Buck and John not being able to report to consider. My dad had agreed to take an impromptu vacation before the Froagans could regroup. Not knowing where they went would give my family time to figure out their next move. They didn't tell the schools, his firm where he and my mother worked anything. So, if the Froagans came calling, and went asking questions, no one would know anything. The neighbors themselves wouldn't be able to say anything either as my family left in the middle of the night.

Leena had come to the rescue once again. She had a home that had been in the family for generations. Absolutely no one knew of it because my dad didn't know either until I told them about it. It was the last thing Leena wrote in her letter. She left the deed in the box. Dad checked it out and it was still standing and also cared for by trusted caretakers. She must've known that my dad would be the one to pass on the Anthoran gene. She left everything to him with instructions to claim everything.

Before I left, my family was planning to go to the home. It was big enough for two families. The pictures alone made me want to go with them. I knew my family would be safe, Jr. would be safe. Leena not only left the house for a rainy day, but she also left provisions in the form of money and trusted allies we could go to if need be. She was living up to the title of hero.

I showered and changed into some sweats and made dinner for myself for the first time in almost a year. Eggs and cheese never tasted so good as they did right now. It was simple, tasty and filling. I walked around my apartment familiarizing myself with the place. I checked that I still had those stones in each room and then I turned on the stereo to listen to some music. I danced to the latest in Techno music. Yeah, I know, I'm a weirdo.

# CHAPTER NINE

As was the custom for fallen soldiers, we had a memorial service for Ensign Sue Larson and Healer Gruha. The crew and I attended, and we wore white bands on our left arms in their memory. Commander Podge said a few words and awarded them with medals for bravery. The medals were placed in a display case for fallen soldiers on the base.

After the service, I was summoned to see the Elders. A driver was sent for me and as she drove us, I wondered what they had decided. I wanted to make sure that the ships that were in Earth's orbit hadn't taken any action. I know that several weeks had gone by since we left Earth and it was driving me crazy not knowing what happened afterwards.

The chambers were brightly lit, and I entered to find that the layout had changed a bit. The elders now sat at individual dais midway between the ceiling and the floor. Elder Chaktar inclined his head to me when I caught his gaze.

"The last storm caused some damage to the building. Our architects have assured us that this new design will withstand storms better." He explained.

"It looks great." I said looking around.

"Warrior Brightblade, we've had a few days to review your report and that of Capt. Lao's, and the rest of your crew. We have carefully weighed all the options available to us and have decided that a trip to Earth so soon after yours would not be possible." Elder Sim stated. Why is she the spokesperson?

"Why? I don't understand. I told you that we didn't get a chance to even see my brother. We don't know if he's safe or not. Where is the team that is watching over him? Have they reported in?" I asked.

"Warrior Brightblade, you must understand that your brother's safety is not the only concern we have." Elder Sim countered haughtily.

"What does that mean?" I asked. My heart pounded a beat rivaling a master drummer at a parade.

"What Elder Sim is trying to tell you is that we do not know where your brother is at the moment. We were able to keep your brother under surveillance as long as his location was known. We knew because you lived there. But after the skirmish with the enemy, your brother's essence signature has vanished. We cannot detect any lifeforms in your former home." Elder Edwards explained carefully.

I fell to the floor in a heap. "What do you mean vanished? What happened to my family?" I ask tearfully.

"We are trying to find out. I'm sorry Fiona." This came from Elder Chaktar.

"Warrior Brightblade, we are very sorry. If your family came to any harm, we will immediately know and travel to retrieve your brother. So far, our sensors haven't been able to detect whether his essence has escaped his body.

I looked up at them hopefully. I stood up again and faced them. "If you haven't gotten an alert does that mean that he's still alive? Could he have been captured and is just being held?" I asked.

"We cannot be sure, but I assure you that we will get to the bottom of this very soon. It is very unusual for the Froagans to capture our citizens. Now upon careful consideration, we are assigning you to accompany a retrieval team to Embeta Twelve. If the Froagans are changing their tactics, we will require more security. You will leave in the morning. Commander Podge will brief you this evening." Elder Chaktar said.

"I understand." I returned and saluted him and left the chambers.

One thing I didn't include in my report was that my family and I decided that they should travel to the Brightblade homestead in California. If Chaktar didn't know about the whereabouts of my family, I was assured that they were safe. I wasn't trusting anyone with that knowledge. I didn't tell Capt. Lao or the others. I only hoped that they hadn't listened in on my talk with the family. Even if they did, they wouldn't have gotten much. Except for Capt. Lao, they didn't understand English.

My family had gotten on board with the spy game as it were. I used Jr. to communicate that they should disappear as soon as they could. The computer was a godsend in that I had Jr. type out what I wanted my parents to do. The deed to the homestead was valid and the accounts had substantial amounts of money for them to survive for a year if my father couldn't get a job. Fortunately, my dad could work from anywhere. Until the Froagans learned of this, they were safe.

Because Leena and the others were original Anthorans, they aged slowly and lived longer than was normal among the humans, it was necessary that they move after several years. It wasn't until their bloodline was sufficiently diluted that they were able to stay put. Leena hadn't married until she was well into her sixties. It must've been quite a surprise for her husband to age while she continued to appear young.

I could fully understand why they lived apart from the humans. The ship had landed in the Arabian Desert originally, and they lived among the Badawī (Bedouin) at first. The Anthorans didn't dwell too long with them and pushed on until they ended up in the mountains with the Incans, however their religious practices were a huge turn off and they finally found themselves in the Americas and they settled in California. Because of their longevity, the Brightblades were able to amass a great deal of wealth. Apart from monies that would sustain my family for a year, Leena had invested in stocks that resulted in a sizeable fortune.

If my dad is as smart as I think he is, he could join the company that Leena's husband started. A meeting with its CEO would guarantee him a place in the company or co-chair. I left that up to him. Leena's husband had agreed to take on her name in order to keep the bloodline going. In California they developed the precursor technology that today is known as a computer chip. My dad's jaw dropped when I told him, and I saw a gleam in his eye.

My family had always been tech savvy and now I know why. My dad may not have inherited any of the powers of the Brightblade clan, but he certainly knew about technology. It was that knowledge that sold him to make the move. I suspected that Laura only went along because she realized that the family was rich, and she would be able to spend as much money as she wanted.

I cautioned them to be careful not to bring any attention to themselves and to follow Leena's instructions to the letter. Per Leena, there was a stipulation in the company bylaws that allowed for direct Brightblade descendants to automatically be on the board of directors of the company. Her lawyers had seen to it that it couldn't be challenged in any way. My father did some research and found that the current CEO was elderly and there were rumors that the company would be up for grabs.

As I entered the commanders' office, I realized that something was up. He was all business. I saw immediately why. Elder Sim was sitting in a chair directly behind the door. Once I was completely in the office, I acknowledged and greeted her.

"Good evening Elder Sim." I said with a slight bow.

"Relax Fiona. This is an informal meeting. Embeta Twelve was my home world too and I wanted to be of service. Commander Podge will brief you on the details."

I turned to face the commander. He sat behind his desk and clicked on the electronic pad on the desk in front of him. "Warrior Brightblade, we have locked on four essences on the planet. We are ready to retrieve them, however in light of what has been happening recently on the other retrieval missions. We must have extra security. Under no circumstances will we allow the mission to be compromised. Your job is to assist in the retrieval and provide security. Use your own discretion in how to proceed if it appears that the mission is in jeopardy."

I nodded and turned to Elder Sim. "Is there anything you want to add?" I asked her.

"Embeta Twelve is a unique planet. Our populace lived mostly in the trees. When one of ours die, we are careful to cremate the remains. We have a thirty-day mourning period where we gather to pay our respects. The more important the person in the community, the more elaborate the proceedings. If you didn't know, there are two races of peoples on the planet. The commander and I are both from Embeta Twelve. Like Anthora Two, we also have a caste system. The blue haired people were the working class, while the silver haired people ruled. We only know that there are four essences not whether they are blue or silver haired. Each and every one of our Anthoran essences are precious. Please bring them home safely."

I inclined my head and assured them both that I would do my very best to ensure the safety of the mission. Commander Podge handed me a thin tablet that contained detailed instructions for the mission and one to the elder. It was understood that my copy had more detailed information and I couldn't wait to read it.

The ride back to the base was uneventful and I got out of the conveyor absentmindedly. I needed to see Lippi and Pua before walking back to my apartment. They would be my crew members. We were getting another navigation officer and he or she would undergo a Froagan check before departure in the morning.

Lippi and Pua had finally moved to their own apartment and decided to share it. They were good friends and worked well with each other. Besides, what happened with the mission to Earth has left them skeptical of everyone around them. I agreed. I told them about the mission, and they told me that they'd already been briefed. I wished them a goodnight and walked home.

The jump to Embeta Twelve was uneventful; long but uneventful. Our new navigations officer was Bel. I was overjoyed. Lippi and Pua were a bit intimidated as Bel was our commander Podge's daughter. Bel worked hard to draw them out and finally they relaxed around her and treated her like one of the crew.

Elder Bitka's daughter was our new healer. Sooragi was personable and passed the Froagan test. My only worry was that if anything went down, I was to make sure that she returned safely.

Embeta Twelve was huge. It was a bright planet and from our vantage point, it looked like a huge orange. As we swung around the planet to the coordinates given to us, we spotted three Froagan battle cruisers in orbit with us.

Captain Lao ordered a complete stop and engine shut down. As we hung there in space not more than a few hundred kilometers from the closest cruiser, my heart pounded in my chest. We watched in both awe and horror as another cruiser suddenly came out of a jump so close to us that its gravitational pull drew us out of our position. Something was going on there. I wasn't sure if we were spotted or if they knew we'd come for our deceased Anthoran citizens.

I looked to Lao for direction, but he was staring at the cruiser, concentrating hard. Out of the corner of my eye, I saw Lippi pointing at him with a horrified expression on her face. I looked at Lao again. The shiny surface of the console reflected his head and what I saw made me instantly mad and sad. I lifted my hand and nearly decapitated him. Lao was a Froagan and he was communicating with the ship that had nearly collided with us.

I don't know how much he'd communicated to the hive mind, but I wasn't going to stay around to find out. I pulled his body out of the seat and took control of the cruiser. I broke out of orbit and shot out into space. I wanted to put as much distance between us and them as I could.

"Did you know?" Bel asked.

"No. I don't understand how he could have been. This must've happened recently upon our return from Earth. We've got to preserve his body until we get back home." Sooragi pulled the body away to the storage area.

"You're captain now." Lippi said to no one in particular.

"Shit, they're following us and gaining." Pua said looking at her console agitatedly.

"Bel, what's the nearest planet to our position?" I asked.

"I've got to consult the charts, give me a minute." She answered.

The battleship pursuing us was getting closer and I didn't want to panic, but I was close. Lao just betrayed us and probably gave away our secrets. I needed to find a way out of our present predicament before I could think about what his betrayal was going to do to our people.

"Captain Brightblade, we are two jumps from Teah Four. Shall I attempt it?" Bel asked.

"Yes, cloak us and jump." I ordered.

In cloaked mode, we jumped to Teah Four and hid among a cluster of a nearby asteroids. Two minutes after we were safely hidden, a battleship came out of their jump. They scanned the area but because they couldn't detect us, they jumped away again. I suggested we stay where we were for a bit longer before we made any moves.

I went to the cold storage area to check on something that was puzzling me. Lao couldn't have been a Froagan all along. He was a wielder. Why didn't he fight? I unzipped the bag and took a breath before I inspected his body, it had started to decompose into that jelly mass the others had when they died.

I gingerly searched the pockets. I found a small recorder in his breast pocket. I pulled it out and went back to the others. Bel plugged it into the cruiser's communications port and a hologram appeared. Captain Lao's image was bloody.

"If you are seeing this Fiona, I am probably dead. This image you see is of Froagan Umak. His mission was to transmit the cloaking device codes to his superiors. As captain I had knowledge of them, and he will have the opportunity to transmit it to the hive mind. I am sorry. I was overpowered by the team interrogating the prisoner we captured on Earth. He had mind controlled all of them. Under a ruse, I was called to come to them where they ambushed me. I am able to make this recording because of my Le'ak. I am fighting his take over long enough to record this. I am losing control and getting weaker. You must fight Fiona. If you can get back home, let them know that war is coming." The hologram stopped suddenly.

"Where did you find that?" Bel asked in a strained voice.

"In his breast pocket. Somehow, I knew that he would not leave us guessing. I don't know how much was transmitted out, but we have to make it home to warn them."

With a collective breath, we took our positions and faced forward. Slowly, we inched away from behind the cluster of asteroids and found two ships patrolling. We ran silent and very slowly passed them until we were far enough away to jump.

I breathed a sigh of relief, when we reached Anthora's orbit. Commander Podge was waiting for us as we quickly disembarked. He took us to a conference room where the other branches of the military was waiting.

"Shortly after you broke orbit, we found Captain Lao's body. The interrogation team are being treated as we speak. None can remember anything from the time they took possession of the prisoner. The bodies that John and Buck inhabited were not Anthoran nor were they human. This Froagan's sole purpose was to hunt and kill Anthorans. He wasn't meant to travel here. He would've been able to transmit to the hive mind had the planet not been cloaked. From what we can piece together, the prisoner had taken control almost immediately after regaining consciousness. For the better part of a week, he had been gathering as much information as he could before he took over Captain Lao."

"Commander, we don't know how much information he had transmitted out before we caught on. We came out of our jump to the planet's orbit only to find three battleships waiting for us. At first, I thought that they had known of the retrieval operation but now, I'm thinking that Lao had been in communication with them even before we came out of our jump. We barely escaped. To his credit, Capt. Lao sent us warning by way of a holographic message." I handed him the recorder.

"Commander, we have to prepare for war." Ensign Lippi added.

The commander raised his hand to get everyone's attention. A murmur had broken out in the room. "Ladies and gentlemen, we have been preparing for this eventuality for thousands of years. Capt. Lao thought he had good intel, but he didn't. Years ago, our defense technicians devised a way to keep the cloaking device codes from even me. They are picked at random by our computers and they change every other day. What he transmitted were outdated; even he didn't know that the computers controlled the codes."

"How about the coordinates to the planet? Even if they don't have a way of compromising the plant, they know where we are." This came from a ground defense captain.

"I can assure you captain, that we are safe. We will not be engaging in war today or tomorrow. We must however find a way of getting back to Embeta Twelve to retrieve our citizens. Warrior Brightblade, the commander and I are assigning you, Ensigns Lippi, Pua and Bel to your new command. By default, you now are promoted to Captain. Tomorrow, two other ships will accompany you to Embeta Twelve. I expect you to bring our citizens home."

I stood at attention and saluted. "Sir, I have a question. Our chronographs are programmed to detect alien DNA, so how is it that we didn't get any alarms concerning Capt. Lao?"

"That's because, the captain wasn't wearing the chronograph. We found it next to the body. We cannot be certain that the technology hasn't been leaked to others on the planet. If they know about the chronographs, we can still make it work to our advantage. Anyone not wearing one will be suspect."

I nodded and looked around the room. Just like me, everyone was checking each other. The commander handed me my orders and I exited the conference room.

I was still reeling from Captain Lao's death and I felt profound sadness. Elder Chaktar assures me that he can be saved, as long as his body is preserved. I couldn't dwell on that right now. I needed to focus on my new mission as captain.

My apartment offered a welcome respite from the chaos going on outside it. We have Froagans trying to break through our defenses to finish a job they started so long ago; I believe none who are following those orders today know first- hand what actually happened. There's also the Froagans on the planet that are trying to compromise our defenses so the job can be accomplished.

My head was spinning, and I wished I could just close my eyes and have it all, go away. I'm now captain of a space cruiser and in charge of a retrieval operation on a planet the enemy is currently patrolling. How am I supposed to get our people off the planet without being pursued or shot down?

A knock on my door caught me mid-pace and I hurried to the door to open it. Ming and Gorke stood at my front door. I ushered them in and shut the door quickly. I led the way to the living room and motioned for them to sit.

"It is good to see you. What are you doing here?" I asked them.

"All kinds of strange things have been happening. Aisha and Jhael have disappeared. Aisha was set to move into her new apartment unit, and they had gotten permission to cohabitate. Ming and I volunteered to help them with the move. This morning we discovered that they were gone. No one has seen them." Gorke told me.

"Was this reported?"

"I reported it to Elder Chaktar only just an hour ago. We'd been searching for them all day." Said Mingh.

"What about Lylah?" I asked them.

"We saw her earlier, she helped us search for a while." Gorke said.

"Where is she now?"

"She said that she would go back to the dorm and wait for us to return." Mingh replied.

"Did you tell her where you were going?"

"We only told her that we were going to see Elder Chaktar."

I stood up. Things were getting more bizarre by the minute. "Okay. I suppose he'll have to deal with this too." I told them. I turned to face my two friends and fired at their chests hoping against hope that I was doing the right thing. I couldn't bear to hit their heads. After, I couldn't even touch their bodies. I called Elder Chaktar.

Twenty minutes later, my apartment was crawling with Ground Defense officers. They questioned me over and over again and my answer was the same. Mingh and Gorke came to me with a story about Jhael and Aisha missing. They thought I would know where they were. What gave them away was the part about them reporting Aisha and Jhael missing to Elder Chaktar an hour before they came to me, and the fact that they weren't wearing their chronographs. At that time, the Elder was with me and a few others being briefed by the commander about Captain Lao's death.

"I really liked them." I said as I watched their melting bodies being wheeled away. A cleaning crew was already working on the splatter on the wall and floor. I'm losing friends left and right.

"We have a search party looking for Lylah and for Mingh and Gorke's bodies." He took me by the arm and led me to the kitchen. I sat down and watched as he made me a cup of tea. "Here, drink this. It'll help you feel better."

I took the cup from him and held it in both my trembling hands. The cup was hot but comforting at the same time. When I finally took a sip, I felt the warmth of it spread throughout my body.

"They are mobilizing and trying to execute whatever it is they have planned. We've been lucky so far. The Jhael and Aisha Froagans are dead, as well as Buck from Earth"

"Elder Chaktar, if they are able to overpower wielders, what do you think is going to happen to the rest of the population? We don't know who they are or how many there are. Heck we even have one in power." I stressed.

"I wasn't going to tell you this until after you'd returned from the retrieval mission on Embeta Twelve. We've gotten most of the public buildings outfitted with the sensors. The commander has given us the go ahead to round up all who has displayed DNA discrepancies. So far, we've eliminated twenty-five."

I almost dropped the cup. "That's impressive. Are they truly Froagans?"

"Yes, and our scientists had been experimenting with how we dispose of them, when they discovered that the Anthoran skin was aware." He didn't say anymore, letting what he just said sink in.

"Aware? Aware how, what exactly does that mean?"

"All along, we'd been destroying the whole body. Then they tried to remove the skin and just destroy the Froagan underneath. The skin was then prepared for burial. The following day, when they came to take it to be buried, someone noticed that the skin was glowing with health. On inspiration, the kept it in a controlled environment and the body miraculously began to regenerate."

I sat up straighter in my chair. "So, what we thought was the end, was just a pause until they regenerate?"

"Yes, and there's hope that the others whose bodies we couldn't find will regenerate as well through a cloning process. The science team informed me that as long as the essences are still aware, they might be able to regenerate those we have in stasis."

"That's wonderful," I said. I gave him a look, but that was an argument for another day. "What is being done to find Lylah?" I asked changing the subject.

"She's had a head start, but we will find her."

"Of the twenty-five the military has captured, was Druktar one of them?" I asked. He was now the only friend I had left from the dorm.

"He is Anthoran, why do you ask?" Chaktar asked me.

"I know that he is an instructor in the communications sector. He has access to the computers and perhaps the codes. If Gorke and Mingh were able to be compromised, he'll be in danger. Lylah, Jhael and Aisha plotted together. He may be their next target."

"We'd taken precautions to protect our people. He and the others working directly with our computers have been sequestered for the duration of the shutdown."

"What shutdown?" I asked with a frown.

"Since we've found Capt. Lao's body, we've shut the departments down. No one goes in or out without a full Froagan check."

"I'm sorry. I've been through a crash course of unexpected situations lately. I know you and Commander Podge know what you're doing."

He reached over to take the cup from me. I was still holding it in my hands, and it was empty. He placed it in the sink and faced me once more. "You have had a long day, not to mention a dangerous mission to face. Get some rest."

Elder Chaktar left closing the door gently behind him. Getting some rest was not going to be easy. I don't even know if I'll ever sleep again. In twenty-four hours' time, I've lost three friends. I would give anything to fall asleep and wake up in my own bed back on Earth. Anything.

# CHAPTER TEN

When sleep finally came, it was almost time to be up to get ready to meet the others. I took a quick shower, dressed and gulped down two cups of what passes for coffee. I got a jolt of energy and intended on using it to get through the pre-flight checks. I probably will need another jolt once we take off, but I won't worry about that now.

Ensigns Lippi and Pua flanked me as we headed toward our cruiser. I wasn't surprised that this time around, we were assigned a sleek, fully loaded battleship. Along with us was the retrieval crew, and a squadron of soldiers. When I embarked and entered the flight deck, someone announced that the captain was on deck and all activities stopped as everyone stood at attention beside their workstations.

"As you were." I commanded. In my head, I danced a little jig as I watched everyone get back to what they were doing. First Officer Tova approached me holding a tablet in his hand.

"Captain, shall I give you report now?" He asked.

I nodded at him and he rattled off that the ship was ready to take off, all personnel were on board and that a strategy meeting was set for as soon as we escaped orbit. I acknowledged him and made for my seat at the helm.

The helm was situated dab smack in the middle of the deck. I was surrounded by technicians. I had a perfect view of everything including the view screen. I could see people on the ground in the hangar preparing for my ship to take off. The mission control station was to the left of me and I could see Elder Chaktar standing there along with the commander and some other officers. I felt a little lump in my throat as I remembered Captain Lao. He would've been sitting in this chair, not me.

The static of the com in my ear caught my attention. The ships' engine purred gently, and I watched as everyone waited poised at their stations for the command to take off. Once we were in the sky, it would be up to me to assume command of the ship and everyone on board. For some reason, I wasn't nervous. I had done this before, at my flight simulation classes. Fleetingly, it occurred to me that they had been grooming me for this instance all along.

"Captain, we are ready to jump." First officer Tova announced.

I reached over to the console in front of me to turn on the ship's loudspeaker. "Ladies and gentlemen, this is Captain Brightblade. Please take your seats, we are ready to jump." I announced to the rest of the ship. I imagined everyone scrambling to take a seat or rushing to a safe spot.

This time, the jump was almost smooth. That was the difference between my old cruiser and this first-class battleship. Mid-way through the jump, I commanded the security tech to engage our cloak. The viewscreen glowed green and then it was sight by radar. We came out of the jump almost where we'd done before. Again, I replayed in my head Captain Lao sitting next to me communicating with the hive minds on the ships that had been in orbit with us.

Embeta Twelve was in the Cheve-Kule star system. It consisted of a vast number of planets and asteroids. It was also one of three life sustaining planets in the system. It was big and orange with three moons. As we approached the coordinates, we encountered a single Froagan battle cruiser. First Officer Tova looked to me and raised an eyebrow.

"Scan the area for other ships." I commanded quickly.

A few minutes later, the security tech confirmed that it was the only one in orbit and that there weren't any others within scan range. I debated on whether we should engage it or not. Then it occurred to me that it would be prudent to wait to see if they spotted us. To engage it now, would put the mission behind schedule and incur unnecessary casualties if any. Also, if we were to do so now, they'd be able to alert others waiting within their mind communicating range. It would be better to engage it on our way out, less trouble for us and less problems for the planet below us by taking the fight away from it.

"First Officer Tova, alert the retrieval team and have our shuttle ready." I ordered. I stood up and felt all eyes on me. "Ensigns Lippi and Pua, you're with me. Healer Sooragi gather your medical equipment." Then I walked off deck to the lift.

Just before I stepped into the lift, I turned to catch my first officer's eyes. "First Officer Tova, you have the helm."

"Yes sir!" He saluted and went to take my seat barking orders to keep communications clear and to continue to scan for other Froagan ships.

Again, Lippi and Pua flanked me as we made our way to the shuttle. It was a smaller version of our previous cruiser but more streamlined. The retrieval team met us at its base. I nodded to them and climbed up the steps into the shuttle. They followed and took their seats. The inside was like a small airplane on Earth with nine seats. Once we were strapped in, I signaled the helm to open the bay doors.

The surface of the planet was nothing I was expecting. The vegetation was enormous. The trees were so big around and tall, that they shamed the sequoias back on Earth. I understood now what Elder Sim said about them living in the trees. They had whole compounds in the trees. The landing pad was on the ground and once we disembarked, the retrieval team took point. The soldiers that accompanied us traveled in the cargo area with seats built into the walls. Six soldiers flanked us.

Because everyone, lived in the trees above us, the sun's light barely reached the ground. Where vegetation was lush and green above, the ground was dark and spooky. Keeping sharp was a no brainer knowing that a Froagan ship was in orbit. They could be hiding in the shadows for all we knew.

I watched as the retrieval team used handheld instruments to track the Anthoran essences we'd come for. They came to a stop at the base of a huge tree. Lippi and Pua the showed us how to access the tree's lift. They led us around the tree to locate an abnormal looking knob. Pressing it was tricky as we were not solid. The retrieval team were the only ones outfitted with mass enhancing suits to enable them to enter the lift. The rest of us floated up. The soldiers stationed themselves around the tree to await our return.

Following their instruments, the retrieval team led the way to Embeta Twelves' version of a funeral home. Like Earth, we were invisible to those around us. The bodies we came for were in elaborate glass containers filled with flowers. Lucky for us, the room they were in was in a closed off room. I watched in awe as the retrieval team revived the original and activated the pod replacements.

Everything went according to plan and our newest Anthoran citizens were compliant enough that we didn't have to explain much. We exited to meet the soldiers outside the tree to find that they were all lying on the ground dead. Fortunately, we thought to bring a giant camo blanket and threw it over us as we made our way back to the shuttle. Once our people were on board, I insisted that we go back for the soldiers. Only Lippi and Pua consented to go back with me. Healer Sooragi and the retrieval team stayed behind to care for the newly retrieved.

The blanket hid us as we approached the giant tree. We came to a complete stop when we came upon two Froagans standing over a soldier holding a laser-like instrument. They were getting ready to skin him. I whispered to my companions to be still. I came out from under the camo blanket to get as close to the Froagans as possible. I quickly scanned the immediate area to make sure no more Froagans were about. It was just those two.

I held my breath as I blasted at their heads. I waited to see if more were coming but none did after about five minutes. Lippi and Pua helped me get the dead soldiers back onto the shuttle. It took us five trips before we got them all onboard.

We were ever vigilant as we hurried back to the ship. First Officer Tova reported that a shuttle flew down shortly after we did, and he was afraid to contact us in case it alerted them. I told him that he'd done well, and we circled back to our jump point. I prayed all the way that we didn't alert our enemies.

The way I saw it, was that the Froagans knew that we retrieved our dead and they also knew that they could get on the planet if they masqueraded as Anthoran in the skins of our dead. I wasn't sure how they knew that we were coming, but they knew and were waiting, probably from Capt. Lao. They improvised once they saw the soldiers, and they knew we were in orbit cloaked. Their best bet was to ambush us on the planet. I could've engaged the ship on our way out, but with six dead already, I didn't want to raise the count. Besides, I still felt uneasy with these new crew members. They didn't know of my Le'ak abilities and I wanted it to stay that way.

During the jump, I got out of my seat to go investigate the bodies of the soldiers. As I neared the cargo area, I turned quickly to find Tova following me. In his hand, he held a weapon looking suspiciously like the one the Froagan Buck and John used on me.

"I don't require an escort First Officer Tova. I just wanted to make sure that our dead is secured." I told him playing it cool.

"Nevertheless, I shall accompany you Captain." He answered.

"We'd better hurry then, we'll be coming out of the jump soon." I said to him.

He continued to follow me and when we were fully into the cargo area, I went to inspect one soldier and found that its skin was wrinkled. That wasn't an Anthoran. I pretended not to notice and went to check the others. They were all switched, and pretending to be dead, except for the two who'd been in the process of being skinned.

"Are the bodies Anthoran Captain?" Asked Tova.

"Yes, I just wanted to make sure that the others weren't already skinned." I explained. I realized that it takes a bit of time for the Froagan and Anthoran skin to meld. By the time we land, it should be fully Froagan.

Tova holstered his weapon and I followed him back to the helm. I took my seat and continued to play it cool. "First Officer Tova, have ready a report of the incident and list the names of our fallen before we dock."

He inclined his head to me and pulled out his tablet. The rest of the jump was uneventful, and I held myself ridged as we disembarked. I watched the bodies being taken away and Elder Chaktar greeted me as soon as I was on the ground.

"What happened up there? We've been alerted to six more essences to retrieve."

"Have a squadron surround the dead soldiers, they've been switched and have Tova taken as well. He is either a Froagan or he's been compromised." I said hurriedly.

Elder Chaktar didn't waste any time as he barked orders into his wrist com. I watched as the bodies were given a sedative and Tova taken in handcuffs. Once that was done, Elder Chaktar took me to a closed off room to talk.

"They were waiting for us sir. I'm guessing that Capt. Lao briefed them. While we were retrieving our citizens, they attacked the soldiers and pretended to be dead. I guess they knew that we'd be back for the bodies because after we got the crew on board, Lippi and Pua went back with me. That's when we caught two of them getting ready to skin a soldier. I killed them not realizing that the others had already been switched. On the jump back, I had a hunch and went to go double check the dead soldiers and that's when I discovered that they'd already been switched except for the two we intervened for."

"Obviously, they are still trying to get as much of their people on the planet, but I can't figure how they are getting their intel."

"What does Elder Sim do in her spare time? It's got to be her. She was very interested in this trip to Embeta twelve. She was with the commander when he briefed me yesterday. Do you think she's gotten to him?" I asked. My stomach was doing things with a queasy result.

"The commander is waiting for you in his office. Be careful, if what you say is true, we have to prepare. Get back to me as soon as possible." He gave me a syringe full of the paralyzing agent to use if need be.

I saluted and left the room. I caught a ride back to the base with Lippi and Pua. They were happy to have friends from back home with them. They told me all about their friends. Chua and Sheyh were blued haired while the other two were silver haired. Chua and Sheyh grew up with Lippi and Pua. Their families were manufacturers of leather goods together.

"Captain, I know something happened in the cargo area. Are you going to tell us?" Lippi asked.

"The soldiers were killed and switched. They were all Froagans. I didn't want to let on because First Officer Tova came back there with me and he had a Froagan weapon. I don't think he's one of them, but he could be in their control. I think when they took over Captain Lao, they programmed him or else he wouldn't have passed the Froagan check for the mission. Elder Chaktar is investigating."

"When is this going to end?" Whimpered Pua.

"I don't know, but we can't give up." I told her. I stepped off the conveyor as soon as it came to a stop. "Look get some rest and come to dinner at my place later. I'll cook something from home."

"See you later!" Lippi replied enthusiastically.

I watched them until they were gone and then rushed to the commanders' office. I breezed through his ante office waving at the clerk at the desk. I knocked on the commander's door and entered the office.

"Commander Podge, sorry to barge in sir," I began and stopped talking. Elder Sim was sitting next to him by the desk and she was holding his hand.

"This is highly irregular, what is it?" He asked. He didn't even look embarrassed while Elder Sim's features looked a little blanched.

I stood at attention and saluted. "Sir I apologize. I wanted to report that the mission was a success and we have retrieved all four of our citizens. They are being examined at the medical facility as we speak. I also wanted to report that there was one Froagan battleship in orbit, but as we were cloaked, we didn't alert them. We ran silent until we could jump home."

"Very well. Please prepare a formal report. Have it on my desk in the morning." He said.

"My apologies Elder Sim. I was eager to give my report." I said carefully.

"No harm done Captain. Let me be the first to thank you for retrieving our citizens safely." She said with a sly smile.

"I was just doing my job Elder. I'll say good night then." I saluted once more turned and left as quickly as I could. I didn't know what she was doing holding his hand, but it didn't sit right with me. He didn't even appear to be out of sorts. I paid close attention to the officer at the desk and decided that he was okay. He could've stopped me from entering the office, but he didn't. It was as if he wanted me to see what was going on in there.

"Good night Captain." He said.

I nodded. "Yes, good night." I waved at him and left the office.

Today was one for the books, I thought as I walked to my apartment. I decided that I was going to scan everyone I meet from now on, especially those close to me.

Lippi and Pua couldn't get enough of my spaghetti and meatballs. At first, they were cautious because they didn't eat meat. I explained that it was a meatless meatball. Once I told them that, they tried it and enjoyed it. I got the recipe for a meatless meat from Mrs. Podge.

Dessert was ice cream. Then it was time to talk. I had so much on my mind, and I didn't know where to begin. Just before we could even get down to it, my doorbell chimed. I got up quickly to see who it was. I let Bel in and shut the door just as quick.

"You have to come to my house now. Something is wrong with Dad." She said. She had tears in her eyes.

"What do you mean?"

"He's acting funny. He has a routine he keeps, and he never deviates. Tonight, he's not doing it." She explained.

I turned to Lippi and Pua and they stood up as a unit and came to the door.

"What exactly is it that your dad didn't do? Where's your mother?"

Mom isn't home. She has retrieval duties she attends to every time we get a new citizen. Dad usually comes home and showers, then he goes to expel in the basement. He never deviates from expelling as soon as he gets home. Tonight he came home and went straight into his study and hasn't been out." Bel explained.

"I thought they cancelled all exposure to the new arrivals until they had been processed." Immediately, my hackles went up. "Okay, but when we get to your house, play along that we had been invited to dinner."

"Dad came home and told her that they were waiting for her at the medical facility."

"Bel, I don't want you to panic. We'll come with you; just play along that we were invited to dinner okay?"

She nodded with a frown and then beckoned us to come with her. I gave Lippi and Pua a signal and they nodded back at me. Commander Podge was a Froagan and Elder Sim had taken his place. That's what was happening in the office when I barged in. Now she's in his skin and God only knows what she's done since.

Bel practically jumped out of the conveyor when we got to her house. She led the way to the front door and entered with us following. "Dad? We've got company." She called out.

Commander Podge came out of his study with an odd expression on his face. He did a double take when he saw us.

"To what do I owe this pleasure?" He asked.

"Don't you remember that we invited them to dinner? Mom told me to pull something out of the freezer she'd prepared already." Bel told him. I watched to see if he was going to raise a fuss, but he nodded and told her that he would appreciate it if we called him when dinner was ready.

"I'm sorry commander, but if this is a bad time, we can do this some other night." I offered.

"It's alright Captain, I've been so busy lately, I must've forgotten. Will you excuse me?" He asked and walked back into his study.

Bel motioned us to follow her into the kitchen. "See what I mean. He's acting weird."

"That's not your dad." Pua blurted out.

Bel looked horrified. I grabbed her by the shoulders to face me.

"Listen to me. I want you to go back to your father's office on base. I want you to search his office building and find his body. Do you understand?"

With tears in her eyes, she nodded and turned to leave. I asked Lippi to go with her. Pua and I looked at each other and squared our shoulders. I took lead.

My first knock on the office door yielded silence, but my second did.

"Just a minute." Commander Podge said.

I grabbed the doorknob tightly in one hand and pushed the door open. Without giving the commander time to react, I blasted him in the chest. He was in the process of adjusting the skin around his head when I shot him. He looked at us with one humanoid eye and the frightening Froagan glassy one. He slumped over the desk spraying blood all over it. I plunged the syringe Chaktar had given me into his neck immediately. I didn't want to take any chances in case he wasn't dead.

I went over to the desk to see what it was he was doing and found that he was holding the commanders' tablet. It was bloody, but I could see that he was communicating with Lylah. Good thing it wasn't video. She was telling him where to meet him. I noted the location and logged off.

Bel burst into the office screaming that her father was dead. She rushed to the body as if to give it a hug, but I pulled her away.

"Bel look at me. Your father is not dead. Did you find his body?"

She was crying freely now. "Yes, I found it in the expel room in the basement."

"That's good. Your father will be just fine. Master Physician Bolka will take great care of him. I want you to contact your mother okay?"

"I talked with her a little while ago. She said she should be home soon that she wasn't needed."

"Okay, now I'm going to call Elder Chaktar and he'll get the medical team to come for your dad."

The call to Elder Chaktar was quick and the medical team was even quicker. For all intents and purposes, business was to go on as usual. I didn't know how Elder Chaktar was going to explain Elder Sim's disappearance if we didn't find her skin. Commander Podge was going to be fine as soon as they returned his essence back to his body. Anthorans had a peculiar quirk; their essences only die of natural causes. That's why we lived so long. If we die by any kind of violence done to our bodies, our essences brings us back. Weird, but hooray for us. Essences dying by natural causes, do not come back which explains why our people are so few.

It was almost two weeks before Commander Podge could receive visitors and I was among the first after his wife and daughter to see him. He looked none worse for wear as they say. I'm glad I was thoughtful when I shot the Froagan wearing his skin. His recuperation time would have taken longer had I gotten him in the head. Head reconstruction took more time than the chest area, especially since I missed vital organs.

"Captain Brightblade, I want to thank you for acting as fast as you did. We couldn't have captured Lylah had you not thought to investigate what the Froagan was doing at my desk." He said.

"I was just doing my job." I answered. It had become my stock answer lately. I was starting to feel uncomfortable again. People around the base heard what happened and those adoring gazes had started up again. I left as soon as I was convinced that he was okay.

I had got great news later too. Aisha and Jhael's skins were found and brought to the medical facility. I hear that they are regenerating, as was Gorke, Mingh and Lylah's skins. This time around, the Froagans had destroyed the original bodies, thinking they had it made. I guess in a few more months, I'll have my friends back. Elder Sim's skin is also regenerating in a secure location in the medical facility. No one is to know that she is there. Word is that she has taken an extended vacation.

A week later, Elder Chaktar came to my apartment. He said that the commander wanted to have a meeting. Dinner would be served, and the meeting was to be at Elder Chaktar's home. He didn't look like he liked the idea of having company at his place, but I guess he didn't have a choice.

"I'll need directions to your home Elder." I told him.

"You won't need it Captain. I was instructed to wait for you and bring you myself." He answered uneasily.

I asked him to follow me to the living room to wait. As he took a seat, I casually looked for his chronograph. He was wearing it, there's that.

"Can I get you anything while you're waiting Elder?" I asked him.

"No, thank you." He replied.

"Okay, then I'll hurry."

I walked away to quickly turn the oven off. I was planning on having a quiet evening at home after a day at work on the base. Now I'm going to have an evening of intrigue and mission briefs, I thought. The life I was re-born into wasn't an easy one, I can tell you that.

Twenty minutes later, I was dressed in a pair of jeans and a lacy tee-shirt. I'd finally had a chance to visit a hair salon and got my hair cut into a manageable length. Now it was just a bit past my shoulders with soft waves. The weather had turned summerlike and I'd gotten a real nice tan. Most Anthorans didn't tan, so I was an anomaly and elicited even more stares when I walked down the streets.

Elder Chaktar was going through my photo albums when I joined him in the living room. He put it away quickly looking guilty. I smiled at him and went to sit next to him and picked up the album. I hadn't looked at it in a long while.

"I see you're looking at my album. This is a custom humans have. We take pictures of each other and keep them. I look at these pictures of my family back on Earth and my friends here and they make me feel content." I explained. When they duplicated my room, they copied my camera. I took pictures until I ran out of film. I had some of the tech guys figure out how to develop the film.

"I see you have a few of these pictures of me. Do you consider me your friend, Captain Brightblade?"

"Yes, I do. At first, I wasn't sure but now I admire and respect you. You've been a great help to me." I answered truthfully.

"Well, shall we go then?" He asked completely changing the subject. I got that he was feeling embarrassed.

"Yes, let's go." I agreed.

The conveyor was waiting for us outside and he was driving. As he drove, I struggled to find a safe and less embarrassing topic to speak on. He seemed to prefer the silence, but I was not having it.

"Elder, do you live far?" I asked because I was curious. I mean he was an original Anthoran and he probably lived like they did in the old days not having been exposed to other cultures.

"Yes, it is quite a distance from the base and the city proper. The commander caught me by surprise. I hope you'll excuse me. I don't live with anyone and I haven't had time to make it presentable."

"You don't entertain in your home often?" I asked. I pictured a bachelor pad full of naked women's posters, clothes strewn all over. "Then I suggest you hire a cleaning service to keep your home presentable." I said looking at him through the corner of my eyes.

"That is a helpful suggestion."

"What time is the meeting?" I asked.

"It is for an hour and a half from now, he said checking his chronograph."

"Elder, may I speak plainly?"

"Of course."

"I meant what I said in my apartment. I really do admire and respect you. I've come to rely on your advice and judgement. The other elders are pretty much who they appear to be, except for the time Elder Sim was an imposter. You are closed off to not just me, but everyone. I was wondering if you considered me a friend?" I twisted my body to face him.

He kept his eyes on the road and his jaw worked so hard, that I thought he would bite through his cheeks. Then he visibly relaxed.

"I do consider you a most valuable friend, but I must explain something to you before we get to my home, to prepare you. The others know about my origins and they've come to accept me. Elder Sim knows now since she is fully Anthoran. I had to tell everyone in light of what had been going on with Froagans imposters everywhere." He stopped talking as we drove through a tunnel.

When we came out on the other side of the tunnel, it was my turn to feel uncomfortable. This was like entering another world. Not having done much exploring or research on the planet itself nor of the originals, this was mind-blowing. Elder Chaktar was a by-product of the original inhabitants living on the planet. The books in the library said that they had died off, but here they were alive and well.

The more the Elder drove into this other world, the more blown my mind was. On either side of the rode we were driving on, were aquariums. There were men and women and children in them. Their bodies were magnificent, with colorful scales. The legends of mermaids came to mind and I wondered if these people once traveled to Earth.

I realized that the whole complex was under a massive dome with artificial atmosphere. The sky was blue, and the sun was shining. We just came from my apartment and it was evening there.

Since he was in a chatty mood. I asked him to give me a quick history lesson. He relaxed even more and told me about a people called Zwazodor. They were the original people living on the planet. When the Anthorans arrived, they encountered an established race of people. The Zwazodorians were cultured and civilized. It was them that helped the visitors stabilize atmosphere under a dome for them to live. At first, they lived in the domes in a less inhabited part of the planet and they co-existed for a long time. Disaster struck in the form of a colossal meteor that struck the planet destroying a great number of the population.

The Anthorans had survived with minimal damage to the domes. The Zwazodor suffered greatly. The meteor damaged the planet's atmosphere and radiation filled the planet. It took both Anthoran and Zwazodorians scientists' years to put the planet to rights again. As they worked together to save the lives of the populace, they terraformed it to benefit both species.

"So, the books in the library are wrong again? I read that the Zwazodorians had gills." I commented. I tried not to be obvious as I scrutinized him looking for the gills the books said he should have.

"The books are unreliable Captain. My people do not have gills; however, our physiology allows us to breath under water. When the planet underwent the transformation, our people decided that it would benefit all if we lived as one people. So, we mated with each other to produce what you see here. Some of us have more Zwazodor genes than others, hence the colorful skin and scales."

I began to understand why our planet was cloaked. It wasn't to keep the enemy out, but to stabilize the planet. With the outer atmosphere damaged by the meteor, the planet was still unstable. The shield around the planet was in fact an artificial atmosphere keeping radiation out. He further explained that there were signs of the planet repairing itself in some spots. He hoped that very soon they could disable the shield.

# CHAPTER ELEVEN

I closed my mouth and turned to look at him once more. I understand now why he was so secretive about himself. He told me that he was a descendant of the original Anthorans, and I took it to mean the refugees that came to the planet, not the real originals. I wondered if he felt any animosity toward all these people coming here to live and proclaiming the planet as theirs. On Earth, we have the history of people coming into whole countries and taking over, like Australia, and the Americas.

"Um, you don't live in a pool, do you?" I asked.

Elder Chaktar laughed. It was something I wasn't expecting and kind of made me feel more nervous. "No, I don't. I live in a proper house, but I do love the water. I'm what you would call a hybrid. My ancestry is full of the original peoples of this planet and the Anthorans. I am half of each which is why I have the ability to wield Le'ak. There are a few of us who turn out to be Anthoran and we stay to ourselves. When the storms come, these are the people I worry about most. This place takes a beating and they don't have anyone to advocate for them."

"Wow, I really wasn't expecting this, and I am honored that you trust me enough to allow me to see it for myself." I said and I really meant it.

"It has taken me some time to trust you Captain. You are attached to a legend that kept the Anthoran race going. Although some of us have the Le'ak abilities, we lack most of them. In the library, the books say that the shining ones threw light, healed others and were oracles, however, not all the abilities were chronicled. You hear thoughts and sense things others don't. That is why people look at you the way they do. They can sense that you are much more."

"Really, you and everybody else must stop doing that and thinking that. I may have a bit more abilities than most, but I am not a hero or anything like that. I am just a person and it makes me so uncomfortable."

"I understand. We are here." He announced.

I looked up at the house and it was just an ordinary house in the Anthoran style. Square shaped and shiny. The windows were up high and once we were inside, I was not surprised to see that there was a giant pool on one side of the house. I approached it slowly and looked down into it. It was just a pool and there wasn't anything in it but water.

"Is the water saltwater or fresh?" I asked.

"You mean like the ocean?" He asked with a confused expression on his face.

"Yeah, like the ocean." I haven't been to the beaches yet but now I am curious to go.

"The water in my pool is fresh water but treated to simulate the ocean. Because of my unique genetics, I cannot tolerate full ocean water. Most of us can't which is why this place was created. Hybrids like myself can live in both worlds. I try to speak for those that cannot speak for themselves." He explained again.

I turned away from the pool to face him once more. "So, who else is coming to dinner?"

"The council, the commander, Boham and Captain Lao." He answered easily. He led the way toward the other side of the house. It was there I saw his problem. The living room area was a mess; not dirty but messy with books and clothing lying on the floor and chairs. The kitchen was spotless as was the dining area.

It didn't take us long to straighten up and get dinner going. He had solved that problem by having it brought in. One of the women setting the table I recognized from the dorm cafeteria. I smiled at her and she returned it with a quick one of her own.

Once the table was set, the women left and the Elder and I were alone once more. While I still could, I thought to get as much of my questions answered. I might not get another chance, so I cleared my throat and hoped for the best.

"Elder Chaktar, do you think we have anymore imposters on the planet?"

He was sitting across from me in the sitting area. It wasn't quite like any living room I've ever known. The chairs were oddly shaped and close to the floor. I sat in one such seat with my knees practically in my chest, while he knelt in his.

"If there are any, they're in hiding. The last count was seventy-four. The last two being Elder Sim and Lylah." He replied.

"Do you think I could convince the commander and the other Elders to allow me to go back to Earth to check on my brother?"

"It is a very distinct possibility. You've proven that you are a very capable soldier and leader. The battles you've participated in shows that you can handle yourself and protect others. I don't think they will deny you another trip." He smiled and stood up. I watched him as he went to the door. His other dinner guests had arrived.

I scrambled to stand up just as Elder Bitka entered the room, followed by Elders Edwards, Ullah and Sim. Elder Sim wore a simple long dress past her knees. Her hair was not covered, and she wore that loose. This was not the Elder I was used to. I noticed that she was nervous.

"Good evening everyone." I announced.

Boham was the last to enter the room. He had a huge smile on his face when he saw me. "Hello Fiona, you are looking well this evening."

"I am, thank you, Boham. It is always nice to see you." I answered easily.

The commander stood silent watching the exchange between us. "Commander, how are you?" I asked him. He was looking nervous as well.

"I am well." He replied.

"Shall we go to the dining room?" Elder Chaktar suggested. He led the way and we all followed.

The seating took a few minutes and then we started eating. The food was delicious and was something everyone could eat. This was something I had once before at the commander's home. It was similar to a lasagna but meatless. The sauce was not red like Earth's lasagna, this version was green and with a hint of hot peppers.

The conversation was light, and I could feel the tension dissipating. The commander and Elder Sim both seemed to relax a bit more and Boham acted like a buffer for everyone.

After serving a tea that tasted like peppermint, Elder Chaktar led us all into another room he hadn't shown me earlier. It was a large room with a huge table in the middle with table height chairs around it. I don't know why I wasn't expecting a conference room, after all, he was an Elder.

"Commander would you do the honors?" He deferred to the man who up till then hadn't said much.

"Very well. Ladies and gentlemen, the reason I called this meeting is to discuss our place in the alliance the planets in our neighboring star system have created. We were contacted by representatives of the ten member planets in the alliance to join. The purpose of the alliance is to fight off the Froagan menace that has plagued the star system for millennia. We'd been stalling for quite some time, and now, they are demanding an answer. In light of our own Froagan issues, I recommend that we should join the alliance. Together we are stronger than if we were to engage our enemy alone." Commander Podge stated.

"The Alliance of Planets is the official name and I believe joining will be beneficial for us; not only if we were to go to war with the Froagans, but especially for commerce. We can finally act like a world again and trade our goods for items we don't have and vice versa." Elder Bitka said.

"Who gets to vote us joining?" I asked. I didn't want to burst their bubbles, but I thought they alone shouldn't decide for the entire planet.

"There will be a general meeting where representatives from each species living on the planet gets to have their concerns heard for or against joining. All our peoples will have a chance to voice their opinion. However, I don't think it will take long to come to a mutual agreement. We need allies." Commander Podge insisted.

"Why are we meeting here? Couldn't we have discussed this in chambers?" I asked.

"That's because we are yet unsure if we've rounded up all Froagan on the planet. This compound is unique in that the Froagans cannot breathe here. Something about the air paralyzes their lungs." Elder Chaktar explained. He looked pointedly at Sim and the commander. I understand now why they were nervous when they first arrived.

"I agree that we need allies, but what exactly do we know about these other planets? Do they have other enemies besides the Froagans? And more importantly, if we join this alliance, will we be obligated to fight against enemies that we have no quarrels with?" I asked. I noticed that Boham and Chaktar were nodding.

Commander Podge clicked on the tablet that had been resting on the desk beside his folded hands since the meeting started.

"We have been invited to visit the closest planet to us to meet with the alliances' representatives. There we will bring our concerns and have our questions answered. Because our whole world is impenetrable to others for obvious reasons, I think it is best that we go." He suggested.

"Commander, I understand all that. My concern is that in light of our recent problems with imposters, how can we protect ourselves. I mean, suppose we go to this meeting to find that it is a trap of some kind. I mean no disrespect to you or Elder Sim, but both of you had been overtaken. If one of you in power go and get compromised, our world will then be in danger." I explained. I know it sounded paranoid, but I believed we needed to think that way.

Suddenly, it dawned on me why I was included in the meeting. They weren't going themselves, they meant to send me! With a recent birthday under my belt, I was twenty-one now. These people never saw me as young, or incapable. They really saw me as the hero they'd been waiting for. How can they afford to place so much responsibility on me?

"Fiona, I see that you finally understand your place in these proceedings. You must understand dear, that of all of us who have abilities, you have somehow inherited them all." Boham said quietly.

"I read in the library that Leena had been enhanced. What does that mean? What had been done to her?"

"It would be unfair not to tell you," Elder Sim began. "For as long as our people have been in existence, the shining ones as they were called back then had been our protectors. Our scientists were given a task when the shining ones began producing offspring without abilities to isolate their genes to preserve Le'ak. Leena and a few others were the products of that experiment. She alone however exhibited all the abilities. You have all of them also." She said as if that answered my questions.

"I get that she was special. What else can I do and who were the others?"

"All of us who can wield are descendants of the original shining ones. However, we have found that once we'd begun retrieving our people, the ones with abilities were incomplete. You started exhibiting abilities almost as soon as you arrived. You and your brother are direct descendants of Leena which means that all is not lost." Elder Sim further explained.

"You will find that as time goes on, more of your abilities will emerge. In every situation that you have found yourself in, you have found a way to resolve it successfully. Your intuition is more than that, it is your oracle abilities manifesting. Your ability to throw light is far more superior than any we've seen, and you suffer no side effects either." Captain Lao said finally joining the conversation.

"What side effects? I've seen you both throw light. I didn't see any side effects." I countered.

"After that sparring exercise, we had with you on base we couldn't wield for the better part of a week afterward while you suffered no such problems. Fiona, you can hear thoughts, see ahead into the future and,

I for one cannot wait to see you move matter, teleport and fly." Elder Bitka actually clapped with glee upon hearing Elder Chaktar list my so-called abilities.

It was at that point that I couldn't sit any longer. I stood up because I was scared, nervous and angry. I felt that all they wanted to do was use me and I also felt that I had no say.

Because I was feeling so many emotions at the same time, something truly weird began happening. Suddenly, I could hear their thoughts and feel what they were feeling. I looked at Boham and I could feel the compassion he felt for me. Elder Edwards was eager to have open trade with the other planets and wanted me to use my influence to gain access into the alliance.

Sim wanted a sample of my blood to study and Chaktar just wanted to protect the people. Commander Podge wanted more soldiers who could wield, Lao wanted to be able to crew with me. It was too much coming at me at once.

"Stop! It's too much at once." I looked at Elder Ullah and there was worry on his mind. With the population growing, food was getting scarce. The ability to import food and seeds to grow more food was a top priority on his mind.

Boham stood up and made his way around the table to stand beside me. I felt a deep sense of calm come over me. He truly felt sorry for me and he wished that he could help me. I leant over and gave him a hug. I felt better for it. I pulled away slowly and looked around me.

"I truly appreciate the concerns you all have. In Leena's time, there were others who shared the responsibility of protecting the people. I cannot do it alone. I get that you all feel that I should be able to step up, but honestly, I don't think I can do all that you are expecting from me. Elder Chaktar, you have abilities as well as experience. Captain Lao so do you. Frankly, you all have something that is useful to protect our people and our world. I will do my part if you do yours."

"What do you need from us?" Commander Podge asked.

I sat back down again. "I would like to hear what the people want and then I'll take that to the alliance. Before I travel to meet with the

Alliance of Planets, I would very much like to visit my brother. Earlier, you said that his essence wasn't detected. I have been thinking about it and I have an idea where my family might be. Will you give me permission to go?"

I watched as the Elders conferred with each other. I saw smiles and nods.

"Captain Brightblade, when you go to represent us at the Alliance, we would like you to go with no worries on your mind, so go visit with your brother, ensure that he is safe and return as quickly as possible." Elder Chaktar said.

Two days later, I sat in a newly outfitted cruiser, jumping dimensions to Earth. I requested only Lippi and Pua to go with me. I told them mostly everything. I trusted them, but they didn't have to know all my secrets.

California was balmy and overly bright. I probably will have to find a way to expel my energies before the day was out. We landed in the wooded area behind the house. We didn't spot any ships in orbit this time neither. I wasn't quite sure how long I'd been gone this time, but I estimated it be somewhere between nine months to a year.

We entered the house through the back entrance and into the kitchen. My mother was at the sink and she was humming. I smiled at her and floated past her to the living room. My sister was sitting next to a young man giggling at him. We floated past her up the stairs. I could hear voices in one of the bedrooms. I poked my head into the room and caught my father pacing and talking on the telephone.

"Roland, the order was supposed to be shipped yesterday. See that there are no more delays." My father clicked the phone off and shook his head. I quickly moved out of the way as he made for the door. We followed him back downstairs.

My sister quickly pulled away from the young man she was kissing. My dad pretended not to notice and sat in the single chair facing them.

"Laura, has your brother come back yet?" He asked her.

"I think I heard him come in through the back." She answered.

"Why don't you go see if your mother needs any help in the kitchen honey?" My dad asked her.

Laura stopped smiling and stood up. "If you'll excuse me." She told the young man and left to go to the kitchen. I signaled Lippi and Pua to stay put whilst I followed Laura to the kitchen.

The minute my brother spotted me, he told Mom and Laura that he was going up to his room. I followed him and signaled for Lippi and Pua to follow us. He immediately went to the wall opposite his bed and pushed a button. I realized that the room had a privacy mode feature which he'd just activated.

"Fiona, you're back! I didn't think you'd ever come back. So much has happened since we got here. Do you realize that it has been a little bit over year? Dad loves it here and so does Laura." He said excitedly.

"What about you? Don't you like it here?" I asked. I noticed that he was careful to relay that the others were happy.

"That man downstairs acts weird around me. He's always watching me, but Mom, Dad and Laura love him. His father works with Dad and they came for dinner one time and he acted like he's fallen in love with Laura."

"I didn't want to say anything but, that man downstairs was talking with your father. His voice sort of echoed when he spoke. I think the whole family is being controlled." Lippi told me.

"So, you have been found out. Jr. have you noticed anyone else acting weird?" I asked him. I wanted to make sure that the whole company wasn't infiltrated.

"I don't think so. Chris and Patrick are new to the company. They started shortly after we got here." Jr. told us.

"Have you been to Dad's office yet?"

"Yeah, the director took us on a tour. His name is Jude Brightblade. I liked him. Everyone was so nice. Dad has a big office and he's in charge of product development. It was like they were waiting for him."

"What about school? Are you going?"

"Yeah and I like it a lot. Laura graduated a few weeks ago. Now she wants to work at the office with Dad."

"What's the company called?"

"Bright Future Logistics."

"Okay. I'm going to do some snooping around to see what else I can find out about Chris and Patrick. Try to stay away from them and be careful not to be alone with either of them, okay?"

"Will we have to move again?" He asked as his eyes grew sad.

I shook my head. "Not if I can help it sweetie. I'm going to try very hard. Now, I understand that this room is very special. Was it like this when you moved in or did Dad fix it?"

"No, when we arrived, the caretaker insisted that this is to be my room. He helped me move my stuff in. He showed me how to use it and told me not to tell anyone, not even my parents and sister. He said that if I ever wanted privacy to use it and nobody can snoop on me."

"Where can I find the caretaker?" I asked.

"Mr. Edwards lives on the other side of the property; he has a cottage there." Jr. told me. I couldn't get over how much he'd grown and how mature he sounded.

"Great. Don't tell the rest of the family that I'm back okay. I want to do some investigating first." I told him.

"Your uniform is different Fiona; did you get a promotion?" He asked as he reached out as if to touch my badges.

"Yeah, I'm a captain now."

"Cool. I have to go downstairs now. I have to do some chores before I can go meet up with my friends."

We watched him disengage the privacy mode and then leave the room. We followed him back downstairs to the others.

Laura was back on the couch snuggling next to Patrick and my parents were sitting across from them.

"Mom, Dad, I'm gonna put the trash out now and then go on to Douglas's. I'll be home by ten." Jr told everybody.

"I thought you were going to stay and have dinner with us?" My mother asked. She looked crestfallen.

"Dad said it was okay to have dinner with Douglas and his family tonight." Jr. explained carefully. He never once looked my way. The kid is very good, I thought.

"Fine but be careful and call us when you get there and when you leave." Mom cautioned him.

"I will Mom." Jr. replied and rushed out.

Lippi and Pua stayed with the family, while I followed Jr. out of the house.

After carefully placing the lid on the trash cans, Jr. walked me over to the caretaker's house.

The cottage looked like a dollhouse and it was cute. There was the faint sound of music coming from inside and I recognized it from home. I deduced that the caretaker was Anthoran, or closely related to one.

A fiftyish looking woman opened the door to us. She smiled when she saw Jr. and then she looked straight at me. "Hello Jr, why don't you and your sister come in?" She asked with a smile.

She led us into the small living room and sat down. Her husband was sitting at a desk and he smiled when he saw me.

"I was hoping I'd get to meet you one day Fiona." He said with a smile.

"I'm so glad that you are Anthoran. Can you fill me in on how you ended up here?" I asked him.

"That's simple dear. We've been here ever since Leena left us in charge of the property some sixty years ago." Mrs. Edwards told us.

She spun a tale of intrigue and adventure. Leena and her husband were ready to move on because her husband was getting on in years while she was still young looking. He was well known as president of the company. They planned to move on to another state when her husband died suddenly of a heart attack. Then the visitors came. Leena was able to warn everyone. She gave them all shields and the option of staying or moving on. The visitors stayed in town for weeks before they attacked her. She fought bravely before she succumbed.

"We know about our essences going back to the home world, but they did something to her. We've always been caretakers of the property and she encouraged us to stay to watch over her descendants. She and her husband had perfected the shields that hides our true identities but didn't get a chance to use it on herself. All the others wear them also. We were the first to use it. She instructed us to keep the technology until someone like you came along."

"Will you trust me enough to give it to me?" I asked.

"Dear, you are the spitting image of our dear Leena. Of course, you can have it." Mr. Edwards said. He got up to go get it. Mrs. Edwards offered Jr. some cookies and I watched Jr. devour them.

"Mrs. Edwards, how long have you and your husband been here on the planet, if you don't mind me asking?"

"We've been here almost two hundred years altogether. We stay to ourselves to keep from being found out and the shield hides us as well. We hope to one day see our home world too."

"One of your descendants is an Elder on Anthora Two. The planet the scientists finally landed on is beautiful beyond words. I'm sure you will be able to see it." I told her confidently.

Mr. Edwards returned with a strong box resembling the one my dad has. He handed it to me, and I took it from him reverently. Inside, I found a longish flat jeweler's box with two sets of hearing aids. Mr. and Mrs. Edwards both showed me their ears. Each was wearing one in one ear.

"These are the final product that they've perfected. I was hoping to give them to your father, but that Chris and Patrick showed up. They are bad news."

I turned to Jr. "Aren't you going to Douglas' house for dinner.?" I asked him. I didn't want to scare him with my plans for Patrick and Chris.

"This is Douglas's house. I come here to learn about Anthora, since you can't be here to teach me." He replied.

"So where is Douglas?"

"That's my grandson, dear, he'll be along shortly." Mr. Edwards answered.

"Wait, I'm confused. Jr. comes here to play with your grandson and to learn about Anthora and my parents are cool with it?"

"Duh Fiona, they don't know that's why I'm here. Douglas is cool and his grandparents teach both of us. He's Anthoran like me too. The rest of his family aren't." He explained to me.

"Oh, I get it. Because you both are cloaked, Patrick and Chris cannot detect that you are Anthoran and my parents are cool with him hanging out with you because you are close. By the way, Jr. did you let them know that you are here?"

"Yeah I did." He said showing me his cellphone.

Suddenly, we heard someone at the door. A few seconds later, a young boy Jr's. age strolled into the living room where we were. His eyes grew like saucers when he spotted me. "You're Fiona, aren't you? Jr told me all about you, but I didn't believe him." He went over to greet his grandparents with hugs. "Grandma, Grandpa, I'm sorry I didn't believe you. I kept coming back only so I could hang out with Jr." He stated.

"Perhaps now you'll take our lessons more seriously." His grandfather scolded him gently.

Douglas went to sit beside Jr. They looked at each other and started speaking in the Anthoran language. Their accents were terrible, yet it was music to my ears.

"Wow, how are you able to teach them?" I asked the couple. They were sitting side by side beaming at the boys.

"Azel, is our native tongue so it is not new to us. Children are easier to teach than adults."

"Grandpa, show her what happens when you take the shield off." Said Douglas.

His grandfather obliged him, and it was my turn to be surprised. A bright and shimmering aura enveloped him. He quickly put the device back in his ear and the aura disappeared.

"What was that?" I asked.

"It is how we appear to other Anthorans here on Earth. When Douglas saw it, we knew that he was Anthoran. It is also how I knew to make sure that your brother gets that special room. I took it out of my ear to test him."

"And I asked why he was glowing like that." Jr cut in.

"Yes, he did." Mr. Edwards confirmed.

"Well, I'm relieved that he has you two to watch over him. I brought friends with me that I left in the house with the rest of the family. I'm going to see what I can do about Patrick and Chris." I turned to glide toward the door with Mr. Edwards following close behind.

"Fiona, you must be careful around those two. I've seen them do something to your sister. They have the power to control minds. They've got your family eating out of their hands."

"Don't worry Mr. Edwards, I didn't come alone, my friends and I know exactly how to take care of them. I just want to make sure that the company isn't compromised, otherwise my family will have to move again." I told them.

"I can clear that up for you dear. We not only keep an eye out for the house and the land surrounding it, but we also keep tabs on the status of the company. Nothing happens there that we don't know about. Patrick and Chris are the only new people. Everybody else and I mean everybody are direct descendants of the original 80 that landed here. My family worked there until about 15 years ago when our youngest daughter met with an accident and was killed. I believe that's the Edwards on the council."

Mr. Edwards had a nostalgic expression on his face as he spoke. I made a note to let Elder Edwards know that her parents are alive and well.

"I thought they were scattered to avoid detection."

"Their children work there, but some of the original who remain alive serve on the board wearing the shield Leena invented. We were able to duplicate it a few years ago." He explained.

He opened the door for me, and I turned to wave at him before heading back to the house. Lippi and Pua were outside waiting for me and I rushed to them.

"I hope it's okay that we wait for you out here. That Chris fellow is really working them over, he's using something to enhance their control over your family. We were starting to feel weird too, so we came outside." Lippi reported.

I pushed past them to see for myself what was being done to my family. I found them in the dining room eating. Dad was sitting at the head of the long table, my mom was sitting on his left, Laura on his right and beside her, was Chris.

"I want you to tell me immediately when Fiona comes back. Make sure Jr. tells you when he sees her." He said. His voice echoed in the dining room and I saw why. The headset on his head must be some sort of enhancement for his mind control abilities.

My mother nodded as did the others. I wanted to be sick. Chris had learned all about the company and the people working for it. Just then the doorbell chimed, and I expected Mom or Dad to go get it, but Chris got up instead. He came back with another man. He was wearing a headset too.

"Patrick, I don't need your help. I've got this. Look around, look at them! Do they look like they've given me any trouble? Laura told me everything, she said that Fiona came back and she killed John and Buck."

"These Brightblades are so much trouble! I hate this planet and I miss my family. I had a very successful afternoon at the office today. I got a full tour of the place. That boy is the only Anthoran here; so, after we kill him, we can leave." Patrick relayed.

I went back out satisfied that my family wouldn't have to leave. Lippi and Pua were staring at a squirrel when I joined them. I took the time to explain what animal they were looking at and then told them that we needed to make sure that there weren't any more ships in orbit.

Pua nodded and walked toward the back of the house to where we landed our cruiser. The land around the house was so big, we could've landed three more cruisers without any problem. She came back a few minutes later stating that there was one ship in orbit.

It had occurred to me that it was weird that we could detect Froagan ships while they couldn't detect ours. Commander Podge explained it to me. He said that all our ships were made of a special metal that enhanced the cloaking mode that even the most advanced radar couldn't penetrate. Now I wondered if that wasn't something similar to what Leena and her husband invented.

# CHAPTER TWELVE

I kept watch over Jr. until he was home for the evening and then we followed Chris and Patrick back to their car. They didn't go very far. They had a hotel room in town.

Yountville was in the heart of the Napa Valley. The Brightblade estate has been there for over 80 years and a curiosity to all nearby. Until recently the house was unoccupied but meticulously kept by the caretakers. Since capturing Leena Brightblade years ago, the Froagan Nation has kept an eye over it as well.

Under different humanoid appearances, Chris and Patrick routinely made trips to Bright Future Logistics to gather information on the Brightblades. When word came that a Brightblade family had moved into the estate, they knew that their quarry had been found. Fiona's family had made their way to the estate.

Orders came for them to kill the boy and be done with it. John and Buck had orders to kill both the girl and the boy. Instead, they killed the girl and left the boy. They hadn't believed that Fiona would come back to protect the boy. That was a mistake.

"If we kill the boy outside of the house, it would attract too much attention. It must be in the house. We've gotten the family controlled. They won't notice that he's gone for at least a week when the Subiac wears off and we'll be long gone by then." Patrick said. He was sitting at the small desk on the other side of the room.

Chris was lying on the bed smoking. "The Brightblades will be no more and we can all go home. Supreme Commander T'aku will be pleased." He said.

"Maybe we'll be rewarded with a view of Leena. I've wanted to get a look at her since I was a young hatchling. Thanks to her, we've been able to get all the information we need to eliminate the Anthorans once and for all. Supreme Commander T'aku will be able to launch an attack of their home world and take over the planet. You were foolish to hack into the security system Chris. I realize that some of it has helped us find the family, but you went too far to get footage of her in the containment case. You mustn't keep it. After we kill the boy you must erase it." Advised Patrick.

"My Uncle works to maintain security of the prisoner. I was careful not leave a trace of my codes, but you are right. I'll destroy it as soon as the boy is dead."

Chris got up off the bed and walked over to the bureau. He pulled open a draw and took out a small metal case. He swiped his hand over it and the lid glowed and opened. He pressed a code into the device in a sequence I quickly memorized. A scene played out that made my blood boil.

Leena was taken in ambush. She was with some others and they fought bravely, but she couldn't save them. She used her Le'ak to kill eight Froagans before they could get close enough to sedate her. When she fell, they placed her body in a case that was filled with a black viscous substance. The next scene showed her in a room. Her body was in some form of suspended animation. The black substance continuously swirled around her body. Every now and then, she would scream as if in pain. Then the screen went blank.

Leena was alive? She'd been a prisoner for over sixty years? If I hadn't seen it with my own eyes, I wouldn't have believed it. Immediately, my thoughts went through scenarios to save her, but I shook my head to clear it. My first duty was to remove the threat to my brother. Saving Leena was something I was going to need help with.

I signaled for Lippi and Pua to follow me outside. We headed back to the cruiser and it was then and only then that I could take a breath and calmed down. Lippi and Pua watched me nervously.

After I was sufficiently calm, I went over to expel in the area built into the cruiser just for me. I paced while my companions prepared dinner, alternately keeping watch over me.

"We have to deal with Chris and Patrick and that ship in orbit. I don't know how much information they'd gotten from my family, but it can't be helped. Right now, our immediate duty is to ensure Jr's safety. When we get back home, we can prepare a rescue strategy for Leena." I said calmly.

"Oh good, for a minute there I thought you were going to try to do this by yourself." Pua stated. Lippi nodded too as she set the small table in the mess area.

"I may have powers, but I'm not stupid. I realize that our enemy had an advantage over us holding Leena captive, but they don't know everything. Leena apparently hasn't told them about the device she and her husband invented. The shielding device has kept the Edwards and the others safe all these years. I realize that it is the same technology that prevents our ships from being detected."

"So how do you want to do this?" Lippi asked.

"Before we do anything, I want to make sure we have enough firepower to make it to our jump point when we leave the planet."

Pua frowned. "Why?" She asked as her frown grew deeper.

"Because after killing Chris and Patrick, I want to lure the ship in orbit away from the Earth and destroy it." I told them.

"Wouldn't that alert more Froagans?" Pua asked.

"Perhaps, but it'll be part of the plan. My brother will be safe because obviously, they can detect Anthorans. If he is wearing one of these, his essence signature will be gone, and Chris and Patricks' superiors will think he'd been killed before their demise." I said showing them the small flat box.

"Oh!" Lippi and Pua chorused together.

I sat down at the table to eat. I was calm and in control. Lippi and Pua followed suit but I noticed that they kept looking at each other nervously.

"What?" I asked them annoyed.

"We were wondering if you thought this through. Destroying that ship could mean war for Anthora Two. How much constant bombardment do you think the shield over our world could take before it started to malfunction, and they get through?" Lippi asked.

"It is inevitable that we'd be going to war. We will soon become part of the Alliance of Planets. Joined with these other worlds, we can turn the tide of the Froagan threat for good. When we get back, I'll be going on a mission to present our issues and to officially join the alliance." I told them.

"Oh, so that rumor is true? We'll be opening up the planet for trade and stuff?" Pua asked.

"Where did you hear that?" I questioned her with a frown. I was under the impression that knowledge of the Alliance of Planets was still secret.

"Embeta Twelve is part of the alliance. Our world joined years ago." Lippi told me.

"Our world, Teah Four, Aveng Three are some of the worlds in the Alliance. Anthora Two would be foolish not to join. Since joining, Embeta Twelve has been successful is fighting off some Froagan attacks." She explained further.

"Some doesn't sound like a good deal to me. We almost lost a squadron and got Captain Lao hurt." The alliance didn't seem that effective if they were going to allow Froagan ships in their orbit, I thought.

"That's because, Embeta Twelve was ravaged and pillaged by the Froagans. They came and destroyed almost all of our ships. We fight them when they land but not in the air. That's why we joined the alliance. We've gained better advantage. The Froagans come to a planet, destroy their defenses and then come back later to do whatever they want. We have allies now we can call upon for help." Pua added.

"When we were there, why wasn't there any help?"

"That's because, we are still rebuilding our defenses, ships and communications capabilities." Lippi instructed me.

"Is that how the Froagans operate? They come to a planet and destroy its ability to defend itself?"

"Exactly. When they come back next, it is to occupy and deplete the planet's resources and enslave its people." Pua explained.

"Will Earth be next?" I asked suddenly afraid.

"Earth has a fighting chance. They are more advanced in warfare. I don't think they will ever attack Earth, because it would take too much effort." Lippi replied.

"How do you know so much?" I asked Lippi.

Lippi's features changed to one of anger. "My parents were part of the space corps on Embeta Twelve. They fought hard and for a while it looked like we were winning when all of the sudden, the Froagan mothership appeared and blasted all of our ships, communication towers and half the militia. They have a secret weapon. Only the mothership is equipped with it. I learned from others that their world was similarly attacked." She replied.

Suddenly, it dawned on me what their secret weapon was. Leena was being held on the mothership and whatever they contained her in kept her Le'ak abilities inert until they needed her. They've been using her ability as a weapon. I tried to recall the images I'd seen on that hologram viewer that Chris had. Leena had electrodes attached to her body. They were using Le'ak through her. It made sense now. They have to hunt down all her descendants because we are the only defense against her!

I stood up and they looked at me expectantly. "We have to get Jr. outfitted tonight and then kill those two and go home. There's much to do." I told them.

"Are you sure?" Pua asked,

Yes. I know what their weapon is, and I know how to stop it."

"Well, are you going to tell us?" Asked Lippi.

I shook my head. "No not now, but I promise I will when we get home."

"I trust you Fiona, I just hope what you have planned succeeds." Pua said quietly.

"We have to get going." I told them. I walked away from the table with my plate. After placing it in the cleansing module, I went to sit at the helm. I wrote up a report of the proceedings thus far and once I was done, I motioned for the ladies to follow me.

Jr. was asleep when we got to the house and it was quiet. While Lippi and Pua kept watch over Jr, I conducted a check on the rest of the family. Mom and Dad were sleeping peacefully, Laura was sitting up on her bed talking on her cellphone.

"But Chris you promised me. I can't stand it here. There's nothing to do in this crappy town. You promised you'd take me with you, you swore to me." Laura said pleadingly, just before her eyes went glassy and her jaw slack.

"I will do as you say. I will keep watch over my brother. I will call you right away when Fiona comes." Then she hung up and slid her body down and closed her eyes.

That was beyond creepy, I thought. They could use their Subiac ability over the phone. I kind of felt sorry for my sister. Once this was over, she was going to need a lot of therapy.

I went back to my brothers' room. He was awake now and he was talking with Lippi and Pua. I quickly looked across the room to find that he had engaged the privacy mode for his room.

"Good, I'm glad you're awake." I told him and pulled out the shielding device. Mr. Edwards said that he only needed to wear one. I helped him put it in his ear. I jumped back when it took the shape of his ear. I hadn't taken a real look at the Edwards' ears to see if it did the same thing. Jr. didn't look hurt. He reached up to touch it and it changed again to look like a hearing aid.

Leena and her husband were geniuses. To remove the device, it changed to appear as a normal hearing-aid, but once inserted into the ear, it disappeared to cover the whole ear, mimicking the shape and color.

"Don't take it off for any reason, not even to shower." I told him.

"Can Douglas have one too?" He asked.

"Yes, I believe his grandparents will give him one. I have to go now; I will try to be back as soon as possible. I'm going to need your help in helping Mom, Dad and Laura. Those two men messed with their minds and once their control wears off, they'll be confused. Can you do that for me?"

I watched as my almost teenaged brother squared his shoulders and nodded. "Don't worry Fiona. I'll make sure they're okay." He said bravely.

I reached out to touch him at the same time he reached for me. "I love you, kiddo. See you soon."

"I hope it's very soon. Goodbye Lippi, goodbye Pua. Come back to see me too okay?"

"We will." Pua and Lippi said. I marveled at the communication device. One would think Pua and Lippi were really speaking English.

We hurried back to the hotel to find Chris watching TV, and Patrick fiddling with a nasty looking weapon. He held it up admiring it. "I can't wait to use this on the boy. It's supposed to not only kill the boy, but his essence too."

I stood in the middle of the room and fired on both of them at once, I went over to each of them to make sure there wasn't any parts of their heads functioning. A few minutes later, and to our disgust, their bodies disintegrated to mush.

"Clean up in aisle four." I said to no one in particular. Lippi and Pua went to work getting the hologram viewer into a smaller version of the box we used to transport John's body.

I did a quick check to see if there was anything of theirs that we could use and found a communicator on the nightstand. I asked the girls to scoop it and the weapon up as well and we left. Fleetingly, I wondered what the cleaning lady was going to think when she found the sludge in the bed and on the floor.

Lippi and Pua both sat at their stations as navigations and security techs. Pua assured me that we had enough firepower to defend ourselves once the Froagan ship began chasing us. I went over in my mind what I would do if it came to a point where we became desperate.

"Uncloak us, Ensign Lippi." I ordered. Immediately, the Froagan ship's lights went on and began to move toward us.

"Light speed, Lippi."

"Yes sir!" She replied. The ship accelerated to light speed with the Froagan ship gaining.

"A little more." I murmured. I wanted the ship to get as close to the sun as it could get. "Ensign Pua, fire everything we have now!"

"Yes Captain." She answered and opened up fire.

We watched our barrage hit the ship once before it's shields went up. There was some damage but not enough to blow it up. They returned fire, but our shields held firm also.

I allowed them to chase us a little further and we'd gotten as close to the sun as we could without disturbing the gravitational pull of the surrounding planets or their orbits. I closed my eyes and felt for my Le'ak. My body knew what it had to do, and I could feel it pulling on the sun nearby.

My body began to vibrate as it pulsed with power. I had Lippi turn the cruiser around to face our enemy. I went to the bay area and buckled myself into the harness the soldiers use when they travel on the cruiser. Then I ordered Pua to lower the shields. I opened the bay doors just a bit, I aimed and fired, along with the cruiser's laser beams. It was over before I could fully comprehend what happened. The ship blew up in a spectacular display of light. It happened so fast, that the only thing that escaped through the bay doors was a container of foodstuff. The back lash threw us thousands of feet away and once we'd gotten control, I ordered Lippi to take us to our jump point for our trip home.

Captain Lao and Elder Chaktar greeted us as we disembarked. I held the box containing the hologram viewer under my arm as we were led to a conference room at the air corps station.

"I trust your trip proved successful, Captain?" Elder Chaktar began.

"Yes sir, it was." I answered. "Before I give you a report, has there been any more Froagan sightings or captures since I was gone?"

"As a matter of fact, we've caught two more."

"Is the base secure?"

"Yes, it is. What's this about Captain?" Elder Chaktar asked with a frown.

We'd gotten to the conference room and I took out the shielding device and placed it on the table. It took on the color of the table and disappeared.

"What was that?" Captain Lao asked as his eyes searched the table.

"Before I explain what that was, I must backtrack to my first trip back home. I wasn't entirely truthful. What Captain Lao reported was mostly true but after the captain went back to the cruiser to wait for me, my father had some artifacts from Leena which he showed to me. It was handed down from father to son for generations. Leena kept the ships' manifest and kept a diary of what happened to the eighty people on board."

When I finished my tale, Captain Lao and Elder Chaktar were silent for a moment. Then the questions began.

"Captain, I understand your caution, however, this was something that could have given us more information we need to combat the threat to us all." Elder Chaktar said.

"I don't understand how knowing that she had made a life for herself and her family could benefit us now. I didn't know half of the stuff I know now." I countered. I figured that I would feed them information in small increments especially if their reaction to knowing that Leena had started manufacturing devices that could shield us made him turn purple.

"We felt that the Froagan threat was too great for a return trip so soon, especially after your family disappeared. We didn't want to lose you too." He explained further.

"Well there is more. Apart from starting the Bright Future Logistics company, she and her husband had developed what I just placed on the table. There are two versions of it. One that could be worn to shield the person and the other a whole ship which is what we already have. I'm beginning to understand some of the enhancements that our scientists added to Leena's DNA."

"You mean that she had found a way to miniaturize it?" Captain Lao asked searching the table again.

"Yes, and had I not gone down to see how my family fared, I wouldn't have been able to get one. Now we can be assured of safety when we travel to other worlds." I told them.

"What else have you to report Captain?" Elder asked eyeing the box in front of me. Now that I was solid again, I can touch it. I opened the box and pulled out the hologram viewer. I nodded at Lippi.

She came around to swipe her hand over it. Just as Chris did it, the lid opened, then she inputted the codes we'd memorized to activate it. Again, I was in awe as Leena's image appeared.

"That's impossible!" Elder Chaktar sputtered.

"And yet, you just saw with your own eyes. She's still alive and what's more, I know why they're keeping her alive. She's been the power behind their attacks." I told them.

"I get it now!" Lippi blurted out excitedly. "That's why they are trying to assassinate her descendants and why they are still trying to capture Anthorans. If they can get more Anthorans with Le'ak abilities, they'll be able to outfit the rest of their fleets."

"It took them this long to figure out how to use her ability to their advantage. Before now, they'd been doing what they've always done, plunder and move on." Captain Lao said.

"Captain Brightblade, you've done very well. The council will meet soon to discuss what we should do next." Elder Chaktar informed me.

"I don't care what they decide, I want to be a member of the crew that's going up against that mothership to rescue Leena." I told him.

"Without a doubt Captain. I will make sure of it." He replied. He got up and walked out of the room.

"Elder Sim will want to examine the shielding device so that we can duplicate it, and the hologram viewer will be placed in a secured area." Captain Lao said. He too stood up to leave.

"That went well." Pua said once we were alone in the room.

"They didn't seem too enthusiastic about going to rescue Leena." I answered back.

"Give them time to adjust. We've just dropped a boatload of information on them. Bureaucrats always take time to argue issues that seem clear to others. By the way, Pua and I want in on the rescue too." Insisted Lippi. Pua was behind her nodding too.

"You bet, you two have been with me from the very beginning. It's incredible that it has been only a short time. I haven't been here a full year yet and look at all we've done together." I told them. Next week will mark a six months since my retrieval and I can't believe that I'd been through training to sharpen my skills as a warrior, space traveled to other worlds and had combat experience with the enemy under my belt.

"Come on, let's go home. I'm tired and I need a shower." I said to them.

"How soon do you think it will take the council to agree on a rescue mission for Leena?" Pua asked.

"I don't know but I want you two to prepare. Practice your combat skills, join the target practice units on base; anything that will give us a fighting chance against the Froagans." I told them.

I headed to my apartment daydreaming about how long I was going to stay under the shower's spray. Elder Chaktar was standing in front of my door waiting for me.

"Elder, has something happened?" I asked him. I could feel my heart pounding in my chest.

"Shall we go in?" He countered. He seemed anxious.

When we were in the living room, I turned to face him. "What is it?"

"I know that you are tired and want only to rest, but if it is not the case. Captain Lao, Boham and I would like to train you further." He said. His tone was serious, and his eyes didn't stray from my face.

"What more is there to teach me?"

"If you recall, the meeting we had at my home, we spoke of your other abilities. We can help you access them. If we are to rescue Leena, then you must be as powerful as she to defeat her if need be."

"I understand Elder, but you misunderstand my intentions. I don't want to defeat her; I want to rescue her. Think of how much more powerful we as a nation will be with her on our side." I reasoned.

"You do not fear that she may have become evil?"

"No, I do not; and if she is, we can deal with her then." I told him. He didn't look convinced. "Elder, is this also a concern with the other elders?"

"I believe so, but as you say, we will deal with her if it is determined that she is evil. The others are waiting for us. Shall we go?"

"Can I change first?"

"Of course, I shall continue to look through your album." He answered. I watched him pick it up and open it.

I rushed to take a quick shower and pulled on a pair of jeans and tee. When I joined him, he was staring at a picture of me as a young girl. I smiled at it too.

"I was fourteen years old in that picture and I was so proud of my new haircut. For so long, my parents dictated how I should wear my hair and I had finally won, and they allowed me to get it cut." I told him.

"You had a fighters' defiance even back then." He commented.

I reached over and took the album from him. "Shall we go?"

Elder Chaktar drove us back to his town he said is called Zwood. He drove past his house and further into the town. It was daytime here and there were people in the aquariums splashing around.

"Do they swim all day?"

"No, we can only be out of the water for a limited amount of time, then we must go back." He explained.

"How long can you be out of the water?"

"The longest I've been away from water is twelve hours; past that, I begin to feel weak and my skin begins to dry up. Pure Zwazodorians have a limit of three to four hours."

"I see why this place has to be maintained. If they had to go to the ocean, would they survive? I mean if they had no choice, would they?"

Chaktar nodded. "Yes, the full ones would, but hybrids like me would suffer some difficulty."

"I'm sorry I'm asking so many questions. I find your people fascinating and I feel that my education of Anthora as a whole is lacking. Besides the Zwazodorians, what other special species live here on the planet?"

"Well, let's see. We have the Nozans who can only live underground, and the other are the Radi. They are part humanoid and bird. Their numbers are few and they have colorful wings."

"Wow, will I be able to meet them sometime?" I thought it was fantastic to have wings.

"A representative of each of our retrieved will be at the meeting to voice their concerns about joining the Alliance of Planets. You'll be able to meet everyone."

"Are we there yet?" I asked. We'd been driving for over an hour now and the scenery was starting to change. The sky was darkening and there were no homes and the road had changed to dirt.

"We're almost there." He answered. He turned unto another road and I could see an oddly shaped building. It was under a dome and I could see light all around it.

Elder Chaktar parked the conveyor beside the building inside the dome and got out. I got out to follow him into the building. The minute I walked in; I knew I was in trouble and took a stance. Chaktar turned to me and smiled diabolically.

"You've come a long way from the shy and confused person we'd retrieved. Now you're becoming a liability we can't afford to allow to continue." He said.

"Where are Captain Lao and Boham?" I asked trying not to sound afraid. But I was, very afraid. I was surrounded by Froagans.

"They are not coming. This is the last place they'd think to look for you. Your elder is most useful. This part of the planet was deadly to us and now we have a way in. The Elder was most challenging, but in the end, my superior Subiac abilities have won. Through him, I can do anything."

Before I could raise my arms to blast him, two soldiers grabbed me from behind. The one facing me held a clear box that held an orb. He opened the box and the black orb floated out and advanced toward me. I thought of what happened to Leena just before it reached me. It engulfed me and I couldn't move my arms. Immediately, I felt weakened. I fell to my knees and knew no more.

I don't know how long I was out, but I was awake now. My arms were no longer bound, and I was in a small cell. The walls of it were made of glass and when I touched it, a black substance rose from it and surrounded me. I felt weak again and unbearable pain. I let out a scream and fell to my knees.

"Ah, you're awake. I was beginning to think you wanted to sleep forever." A Froagan said. I looked up at it.

"What have you done?" I asked with a pant.

"You will address me as Captain Se'vork. You thought you were so cunning. We'd been orchestrating everything from the start. First, we had to get you here to give these pathetic people some hope. Did you really think we didn't know you'd come back for your brother? We used him as bait to get you to the homestead. We found no others with power, but now we know better. We know that Leena made a shield for them that keeps us from detecting them. Our scientists are working on a way to see through this shield and then there won't be a place in the entire universe for your kind to hide. The boy doesn't have any power, so our agents were instructed to kill him. They succeeded before you destroyed their ship. Now that leaves you. You see dear girl; you've been the prey all along."

"What are you talking about? You didn't know I existed until recently." I felt relieved that they thought Gary Jr. was dead.

"Leena is weakening, perhaps dying. We need another powerful Le'ak wielder and that's you. You're young and strong and will last for a long time. In the meantime, we are in the process of duplicating your powers and then we won't need you any longer. The Froagan nation will be the most powerful force in the universe."

"Why are you doing this? You already are a powerful force. Why can't you leave us to live in peace?"

"Revenge is our way. Long ago, we lived in peace on our own planet. Beings like you came and warred with us. They left us a weak and dying world. Because of our unique physiology, we cannot exist on any of the worlds we've scouted. Our ships are our home and we have made it our mission to hunt you down and kill you. Only recently we discovered that we could use you to be more powerful. That is more palatable than killing you."

"We have no such record in our archives." I told him.

"Why would you keep record of your treachery? Is it not better to have the populace believe that you are innocent?"

"Look, what my ancestors may have done has nothing to do with us as a people now. What can we do to have peace between us?" I couldn't believe I was trying to negotiate with it.

He hesitated, but then he shook his head. "My orders are to bring you back to the mothership. You're to replace Leena. We are not without mercy. We will allow her to die peacefully." He replied.

The black substance swirling around me thinned and then disappeared. The pain stopped and I could stand once again. I dared not touch the walls, I didn't want to activate that thing again. I had to think, and I needed to do it quickly.

"Have you killed the Elder?" I asked.

"I used Subiac to control him and speak through him. He is resting. I will need him to get off the planet." The Froagan replied.

"Are all the Elders under your control?"

"For now, just Chaktar. Your warriors have been successful in finding us out. There is only me and my men. Once I leave the planet with you, we will be back to finish what has been in motion for millennia."

"What were my ancestors called? Were they originally Anthorans?" I asked. This Froagan obviously was babysitting me, so I figured I might as well get as much information as I could.

I watched him get comfortable in the chair he was sitting in. He wasn't wearing a humanoid suit and I had gotten used to seeing his true form. This one was skinny, and he wore a uniform.

His loose-fitting uniform was a metallic white color. His legs were longer than his torso. His head was big, and his eyes were large, glassy and unblinking. I guess because they hardly needed to speak with one another, what with the hive mind connection; his mouth was a small slit under a flat nose.

"For generations my people have searched for The Lipasot. After they destroyed our world, they came to settle on Anthora and even mated with them. While they were pretending to be gods on your world, we were gathering our strength. We hunted your kind all across the universe and when we came across Anthora, your numbers had greatly diminished and easy to kill off."

I was about to ask another question when another Froagan came along. He spoke to him in their language, but the meaning was clear. They were getting ready to make their move. The other soldiers came and there were six of them besides the one who appeared to be in charge. He broke away from the others to approach my cell.

"Soon you shall join Leena; after she dies, you will take her place." He said. I was afraid to make any sudden moves. I watched them gather what supplies they had packed up.

They were in high spirits, after all, if what they said is true, they'd completed their long and complicated mission. They have me.

The Edwards back on Earth said that they had captured Leena sixty odd years ago, which was considerably less in Anthoran time. They didn't have her that long. They also said that they did something to her that when she dies, her essence would also.

This black substance hindered her ability to throw light, but I wondered if it also hindered her other abilities if she has them. For only a brief moment, I was able to hear Anthoran thoughts; Boham hadn't thought was possible. They also mentioned that I could fly. I didn't think they actually meant fly, but perhaps levitate; much like floating when on other worlds.

I was beginning to feel inadequate. I can throw a mean light, but I don't know how to access the rest. How can I save myself, much less Leena?

# CHAPTER THIRTEEN

The one in charge swiped his hand across the lock on the door to my cell and immediately the black substance appeared on the floor and slowly crept up my legs and finally to engulf my body. I didn't feel any pain this time, but I felt weak again and then nothing like I was in a bubble.

From deep within the black shroud, I could hear Elder Chaktar ordering for a cruiser to be prepped for me. I didn't understand why no one thought it suspicious that I was bound. I could see and hear everything that was going on around me through the cloudy substance, but I couldn't do anything about it.

Somehow, the cruiser was prepped, and I was on board. I could see the Elder on the ground, and Captain Lao was standing beside him. I tried to move and was hit with a wave of pain so severe that I thought I'd lose consciousness, but I didn't.

I could feel the cruiser take off and once we broke orbit, I began to feel better. Space was my friend; I could feel the sun nearby. I began to draw on its power. I didn't want to draw too much or else, I'd start to glow. I knew instinctively that they wouldn't hurt me; they needed me to replace Leena. I didn't have conductors or electrodes attached to my body, so I could probably use my Le'ak, but I won't, not yet.

The Froagan in charge, said something and I knew were about to jump. It was almost smooth. We came out alongside the mothership and they cheered. The mothership welcomed our cruiser like a long-lost baby as it settled inside its bay area. Still in the fog, I was transported to another cell and when the cloud dissipated, I grunted in pain.

Across from my cell, was Leena's. She was conscious. We stared at each other. She didn't look bad for someone two hundred plus years old. All Brightblades had either blond hair or red. My brother and I were the only ones in our family to have red hair, Dad and Laura were blonds and Mom was a brunette. Leena's red hair had streaks of white in it. I smiled at her and she nodded to me.

"You will take her place when she dies." The Froagan said to me. I turned to look at him, he was still wearing a humanoid skin.

"How long does she have?"

"We do not know. Her life force has changed and nothing we've done made her improve." He explained.

"What does that mean?"

"The monitors we have attached to her, show that she is weakening and her Le'ak is lessening."

I looked toward Leena again and this time I felt a profound sense of grief. "Can she speak?"

"She hasn't for a long time."

"Leena," I spoke loudly for her to hear. "My name is Fiona Brightblade. I am your great, great, great granddaughter from Earth. I'm so happy to meet you."

"They told me that they'd found my replacement. I'm sorry child." She replied. Her voice was shaky.

I cried freely now. I felt such sorrow; I didn't know how to contain it. Suddenly, I could hear her thoughts in my head. "Do not let on that you can hear me child. Nod if you do."

Through my tears, I nodded. "What have they done to you?" I asked her in mind speech. I didn't know I could do that. I continued to cry to hide our communicating. Besides, I couldn't stop crying. I was overjoyed to finally meet her and saddened that she was dying.

"I must tell you something very important. This you must keep to yourself; no one must know this." She thought.

"I promise, but can't they hear our thoughts too?" I asked her.

"Their frequency is different," She replied. What Leena told me gave me courage. While they scanned my body to measure me for my own Le'ak conduit and electrode prison, Leena and I prepared.

The black cloud swirled faster around Leena collecting parts of itself from her body. Then it floated away from her body after which she slumped over in her specialized seat. She was held in a chair that had tubing going in and out throughout her body. I asked her if it was painful and she said that the tubing was sustaining her body with nutrients and taking away waste. They never allowed her to leave the containment cell or the chair.

She never got hungry and she slept fitfully. The conduit collected her Le'ak and stored it. When they needed it, they combined it with a powerful laser beam of their own devising that became a million times more powerful. They destroyed with precision.

I watched them go into Leena's cell and systematically disconnected her from the tubing that fed her body, and the conduits that collected her Le'ak. Once that was done, I watched her wounds bleed and then seal up. She closed her eyes and told me that she was going to be okay.

They left her lying in the chair. The technician used a small box to collect the black substance. He scanned her body and once he was satisfied, he left the cell and locked it.

He then approached my cell carrying the box. The black goo engulfed my body once again and when he opened the box another inside joined the one around my body. I felt a twinge of pain that made me grit my teeth. Another tech joined us in the cell and together, they started to place the electrodes on my body. The painful part was next, and I was grateful that the goo knocked me out.

When I came to sometime later, I was in a chair identical to Leena's and my arms were locked onto the armrest. I couldn't help the scream that escaped my lips. The newly inserted tubing hurt terribly.

Those bastards thought it would be fun to have Leena watch as they leeched me of my Le'ak. It was painful, not at all like expelling. Through it all, she kept me company; and so, did Ra'el and Suna.

Ra'el and Suna were sentient beings whose natural form is viscous. They too are prisoners of a sort. The Froagans discovered them on one of their conquering sprees on a planet many thousands of light years away. They too were a peace-loving people existing in huge communes. When the Froagans came, they didn't find anything they could take from the planet itself until they discovered that the Chal'e could disconnect from the greater to be singular. Their experiments with the beings taught them that they could inflict pain; something they were very interested in.

The Froagans proposed an alliance in return for something the Chal'e didn't have. The Chal'e dreamed of space travel but lacked physical form to do so. With the promise of helping them obtain the stars, envoys disconnected from the whole to travel with the Froagans. Thus, began the Chal'e and the Froagan alliance and plans to eradicate the Anthorans.

Ra'el and Suna didn't exactly speak with me; it was more like I felt their meaning. They took turns joining with Leena. It was how they learned what the Froagans were truly doing. They knew of the Lipasot. Their version is quite different from what that Froagan told me.

The Lipasot traveled the universe as explorers. When they came to Ra'el and Suna's planet, they stayed to study and gather information. They were scientists and research specialists. They helped the Chal'e in any way they could to give them knowledge of the heavens. They explained that it was not their way to interfere with their natural development. They promised that sometime in the future, that they would obtain the stars. With their Le'ak, they terraformed a small portion of the planet as a monument and left.

The Chal'e still yearned for the stars and took their chance with the Froagans. It wasn't until they found Leena that they understood how treacherous the Froagbans were. They meant Leena no harm and tried to be less painful to her but Ra'el was weakening. He couldn't control the pain he inflicted on Leena. Suna was still in her infancy so she was better at controlling how close to Leena she got. Ra'el was ancient and his lifeforce was coming to its end. It is his weakness, the

Froagans are reading on their instruments. Leena was weaker, but not dying.

The technician stepped back to admire his work. I looked like a pin cushion. He activated the mechanism that would from now on feed my body and I watched in horror as a greenish liquid flowed into my body. Immediately, I felt stronger and refreshed. "Leena, is this supposed to feel good?" I asked in mind speech.

With her eyes still closed, she answered. "Yes, they do not understand that keeping our bodies healthy keeps us strong as well as our Le'ak. Suna will have to give you some pain every now and again to keep our enemy from knowing all."

Suna apologized as she inflicted her pain, swirling around my body. I screamed and tried to control it. She instructed me to let her do it and it subsided.

The tech left us and went to scan Leena once more. He left her soon too and then we were alone.

We could hear them announce something and I only hoped that it wasn't the order to jump to Anthora Two. They'd leeched me almost dry and I didn't know how much Leena had if any.

"Do not worry. When they jump, they always feed me. You will be able to replenish your reserves soon. Their laser burns most of the Le'ak quickly so they need to have a steady supply ready. Ra'el's weakness also weakened my ability to gather the sun's power. This part of the ship always faces the sun. Gather as much as you can while I do the same." Leena said to me.

While we waited to reach whatever destination we were heading to, Leena and I got more acquainted. I told her all about my life on Earth and what little I garnered from the Edwards in regard to the company she and her husband started. I told her about my family and how they came to be living at the homestead.

"If it weren't for your forethought, my family and more importantly, my brother would have died."

"It was my duty to ensure safety for all of us. The original plan was to wait for retrieval, but it never came. When we fled Anthora, it was dying. The Froagans are destroyer of worlds. They thrive on it. The plan for retrieval was our last resort to ensure that not only the Anthorans survived, but us as well. The Lipasot meant only to guard the Anthorans, but one of our ancestors fell in love and so we stopped roaming the galaxies and stayed. When the Froagans arrived, we tried to stay hidden and intended only to observe. They were a species we've encountered before. Finally, we knew that if we didn't intervene, the Anthorans would perish. They possessed power that was not theirs to use."

"Wait, are you saying that we are not Anthoran?" I asked. I was confused.

"Those of us that possess the abilities are part Anthoran and part Lipasot. You and I probably are the only true ones left of our species. I was born on Anthora, but my species is Lipasot. Like many of the Anthorans who mixed with us, some of them carry the genes of the Lipasot, hence the abilities. I sense that there a many such people on Anthora Two."

"Where do the Lipasot come from?"

"Our home world, S'evotgro, no longer exists. Our sun was dying, and we left to find a new home. Like the Anthorans did when the Froagans destroyed their planet, we traveled away in different directions. Those of us that arrived on Anthora were lucky. We sensed that some of the others did not survive."

"Did the Froagans have a Lipasot on board the mothership you destroyed?" I asked sensing a sadness in her.

"Yes. It was with his consent that I destroyed the ship."

"When the Froagan captured me, one of them told me that the reason they were hunting the Anthorans is because the Lipasot destroyed their world. I don't know what to believe." I told her. I was beginning to wonder if perhaps her mind was gone. Being held captive that long could do damage to ones' ability to reason. Elder Chaktar had also suggested that she might have turned evil.

"Fiona child, I have come to my full potential once they started using me. Memories that had been locked away in my genes have been restored to me. I have full recollection of our history. We visited their world and found a power hungry and war-like civilization. They warred with each other. They destroyed their own world. We tried to help them, but they only wanted our Le'ak. They chased us when we left and have been ever since."

"How can you know for sure that those memories are real?" I questioned her further.

"The Lipasot were the scientists that stayed to ensure the populace escaped. It was us who enhanced Anthoran genes. In all the worlds, Anthorans are dear to us."

"Why?"

"We had found a people we could co-exist with and a people whose physiology is similar to ours. When our sun died, we had no way of ensuring our species would continue until we found Anthora."

"Why don't I have this foreknowledge?"

"You will soon. Once my full capabilities were restored, I found that I could tune in to the Froagans' frequency. I knew they were searching for you. I wanted them to find you so I could meet you. I hadn't communicated with my kind in a long time."

"When will I be able to understand them? I don't want them to use me to destroy Anthora Two."

"They are heading for a planet nearby. They are waiting for me to die before going to Anthora Two."

"But you're not dying, are you?" I asked fearfully.

"No, I am not. Ra'el has consented to help me appear dead. He will enshroud my body and all life functions will appear to cease. Then they will connect you to their weapon. They intend to test you on that nearby planet."

"What will they do to your body?" If they thought she was dead, wouldn't they destroy her body, I thought privately.

"Do not worry, they will store my body until they return to Anthora Two. It is their intent to exhibit it to bring fear to the populace, like they'd once done. We must prepare to act then. I must rest now and gather my strength." Leena closed her eyes and to all, appeared dead. Ra'el disengaged from Suna and melded with the walls of my cell.

Captain Se'vork waited while a medical tech performed a check on us. He first inspected me and then went on to Leena. When he opened the cell, Ra'el joined her. The tech felt for a pulse and shook his head at the captain, then he pulled away the last of the tubing from her body. Another tech joined him and together they transported her away.

The tech came back to connect me to their weapon. Suna helped me control the pain. The attachment hooked up to my brainstem felt uncomfortable and as long as Suna stayed with me, it wouldn't hurt. I realized that Suna's task was to keep me comfortable. She absorbed the pain. I asked her if she was feeling any pain and she replied that it was a mild discomfort. She further explained that the pain Leena and I experienced were the byproducts of when Ra'el or her disengaged from us and that it was necessary for the enemy to think otherwise.

They couldn't stay connected to us for long, they needed to disconnect to maintain their identity. If they stayed connected too long with something else, they would forget who they were.

I now understand what Leena tried to explain about the memories. If asked, I wouldn't be able to fully explain how it was happening, but I felt a surge go through me and then a door opening inside my head. I saw S'evotgro in all its splendor.

I closed my eyes to savor my memory visions. At first, I was in orbit circling S'evotgro and what I saw was breathtaking. The planet was a huge ball of blues, greens and oranges. The giant sphere of its nearby sun invigorated me. The planet was the closest to it, saturating it and its inhabitants with its rays. The abilities given to the people, whether it was a form of protection, I cannot say was indeed a gift. It had three moons. There were two other planets circling the sun, but they were so far away, they appeared like dots. How I knew they were planets; again, I cannot say. I just knew. Then, I was plunging toward my ancestral home world. It was as if I was actually there in my memory. I felt the resistance of wind against my body.

The atmosphere was pleasant, the weather balmy. My first glimpse of the sky made my heart glad. It was blue, tinged with purple. I had arrived in the evening. Buildings and homes were all white; circular in shape littered the ground. I saw mountains, forests and flowers of every description. The trees were majestic with their deep green leaves. I saw animals that were truly alien, yet commonplace to S'evotgro.

Then I was heading toward one of the buildings. Inside, I was part of an assembly of people all red headed. We were in a meeting of some sort. The facilitator spoke of the imminent death of our star. A murmur went through the crowd. Two other beings stood up to join the one speaking at the podium. One of the two lifted his hand to get our attention.

"We have known that this day would come. What we are doing about it will ensure our survival. Our closest worlds are not suitable for us; we must venture further away to find a world ideal for us. Our ship arks are almost ready for travel, and we will travel in four directions. Our arks will sustain us for two hundred life cycles until we find a new home. The other option is to stay until a new sun forms, however, the danger involved is unknown to us. We do not know how long it will take, nor do we know what effects on those that remain will be. It has always been our belief that we live by the sun and are subject to its every phases. If it dies, it is doubtful that we will survive."

A new murmur went through the crowd. "I'm too old to travel the stars, I'd rather stay and die if I must." An ancient murmured next to me. I watched as she pushed her way through the crowd to leave.

"Ama, I don't want to lose you, you must come with us." A young man said as he rushed after her. When he caught up to her, he clasped her hand pulling her to a halt. He turned her to face him and took hold of her other hand.

"Ama?" He asked pleadingly.

Ama looked at him with great sadness. Her hair was gray with red streaks. "No, my son. There are others who feel like me. We are too old. It is better to allow our young to go on and survive for us. Take with you our knowledge, our gifts and culture." Ama said.

Her son let go of her hands and watched sadly as she made her way through the crowds and out the door. He observed many other ancients do the same with their children pleading with them as he was.

I was moving again. This time I was aboard one of the arks. I had a feeling that we had been traveling for a long time. I wandered among the peoples in the ark and found Ama's son. He was an officer on the ark and was sitting at his station. I spied his name on his uniform shirt. His name was Lugo and he was a science officer in charge of the arks' propulsion systems.

Another officer announced the demise of another ark and then an encounter with a hostile vessel. The feeling I got was that there were only a few arks left, all the others had encountered some sort of disaster.

Again, the scene changed, and Lugo and the other ark officers debated on whether to land on the planet below them. After a study of its atmosphere and determination of whether it could sustain them, The Orda sent a team to go investigate.

The planet was Anthora. The people were peaceful and excited to have us visit them. The team stayed for a period of a month on Anthora gathering information. Another period of time later, The Orda, landed with its cargo. The Lipasot brought with them their culture and knowledge. Although the Anthorans were advanced in their own right, they welcomed the Lipasots' knowledge.

In my prison chair, I experienced hundreds of years pass as the Lipasots and the Anthorans lived in peace and harmony. Although our lifespans are longer than that of the Anthorans, we started to die off.

Lugo Brightblade was the originator of Leena's and my lineage. The commander of the Orda was the first to marry an Anthoran and the others followed suit. However, because of our unique need to be close to the sun, our people lived in the higher elevations of the planet and with our ability to channel the sun's rays and use it, we became the shining ones.

I was jolted back to the Froagan mothership when a tech came to fine tune the attachment to my brain stem. This was a pain, Suna could not contain completely. As I cried out, part of me wondered how much more horrible it could've been had she not absorbed some of it. Finally, he was done and via communicator, indicated to the commander that I was ready.

The ship was orbiting a small planet. Leena was right when she said that our cabin cell was always positioned to be near a sun. These Froagans knew its importance and meant to use it for their own devious goals.

When they fired on the planet, part of me relished the release of my Le'ak, while another felt revulsion for the destruction, I was helping cause.

When it was over, these sadistic monsters replayed the damage on a viewer for me to see. I was relieved that no one was killed and the commander himself gave me a report, confirming that none were.

"Rest assured that this was only a test. That planet was uninhabited. It is where we build our ships. What we've just done was seal up one of our mining tunnels." What he said made me feel better, but I wasn't going to let him know.

"What have you done with Leena's body?" I asked him.

"It is being prepared. We mean to keep it preserved until we go to Anthora Two. Your pathetic peoples believed that she was a hero when she destroyed the mothership and killed Supreme Commander Oftha. I want them to see how low she had been brought. With your Le'ak, we will break through the defenses and capture as many as we want. Our mothership and a few other battle ships are the only ones that have a wielder on board. The Froagan Nation will rule the universe, and no one will be able to oppose us." He said the last so passionately that his spittle splattered onto his uniform.

I closed my eyes to him and heard as he left my cabin. I didn't know if Leena was truly gone, but I had to try to reach her. After this test, the mothership's next destination was Anthora Two and I wasn't sure how far away we were from it.

"Leena, can you hear me?" I pleaded.

"Yes, I hear you child." She answered.

"Are you okay?"

"Being dead, is the most freedom I've had in a long time. They've placed me in a cabin all to myself, but still a prison." She answered.

"Do you know how far we are from Anthora Two?" I asked her.

"I've been to the planet they've tested you on before, it should take at least three solar cycles to reach Anthora Two. This mothership hasn't been to the planet for a long time. Only their scouts have, and I've always heard the same report. They aren't able to penetrate the outer defenses of the planet. You must tell me how the planet is being protected."

I felt a nudging in my brain. Suppose Leena *was* evil? Look at how long it took to get me where I am. These Froagans have had decades to work on her. Their plan to capture me was ingenious and it took a lot of patience. How was I to know that she wasn't part of their plan?

"I'm not sure exactly how Anthora Two is protected. My training hadn't extended to that level. I do know that the planet itself experiences very severe storms that distorts the defenses." I told her. It was better to have her feel that I was still on board with her plans. Telling her about the storms was just a tiny nugget, she and the Froagans might use against the planet.

"How often do the storms occur?

"I've been on the planet almost a year, and I've only experienced one." I told her. Now she was making me nervous.

"Someone's coming, we'll continue later."

I felt her disconnect, but not completely. I was getting enough to hear what she was hearing, but not her thoughts. What I heard made me want to destroy the ship and everything and everyone onboard if I could. I've learned to trust my intuition. She *is* evil and had cast her lot with them a long time ago. In exchange for her freedom, she was willing to destroy a whole planet and its peoples.

She lied to me when she said that she would help me; and the Froagans knew that she was not dead or dying. It was an act to fool me to further destroy my moral. She was one of them now.

I was becoming agitated. Suna tried to help me. She soothed me and gave me the impression that all was not lost. I tried to communicate that Leena was evil, that all was. I watched as a bluish fluid flowed into me and then I knew no more.

I couldn't be sure how long I was out and was surprised that they even allowed me to rest. Suna gave me the impression that they've just recently started inducing sleep. They are making sure that I stay as healthy as possible. I was still a little groggy, but I could tell that there was activity all around me.

The wall facing where I sat moved. My cabin was alongside the bridge the whole time; made sense come to think of it. How else can they calibrate their weapon if said weapon was several decks below? They needed me right there with the techs manning the weapons' stations.

I wanted to vomit when I spied Leena sitting in a chair beside the commander. She smiled and waved at me. If my hands weren't bound to the chair, I would have disintegrated her. Elder Chaktar was right, she was evil.

"Don't look so surprised Fiona. Did you think the viewer was just given to you? We've been orchestrating things from the first. I'd grown tired of living with the humans. On Anthora our kind were gods. Earthlings thought me an oddity and nothing more, but out here, in the vastness of space, I can be."

"I'm ashamed to be related to you." I spat out at her.

"Along with my new friends, we'd come up with the only way to capture more of our kind. You are among the few we've captured so far. It took us a while to figure out that only a very precious few of us carry the full Lipasot genes. Those of us with red hair are very special. Have you discovered what we can do yet?" She asked.

I was so angry that all I could do was cry. I cried for the hopelessness of it all, and I cried for all those people that would die if I didn't find a way to defeat Leena. I've come to understand that she had become power hungry and while the Froagans thought they were using her;

*she* was using them. Right now, she was all that stood to stop me from saving my home and the people I've come to care for.

"How could you betray your own kind like this? The Anthorans revere you. Should you get past the planets' defenses, they won't fight you. They won't know that you mean to destroy them until it's too late." I told her.

"That's exactly what I'm banking on dear girl. They consider me a god, that is how easy it will be to destroy them." She stated in a gloating manner.

"You've lied about everything?" I couldn't help but ask.

"No, not everything. Opening up secrets locked away in our genes and DNA, was a byproduct of the Le'ak magnifier, which by the way, I invented. I was entertained for a while until I discovered that on S'evotgro, our full potential had not been realized. We have power! I for one don't intend on sitting on it when I can use it and be great." She said further as she sat up straighter and regal in her seat beside the commander.

"You intend on destroying a whole race of people? How can you live with yourself?"

"My dear, I've lived a long life being afraid. I want to be free to live, travel and see the stars. These people don't matter. They are of no use to me anymore."

"Aren't they the last of our kind? These people you've aligned with have been hunting us for hundreds of thousands of years. You can't just end them."

"Oh, you misunderstand me, I'm not going to end them, you are. Didn't they tell you? My Le'ak has indeed been weakened which is why we needed to find you. You are as powerful if not more so than I was in my youth. No, my dear, I will be *directing* the show." She said smugly. "Look around you, doesn't this vessel look familiar? The Froagans came upon it while scouting. This was an ark our people used to find a new home. On board were a few living red headed people that they've used to exhaustion. They came after me, once the very last one died. Good news is, all is not lost. We have you now."

I wanted to learn more of their plans, but it seemed that we had arrived. I saw Anthora Two through the view screen. It was hazy but still the home I've come to love. I watched as everyone on the bridge took their positions. None wore humanoid disguises and Leena was right there with them. I listened to Commander Se'vork as he gave orders ship-wide to ready cruisers that would go down to the planet. On occasion, Leena leaned over to confer with the commander. In my prison chair, I could do nothing but watch and listen.

Suna swirled slowly around my body, she kept me reassured that I would be okay. My head hurt and yet I could feel my body continuously grabbing hold of the sun's power just over the horizon of the planet. Leena's eyes glowed as she too harvested power from the sun.

From my vantage point, I watched several cruisers shoot out of the mothership to circle around the planet. I realized that they meant to use the wielders on board to break through Anthora Twos' defenses. My amazement was complete as I watched the cruisers fire upon each other. The commander shouted commands for them to cease fire but to no avail. They kept firing until all the ships exploded in a fiery ball.

What happened next will give me nightmares for the rest of my life. Leena stood up to face the commander. She smiled as she sent a steady stream of scorching Le'ak at him. Then she systematically turned on each individual crew of the bridge and fired on them.

She calmly walked over to me. "I'm sorry child, I couldn't let you know the whole of my plans. I've been in contact with the others on board the cruisers. They were ancients who insisted on dying this way. They wanted to ensure that we lived. They've been captives for over a hundred years after their ark was captured. I've gotten to know them well and I will ensure that future generations know of their sacrifice." Then she came around to unhook me from all the connections.

Leena helped me get down off the chair. I couldn't resist the urge to destroy it. She smiled at the smoldering remains.

"I don't understand what just happened, but I'm glad that you hadn't betrayed us." I told her. I couldn't bring myself to tell her all the awful things I thought of her.

"I will let you in on a little secret. I wasn't sure if I could pull it off either. I had started to believe what they told me. I almost bought into the whole idea of being a god. These Froagans lived and breathed power. You saved me, child. I really don't know if I would've backed out and done the right thing. I began to doubt them when they came into the room and filled me in with the rest of the plan."

"You wouldn't have gone through with it. You didn't completely disconnect from me when they came to you. I heard everything they said they would do. I believed it and I'm sorry."

She hugged me then, the puncture marks on my body had sufficiently healed. I held tightly onto her. I was so relieved.

"Come we have more to do." She said and pulled me along.

Out on the decks, we went into cabins and staterooms to finish off those that hadn't died. She explained that she had rigged the weapons to send out a massive signal that distorted the Froagans. The signal left them paralyzed and unconscious. She further told me that the Froagan nation was experiencing a decline in their numbers. They were down to two motherships, one of which was the ark that we were on and the other had been damaged in an epic battle with another ship they'd come across.

The ship had been left to float in space. They weren't quite sure if there was anyone left alive aboard it. The next phase of their plan was to mate our people with theirs to increase their numbers and to also gain the Le'ak abilities.

We came across a cabin that had four children in it. They were clearly mutants who they'd experimented with. Leena said that they were her own offspring. They were in great discomfort as their infirmities were numerous. I closed my eyes when she mercifully put them out of their misery.

It took us over two hours to complete our sweep of the ark. In one corner of the mess hall, we found the only markings that told us what the vessel was. The Verna had been home to two hundred fifty-five thousand souls.

I asked if she recovered anything in the computers and she said if there were anything left, it would take time and help. We returned to the bridge and I wasn't surprised that the bodies had turned to mush and were turning to mist. She had thought of everything. She reached over to where she had sat and pulled out two masks, then pushed a lever that depressurized the entire ship. Once that was done, oxygen filled it up again and we took the masks off.

"Now, if you don't mind, I'd like to go home."

"I don't know if we can contact the planet." I told her.

"First we get on the cruiser you came in on and fly down."

I nodded and followed her off the bridge.

# CHAPTER FOURTEEN

Elder Chaktar shook his head to clear it. Captain Lao watched him struggle to get control of himself. He'd known something was wrong when he asked him to meet him in the hangars. When Fiona appeared with two techs, he didn't recognize he was sure of it. Elder Chaktar had absolute authority; he alone authorized missions into space.

Fiona wasn't acting like herself. She held herself ridged and wouldn't acknowledge him. They were a premier team and went on missions always together. Why wasn't he in on this mission?

It was during the countdown that he realized what happened. Fiona was being kidnapped right before their very eyes and no one could help her. Elder Chaktar started violently after the takeoff and so did the crew around them. They were being controlled.

"We must go after her." He insisted.

"If we go after her, we'll only invite war. We can defend ourselves, but at what cost? Fiona isn't as helpless as you think she is. Whatever purpose they've taken her for, she'll find a way to prevent it." Chaktar replied confidently.

"So, we do nothing?" Capt. Lao asked. He was agitated and paced while he watched the crew come to themselves.

"I didn't say that. Rest assured that they will be back. Until they do, we prepare. Alert our elite forces and have them meet us in Sector X." He ordered.

Capt. Lao stopped pacing to stare at him and then he smiled. He saluted and rushed off. He was excited to finally be doing what he and the others have been training to do.

"Your orders sir?" A ground defense tech asked the Elder.

"Stand down soldier and carry on." Elder Chaktar said. He gave the empty hangar one last sweep of his eyes and turned to leave. The tech saluted and went back to his duties.

Exactly one hour later, Sector X's assembly hall was full. Men and women who had been secretly training with their Le'ak sat waiting for the Elder to speak. The hall was quiet, all eyes were on him as he approached the podium. The assembly hall in Sector X held four hundred but there were close to nine hundred packed into it. Air conditioning blasted to keep everyone comfortable. As far as he could see, a sea of Le'ak wielders sat or stood waiting for him to speak.

"We've trained for this day for hundreds of years. We've been set apart and lived our lives in secret for this very cause. The survival of our world and species is on us. We will prevail. We will eradicate our enemy once and for all."

A cheer rose up across the room. He waited for them to calm down before he continued. "Fiona Brightblade has been taken. Under the enemy's mind control I helped them take her. She was supposed to be the hero we all were waiting for. She alone knows the full extent of their plans, but that doesn't mean that we can't act. While under their influence, I was able to catch a glimpse of why they took her. Upon returning from her last mission, Fiona found out that Leena Brightblade was still alive and had been held captive all these years. She was being used to power their weapons with her Le'ak. However, she is dying, and they needed a replacement. Fiona is the replacement they have been searching for." Now a murmur filled the room.

Elder Chaktar held up his hand to regain their attention. "Because I've been compromised, I am stepping down. Commander Podge will take over while I act as consultant." He stepped back to allow the commander to step forward.

"We are saddened by these turns of events; however, our mission is clear. Anthora Two will not be destroyed nor will we take to the stars to start over again. We have the means to fight. The battle that is sure to come to us can only be won by Le'ak. Our enemy has taken one of our own, a powerful wielder whom we must defeat. My orders are as follows; go get your families to safety, then go man your stations. I will direct you via commlink. Go quickly, there are conveyors outside to take you to your individual towns!"

Twenty minutes later, in a small conference room, the Elders, Captain Lao, and Fiona's original crew sat waiting for the commander to speak.

"Forgive me my friends for this last-minute gathering. There are truths that must be laid bare tonight. We've known for hundreds of years why the Froagans have hunted us, however, we've only gotten confirmation when Elder Chaktar mind melded with them; while they used him to speak through, he had a chance to access their thoughts. It is a skill few of us has mastered. Leena Brightblade is alive but dying and they intend to use Fiona as her replacement if they hadn't already done so. She is the most powerful of us, equal to Leena. While she fights in space, we will fight on the ground. As you know, the defenses around our world is weakening. It will not take much effort for them to break through. Once they do, it will be up to us to fight."

"Why can't we take the fight to them?" Lippi asked. Next to her Pua was nodding.

"The footage of Leena showed us why they had her, and why they want Fiona. They somehow managed to combine her Le'ak with their weapons. If we go out in space, we will be destroyed before we even gear up to fire. I do not know what condition Leena is in, or if she is still alive, however I do know Fiona. She will not let them succeed, but on the off chance they land, we will be ready. Our advantage is that they don't know of the wielders we have nor that we have an army of them."

"But that means that you are willing to fire on them and possibly kill them?" Pua asked.

"We must do what we must." Commander Podge told them.

He straightened his uniform jacket, saluted them and left the room, leaving Fiona's friends to stare after him.

"Isn't there anything we could do?" Bel asked looking around the table.

"Isn't there anything we can do?" Bel asked looking around the table.

Captain Lao banged his hand on the table. He was angry. "Elder Chaktar you still have command over the air corps, you can at least have one cruiser on standby to go up there. Could you not?"

Elder Chaktar smiled reassuringly at those sitting around the table. "If it seems that the fight is desperate, we will go up. Destroying the ship will be our last resort."

"Now that's what I'm talking about!" Pua announced.

"Until then we man our stations." As a unit, they stood up and filed out of the room.

Captain Lao, Bel, Pua and Lippi hung back. They felt it would be up to them to ensure that Fiona was returned to them alive. Together they went to their stations. The Elders would probably put them under the prison, but they'd worry about that later.

A planet wide alert went out, when the cruiser that Fiona was taken on appeared in orbit. Wielders all over the planet awaited orders from the commander holding their collective breaths.

Communications between the cruiser and the planet was sketchy but, they would allow it to land. There in orbit was also the mothership.

Under heavy guard the cruiser landed. When Elder Chaktar and the commander heard Fiona's voice, they were relieved, but cautious.

Fiona and Leena Brightblade stepped down from the cruiser alone. Fiona instructed Leena to raise her hands in surrender. With hands lifted they slowly approached the captain and elder.

"Elder Chaktar, I would like to introduce to you my great, great, great grandmother Leena Brightblade. She and I would like to sit somewhere cool, have a meal and give report if that's okay." Fiona said slowly.

"How do we know that you aren't imposters?" Captain Lao returned.

"That's easy, grandma and I here, just killed everyone aboard the mothership and destroyed the cruisers that had surrounded the planet. Captain Lao, I've used a lot of Le'ak this day and my arms are feeling shaky, I would like to put them down please."

"Prove that you aren't imposters." Elder Chaktar challenged them.

Again, Fiona answered. "My grandmother wouldn't know anything about you, but I do. For instance, Captain Lao, it was Boham who you met on Earth. Elder Chaktar, you have an Olympic sized pool in your house."

Pua shoved the men out of her way and rushed to hug Fiona. Lippi followed her and they hugged and cried, while Leena watched and slowly brought her arms down.

In the same conference room, they'd left a few short hours ago, Leena Brightblade told her tale to an assembly of Anthorans and Lipasot descendants.

For those who could not fit in the room, town halls all over the planet was outfitted to have the rest of the world know what happened to their hero via loudspeakers.

"My children, I am gratified to know that some of you made it to other worlds, but sad that you didn't get the chance to know of your ancestors who had sacrificed a great deal. We had hundreds of arks that left S'evotgro to find new homes. Fiona tells me that Anthora Two is home to many of you.

I had been through many hardships and sometimes I confess to losing hope that I would ever see my family or those of my kind. Today, I am assured that many of you that are descendants of those from Earth are here. Because of that assurance, I have hope that we will eventually find the remnants from the other arks. In the coming days, I will be available to answer questions about our kind. The Elders are gracious enough to allow me time to adjust and enjoy being free. Being a captive has taught me how precious life is and the strength of hope. The retrieval process was our last ditched effort for survival, and I am glad that it was a success."

The cheer that went up after Leena's speech could be heard around the world. Anthora Two had regained their hero, but also a freedom they'd not dared to hope for.

Anthora Two joined the Alliance of Planets and with Leena's help removed the deteriorating shield around the planet. Anthora was free to take to the stars, trade with other worlds and be free.

With the Elder's help, a memorial was erected to honor those brave six Lipasots who gave their life to save Anthora Two. Their statues grace the six major towns on Anthora.